P9-CQD-481

"I'm likely more different than any man you've ever known."

His arrogance infuriated Dianna, all the more since he was right. There was none of the indolence about Kit that she remembered from her father's friends. "Do you think I would have willingly come aboard if I had known you were here, too?"

"Perhaps leg shackles and a Bridewell guard colored your choice." Kit caught himself wondering if her wounds had healed yet, and what the curve of her ankles must be like. "Either one of us is lying, or we've both been played for fools."

"You lied readily under oath!"

"I don't lie, my girl, not under oath, and not for the likes of you." Kit wanted to grab her by the shoulders, to shake some sense into her foolish, overbred head. "I told the court exactly what you told me, that you had killed your uncle...."

Dear Reader,

This month we bring you award-winning author Patricia Hagan's latest Harlequin Historical, *The Desire*. The novel is the sequel to *The Daring* (HH#84) and tells the story of Belinda Coulter, a troubled young woman who finally finds happiness as a Confederate nurse, only to come face-to-face with a man from the past.

Columbine is the second book by Miranda Jarrett, one of the first-time authors introduced during our 1991 March Madness promotion. The story sweeps from busy London to the wilds of Colonial New England, where a disgraced noblewoman finds a new life full of hope and promise.

Theresa Michaels's *Gifts of Love* is an emotional tale of a grieving widower and an abandoned woman whose practical marriage blossoms into something far more precious than either of them could ever dream.

Lucy Elliot has been writing books for Harlequin Historicals since the introduction of the line. *The Conquest,* her eighth book, is a sequel to *The Claim* (HH#129). It's the story of a tempestuous Frenchwoman and a cool-headed American soldier who fall in love against the backdrop of the American Revolution.

Four intriguing heroines. Four unforgettable heroes. We hope you enjoy them all.

Sincerely,
Tracy Farrell
Senior Editor

Columbine

Miranda Jarrett

Harlequin Books

TORONTO • NEW YORK • LONDON
AMSTERDAM • PARIS • SYDNEY • HAMBURG
STOCKHOLM • ATHENS • TOKYO • MILAN
MADRID • WARSAW • BUDAPEST • AUCKLAND

If you purchased this book without a cover you should be aware that this book is stolen property. It was reported as "unsold and destroyed" to the publisher, and neither the author nor the publisher has received any payment for this "stripped book."

Harlequin Historicals first edition October 1992

ISBN 0-373-28744-5

COLUMBINE

Copyright © 1992 by Susan Holloway Scott.
All rights reserved. Except for use in any review,
the reproduction or utilization of this work in
whole or in part in any form by any electronic,
mechanical or other means, now known or
hereafter invented, including xerography,
photocopying and recording, or in any information
storage or retrieval system, is forbidden without
the permission of the publisher, Harlequin Historicals,
300 E. 42nd St., New York, N.Y. 10017

All the characters in this book have no existence
outside the imagination of the author and have no
relation whatsoever to anyone bearing the same name
or names. They are not even distantly inspired by any
individual known or unknown to the author, and all
incidents are pure invention.

®: Trademark registered in the United States Patent
and Trademark Office and in other countries.

Printed in the U.S.A.

MIRANDA JARRETT

is an award-winning designer and art director whose writing combines her love of history and reading. Her travels always include visits to old houses and historical restorations.

Miranda and her husband, a musician, live near Philadelphia with their two small children and two large cats. She is still trying to figure out how to juggle writing, working and refereeing disputes among preschoolers in the sandbox.

For Kempy
who gave me nightmares long ago with tales of
Hannah Dustin

Chapter One

London, 1704

Twenty paces to the end of the red Turkey carpet, twelve more across its width, then twenty paces back to the fireplace....

Over and over Kit Sparhawk counted his steps as he tried to control his impatience. It was nearly nine o'clock now, the pale winter moon framed high in the arched windows of Sir Henry Ashe's drawing room. Only Kit's promise to Jonathan kept him there, and his jaw tightened at the last memory of his brother, delirious with pain and fever. In Jonathan's place, he had travelled eight weeks and six thousand miles. Another four hours in a baronet's mansion should make little difference. He owed Jonathan that much. Yet it still rankled Kit to wait at all for Sir Henry. Gentry or not, the man was a rogue, fat and florid and too cunning by half for a partner in trade. A sly, cheating son of a—

Eighteen, nineteen, twenty steps, turn...

Once again Kit forced himself to swallow his irritation, counting the footprints his boots left in the deep
plush. The bank drafts were there on the desk, waiting for the signature that Sir Henry never quite found
time to give. Tonight Kit wouldn't leave until he did.
He'd had enough of the baronet's excuses to last a
lifetime. He struck one fist into the palm of his other
hand, remembering how Sir Henry had tried every
trick he could to avoid paying what he owed. God
knew the colonies weren't free of scoundrels—Kit's
own past was hardly spotless—but in the three months
he had been in London, Kit had not met one man he'd
trust beyond an empty handshake.

He dropped into one of the silk-covered armchairs
and stared moodily into the fire. Praise Heaven he
would be sailing again in less than a fortnight, and
leaving London well behind. His thoughts rolled
ahead, as they always did, to home—to his sisters and
Jonathan and Plumstead.

A woman's scream, high and shrill with fear,
pierced the house's silence. Without thinking Kit was
on his feet and through the door. All was still in the
front hall, the flame in the blue night lantern casting
eerie shadows across the portraits that ringed the walls.
Kit hesitated by the staircase, listening. He had no idea
from where the scream had come or where to turn
next, and he cursed the vastness of the mansion.

Suddenly one of the panelled doors opposite flew
open and a small figure in white hurtled through it and
into Kit. Automatically he caught the woman and
steadied her. In that split second his senses registered
the slipperiness of silk over soft flesh, round breasts

crushed against his chest, a tangled cloud of dark hair redolent of lavender.

"Stay now, lass, and let me help," he said gently. Her face was white with the terror that filled her eyes, and her breath came in ragged shudders. Her feet bare, wearing only a night shift, she scarcely came to his shoulder.

"I've killed him," she whispered hoarsely. "I left him there, still as death itself. Oh, Mother of God, what will become of me now?"

"Hush, sweet, there's not enough of you to kill a butterfly, let alone a man," said Kit as he stroked the hair back from her forehead. Despite the fear that marked her face, he saw she was very pretty and young, perhaps twenty. Who could she be, he wondered. Sir Henry had no daughters, and this was decidedly not Lady Frances. Nor could she be a servant: there was a delicacy to her that spoke of ease and wealth, and her speech was that of a lady.

"But I swear by all that's holy that he *is* dead, and by my hand!" With a little sob she buried her face in Kit's shirt, and protectively he slipped his arms around her shaking shoulders. He knew he should go find the man she claimed to have killed, but he was reluctant to leave her just yet. She seemed so small and vulnerable in his arms, as fragile as a wounded sparrow.

Suddenly the girl broke free and stared up at him with wild eyes. "Who are you?"

"Christopher Sparhawk, lass, though most call me Kit." In the uneven light, he now saw how her shift was torn, the costly lace at the neckline ripped across the twin curves of her breasts. She was aware of his scrutiny and, shamed, she tried to clutch the torn edges together. Red marks that would darken to bruises stained her throat and shoulders, and Kit felt a surge of anger at the man who had done this to her. Some cut-throat intruder, a thief perhaps, that she'd unwittingly surprised: who else would treat a lady so? Instinctively Kit felt beneath his coat for the long knife he always carried, even now in London.

Slowly, so as not to startle her further, he extended his other hand to her. There was no mistaking the desperation in her eyes, and he felt sure she wanted to trust him. "Please, let me help you. Tell me what has happened, and then we'll go to Sir Henry."

"You're one of his friends, aren't you?" She backed further from him, her chin tucked low with wariness like a hunted animal. "No, stay where you are! I should have known he'd not come alone. I've heard what's said about him, how he likes to watch others before he can take his own pleasure. A guinea he gave to a footman last month, as if he could buy that silly knave's silence for what had passed on Lady Frances's dining table! Perhaps he's paid you, too, then, to be a party to his debauchery?"

Her gaze swept over him, noting the expensive cut of Kit's calamanco coat and the linen ruffles at his throat. "But, no, you're a gentleman. You came for the sport alone, didn't you?"

"Nay, I came to talk matters of trade, nothing more," said Kit uneasily. God, she meant Sir Henry. It couldn't be anyone else.

Her laughter was choked with bitterness, and tears glistened in her lashes. "Trade, was it? Where did he promise you could have me, then? At his counting house, on his desk, with all the clerks to gawk and cheer at my shame?''

The tears spilled over, streaming freely down her cheeks. ''Oh, how I wish I were the one who was dead!''

''Nay, lass, never wish that,'' said Kit as he stepped toward her again. But before he reached her, his eye caught a movement in the shadows. Quickly he wheeled around, and the girl followed.

''Sparhawk! By all that's holy, I'm glad you're here!'' exclaimed Sir Henry Ashe, leaning heavily against the doorframe for support. ''Mark all that you see, man, and be ready to swear to it!''

The girl's hand fluttered to her mouth. ''You're— you're not dead!''

''Aye, and no thanks to you, you murdering slut!'' growled the baronet. His wig was gone and across his shaven head was a gash that bled profusely across his face, and his shirt and coat were soaked red. ''Strike me with a candlestick and leave me to die like a dog!''

''You frightened me. You would not listen—''

''Ungrateful baggage, after all I've done for you!''

''Oh, such fine things you've done for me, Sir Henry!'' the girl cried bitterly. ''You took my trust and respect and my innocence, too, and treated them as if they were worth no more than a handful of dust!''

''Enough of your lies, you little chit!'' His mouth twisted with rage, Sir Henry raised his blood-streaked fist to strike her. The girl squeezed her eyes shut and braced herself for the blow.

But the blow never fell. Instead Kit grabbed Sir Henry's wrist, holding it so tightly over the man's head that the baronet yelped with pain and frustration.

"The devil take you, Sparhawk, let me go! How dare you interfere in my personal affairs!"

Disgusted, Kit released Sir Henry and watched him retreat, rubbing his wrist. Kit could feel the girl hovering close behind him, her hands resting lightly on the back of his coat. She needed him to protect her, and he would not let her down. "If you call beating this young lady part of your personal affairs—"

"Lady!" Sir Henry spat out the word contemptuously. "This jade's no more a lady than I! She's a wicked, cunning little creature, and don't let her tell you otherwise."

"Hold your tongue, Ashe." Kit struggled hard to control his anger. He was a large man and a strong one, and Sir Henry was neither. If he gave in to the impulse to strike the baronet's fat, choleric face, he'd likely finish the task the girl had begun with a single blow. "From what I can see, you've precious little right to call yourself a gentleman."

"Take care what you say, sir, or I'll demand my satisfaction!"

"Don't tempt me, Sir Henry," snapped Kit. "Pistols or swords make no difference to me."

Furiously Sir Henry blotted at the cut with his folded handkerchief, peering up at Kit with his other eye. "You would defend her, Sparhawk? Be her gallant? God's blood, are you her lover, too?"

"No, blast you! I don't even know her name!"

"Then permit me to introduce you to the little strumpet you've staked your honor on." Slowly he circled around Kit until he faced the girl. To Kit's surprise, she did not flinch when Sir Henry took her hand and drew her forward. "Lady Dianna Grey, meet Christopher Sparhawk. He's from the American colonies, and more accustomed to red savages than London ladies like yourself, sweetheart. He can't see beyond your pretty face to the black, rotten heart you keep inside."

The girl twisted back to look beseechingly over her shoulder at Kit. "Go now, Master Sparhawk," she said hurriedly. "You need hear none of this. Sir Henry was right. This is not your affair. Aye, you've been kind, but there is no place for kindness here. Go, please, I beg you!"

Before Kit could answer, Sir Henry jerked her sharply by the arm. "Oh, he's not going yet, Dianna. I'll wager he won't leave you. What did you say to make him your champion? Did you tell him I'd seduced you? Did you play the poor, piteous orphan, the wounded dove?"

Bewildered, Kit watched the emotion drain from the girl's face until her expression was wooden as a doll's. He told himself he should take her in his arms and away from this house at once, but her reaction made him pause, uncertain, as Sir Henry continued.

"The dove it was, then. A pretty tale, that, and so much easier to tell him than the truth." Sir Henry lightly stroked the bruise on the girl's jaw, and she quivered beneath his fingertips. "But then, you can't help yourself, can you, Dianna? You like to meld your pleasure with pain, same as I do, don't you?''

Sickened, Kit did not want to hear any more. He had known of men who claimed enjoyment in hurting their partners, but never a woman who enjoyed it, too, nor had he seen the results of such practices on a woman's body. He'd been so eager to rescue her that he'd read her all wrong, seen only what he wanted to see. And she had let him hold her, so fragile and tempting, torn silk, skin like velvet, and her hair tousled, as though she'd just stumbled from her bed....

God, he'd been such a trusting fool, a naive idiot come stumbling from the Massachusetts forest, just as Sir Henry had said. So why did he feel so damned disappointed?

"*You* are your father's legacy to me," continued Sir Henry smugly. "The best he had to leave, too, considering how the money lenders chased him. Poor Jack Grey! It was perhaps for the best that he broke his neck."

The girl winced as if she'd been struck again. "Don't slander my father! He was a good man and loved me well!"

"Of course, he did, just as I love you, niece. But tonight you went too far." The baronet's hand tightened around her jaw, and his voice grew harsh. "You would have killed me, you little chit, and I cannot forgive you that."

The landing above them echoed with clattering footsteps and shadows danced from a dozen candles. Lady Frances swept down the staircase, her purple wrapper flapping loosely. Behind her followed two hastily dressed footmen carrying candelabra, one still shoving his shirt into his breeches. Lady Frances peered crossly first at Kit, and then the candlelight found her husband, covered with blood. She shrieked and ran toward him, arms outstretched. "Oh, Henry, what has happened to you?"

"It is a long story, Fanny, of no matter to you at present." While his wife hung around his neck, Sir Henry's gaze never left the girl.

"But you are injured, Henry, you are bleeding!" cried Lady Frances, and frantically she gestured to one of the servants. "Wilson, quickly now! Summon a physician for Sir Henry!"

Sir Henry shook off her embrace. "My dear, first we shall need a magistrate," he said, his voice icy calm. "Our niece has tried to murder me."

Chapter Two

Dianna sat curled on the edge of the rough, wooden bench, her feet tucked beneath her petticoats and her fur-lined cloak pulled tightly around her. She was a lady, she reminded herself fiercely, a gentlewoman of breeding who could trace her family back to kings and queens. Nothing anyone did or said could change that. No one could take that from her. And here in the chill of Bridewell Prison, it was all she had left.

In the center of the cell was a small, smoky brazier, but Dianna hung back, uncertain what her reception would be from the other women who clustered close to its meager warmth. They were debtors and drunkards, prostitutes and thieves, but she was the only gentlewoman. And the only one of them charged with murder.

Dianna sighed softly. She'd been here scarcely a week, and already the desolation of the place seemed to seep into her bones with the cold. But what lay ahead would be worse. From listening to the other women, she had come to understand what a sentence of transportation meant. In the spring, they would all be chained together and herded through the London streets to a convict ship bound for the southern colonies. She would be auctioned off like some heathen African slave, sold to a planter to work in his fields until she dropped from exhaustion. And the judge who sentenced her had pompously claimed to be merciful by not sending her to the gallows!

It shouldn't have come to this. Her lawyer had assured her that Sir Henry's case was not a strong one, his wound not severe enough, and that the matter would likely be dismissed as a family quarrel. But that was before Master Christopher Sparhawk had testified. He'd sworn she'd tried to murder her uncle, and the judge had listened. Inwardly she winced when she remembered how, that awful night, she had trusted him, how he had seemed like a fairy-tale hero come to save her. Taller than any man she'd known, he was a handsome, golden giant with kindness in his eyes and touch. Yet once he learned her name, she had watched the kindness vanish and his expression harden. There was no point denying her uncle's lies, for no one ever believed her. She had seen it happen before with other people, and though the stranger's rejection hurt her, she was not surprised by it. She had been foolish and weak to believe he was any different from the rest. But oh, how easily he had stood before the judge to damn her with those few careless words!

She pressed her cheek against the cold stone wall and squeezed her eyes shut. Like everything else, it all came back to her handsome, charming father. Dianna's whole life had been the Honorable John Grey, and she had loved him without question. The fifth son of the Marquis of Haddonfield, her father had al-

ways lived as if he had all the prospects of the eldest
heir instead of the youngest. He was witty and amus-
ing, with a gift for music that he'd passed on to
Dianna, and because he was such good company, he
and Dianna had been welcome at court and in every
noble house in England. But then came the Septem-
ber morning when his bay gelding had balked at a
stream. Dianna's father was dead the moment his
forehead struck the ground. The bankrupt estate of
the Honorable John Grey left Dianna nothing except
gambling debts and mortgaged properties and the
condolences of fashionable friends who disappeared
as soon as the will was read.

Of all her grand relatives, only her uncle, Sir Henry
Ashe, had offered her a home, and he had expected
considerably more than gratitude from his impover-
ished niece. By the time Dianna realized the truth, the
rest of the world had already guessed, and no one believed she'd gone to Sir Henry quite as innocently as
she claimed. After all, she was twenty-two, whispered
the gossips, too old and too poor to make a fashionable match. What better could she hope for than the
protection of a wealthy gentleman like Sir Henry?

Against Dianna's will returned the memory of his
squeezing hands upon her breasts, his mouth wet upon
her throat, her own cries of terror as he struck her
again and again in frustration at her refusal, and then
her fingers blindly grasping the cool metal behind her,
the polished whorls of the heavy silver that caught the
firelight as she swung it through the air—

With a noisy creak, the barred door to the cell
swung open and the turnkey peered inside. The other

prisoners shuffled to their feet and stared at him belligerently.

"Ah, Master Will, 'ave ye come for yer sweet Jenny again?" taunted one woman as she swung her hips lasciviously and hiked her dirty petticoats up her leg. "Ye 'ad a taste o' what I can give ye, pretty fellow, and there be more a-waitin' if yer game!"

The other women hooted and whistled at the proposition, but the man ignored it. "Dianna Grey be wanted below. She be here, ain't she?"

With every eye on her, Dianna slipped off the bench and stepped forward, and the others shuffled out of her path. The turnkey squinted at her and automatically touched his forehead and ducked as if she were still a grand lady instead of one of his prisoners. "Ye come wit' me, my lady. Master Potter, the keeper, wants words wit' ye."

"La, so it's words old Potter be wantin' with our gentry!" jeered Jenny. She caught Dianna's sleeve. "I fancy 'e'll be puttin' his tongue to other uses. Garnish, m'lady, garnish be what 'e expects from his guests 'ere, an' you'll be no different. On yer back on th' floor, you'll be no different from th' rest o' us!"

Her cheeks flaming, Dianna tried to ignore the woman's warning as she followed the turnkey, leaving the jeering laughter behind. The warder's quarters were scarcely better than the prisoners' cells, but at least he had a fireplace and a fire. Potter himself rocked back on two legs of a mouldy armchair, his feet propped up on the table that served as his desk. In one hand was a tankard of ale, in the other some sort of formal document at which he was scowling, his lips silently forming each word as he read it. For several long minutes, Dianna and the turnkey waited, until finally the turnkey noisily cleared his throat and Potter looked up.

"So this be the Grey wench, then, Allyn?"

Dianna drew herself up with what she hoped was dignity. "I am not the 'Grey wench'. I am Lady Dianna—"

Potter slammed the tankard down on the table, sloshing foam across the other papers. "Shut yer trap, hussy, or I'll toss ye down amongst th' men. They'd make short work o' a little mouse like yerself, they would. Or maybe me an' Allyn'll jes' take turns with ye ourselves. Ye be a bit scrawny for my tastes, but I ain't never had a *lady* before." He gestured impatiently. "On with it now, wench. Up with th' petticoats."

Her mouth suddenly dry, Dianna could only shake her head in mute refusal.

"Please yerself. It's naught to Allyn if he must do th' task hisself." Potter reached into the basket beside his chair and pulled out two iron rings connected by a heavy chain and tossed them to the turnkey.

Swiftly Allyn bent and grabbed one of Dianna's ankles. She jerked free and kicked his arm as hard as she could. The turnkey growled and swore under his breath, but deftly caught her leg again. This time he shoved her onto the floor and straddled her flailing legs as he clamped the irons around her ankles. Rubbing his arm, he let her go, moving quickly out of the range of her feet.

Panting from both fear and exertion, Dianna sat up and stared at her feet. Around each slender ankle was a dark band of iron. She struggled to rise and tripped on the short chain that held her legs together, pitching forward onto her hands and knees. While Potter and Allyn laughed, she awkwardly tried again, finally managing to stand.

Angry humiliation made her temper flare. "How dare you treat me this way! You're insolent rogues, the pair of you! My father never even chained his dog!"

"Aye, but th' dog was likely better bred, eh, Allyn?" Potter guffawed. "Eh, let her be. She's no matter t' us anymore anyways." He leaned over Dianna and waved the letter he'd been reading in her face. "You be leavin' us tonight, my lady. That fine gen'leman ye tried t' murder wants ye gone at once, and off ye shall go with th' tide."

"But why would Sir Henry want me gone so soon?" Dianna's voice rose with panic. "What harm could I bring him where I am now?"

"Mebbe his lady wife caused a row and wanted ye gone. Mebbe he can hear yer yappin' all the way to 'is country house. How should I know why he done it? Ye should be thankful he didn't jes' 'ave you throttled. Fer the coin he offered, he might 'ave, y' know."

"But tonight! I'm not ready to leave, not so soon—"

"Awh, yer fondness touches me, m'lady," said Potter, smirking. "But ye wouldn't 'ave suited me in the end. Guards!"

Dianna stared at him, unwilling to believe his words. As long as she remained in England, even though in prison, there was still a chance that she would be freed, that all this would turn out to be some awful mistake. "You're lying, I know it! There are no ships to the colonies until spring, until April!"

From behind, two soldiers hauled her roughly to her feet. She twisted and turned, but even in her frenzy to break free, her strength was soon exhausted and the soldiers dragged her stumbling down the stone steps and into the courtyard. After a week in Bridewell, the sky overhead seemed impossibly blue, the sun blindingly bright, and, squinting, Dianna tried to shield her eyes.

"Come on now, up wit' ye!" One of the soldiers prodded her with the butt of his rifle. She whirled around and tried to strike him, but instead he deftly caught her around the knees. Hoisting her effortlessly across his shoulders like a sack of meal, he tossed her into the back of a closed sided wagon. With a *thump* that knocked the breath from her lungs, Dianna landed on the rough-planked wagon bed, her nose jammed into a pile of ancient straw reeking of chickens.

"Don't be thinkin' of tryin' to escape, ye little baggage. Th' driver's got a pistol bigger'n you, an' he ain't 'fraid to use it. Never lost a pris'ner yet, and he won't be beginnin' wit' ye." The soldier slammed the gate shut and turned the key in the padlock with a clank. At once the wagon lurched forward and jostled unevenly across the rutted courtyard.

Unsteadily Dianna sat up and leaned against the wagon's rocking sides. From what she could glimpse through the slats, the wagon was travelling through streets she'd never seen before, narrow, crowded streets lined with ginshops and dilapidated taverns. Dianna shivered, and not from the cold alone. She'd fare better in China than in this part of London. Not that she had any hope of escaping. Even if she could somehow elude the guard and shed the iron shackles, she had no friends or family to turn to, no money, not even any clothes beyond those she wore.

With a sigh she reached down to rub her ankles. The heavy cuffs had shredded the silk of her stockings and left the skin beneath raw and bruised. The lace on her petticoats had been caught and torn by the chain and now, stained with mud, it trailed forlornly beneath her skirts. She had worn the same gown since her trial, and the white lace cuffs and kerchief around her neck were also creased with soil. At least the black mourning she wore for her father hid the worst of the dirt.

Finally the wagon slowed, then stopped. Dianna could hear the mewing of gulls overhead, and the air was heavy with the pungent scent of the river. She peered through the slats and saw the forest of masts and spars that marked the ships at the quays. So Potter had been right after all, and she would soon be carried away from England. Her heart pounding, she struggled to control her panic.

The driver opened the wagon's gate, and clumsily Dianna climbed out. The man said nothing as he took her arm, but the long-barreled pistols he wore belted across his chest were warning enough, and the curious crowd along the waterfront melted away in a path before them. In a way, Dianna was grateful for the guard's strong grasp, for she wasn't sure she could walk without his help. With each step the irons dug farther into her ankles, and she pressed her lips tightly together to keep from crying out from the pain. Slowly the guard led her up the gangplank of a ship bustling with final preparations for sailing, and down the narrow companionway to the captain's cabin.

Captain Abraham Welles stood leaning over his desk, reviewing orders with his first mate. He frowned at the interruption, and his scowl deepened as the guard explained his errand.

"Damn it, man, they told me you'd come tonight, not here with the sun bright as brass!" he exclaimed impatiently. "I've no time to deal with the wench now."

"I'd my orders, sir," replied the guard. "I'll not take 'er back."

"I didn't ask you to, did I? She's here and there's no changing that." Welles sniffed, then motioned irritably to the mate. "Harper, take her below with the others. And find her a bucket of water, too. She stinks like a ruddy henhouse."

"Aye, aye, Cap'n Welles." The young seaman came forward and nodded respectfully to Dianna, but the guard still clung to her arm.

"She's a bad 'un, Cap'n," he explained doggedly. "Taken for murder, she was. Best I stow her below for ye."

Dianna caught the startled glance Harper shot to Welles, and the way the older man's bushy eyebrows came sharply together. "I never murdered anyone," she began. "It was not my—"

"Silence, woman!" roared Captain Welles. He stalked around the desk, and to Dianna's embarrassment, jerked up her skirts to her knees. "Good God, so they've got you in chains, have they? What do they take me for, a blasted slaver? Free her, you black dog, then off my ship before I have you thrown into the Thames with the rest of the offal!"

Muttering to himself, the guard unlocked the shackles and stomped from the cabin. The mate followed, carefully closing the door behind him, and Dianna was left alone with the sandy-haired captain. His arms crossed, Welles leaned against the front of his desk, still scowling as he studied her.

Dianna waited, watching him warily in return. In Bridewell, she'd heard plenty of stories about shipmasters who treated the female convicts in their care as their own private harems. True, he'd had the shackles removed, but Captain Welles was still a man, and thanks to her uncle, she knew too well the folly of trusting men.

"You haven't the look of gallows-bait, I'll grant you that," said Welles at last. "No, nor slattern, neither, and God knows a mariner sees his share of those."

Dianna bristled and drew herself up proudly. "I'm no slattern, sir, but a lady. Lady Dianna Grey."

The captain's laugh was harsh. "Oh, no, my girl, you've lost your claim to that nicety. English law says you've tried to murder a man, and it's only through the mercy of the Crown that you'll not be strung up by that pretty neck of yours. On my ship there's no place for lords and ladies and other such trumped-up gentry."

"I'm none of your trumped-up gentry, any more than I'm a rascally Yankee sailor like you!" cried Dianna. "My family is older than Queen Anne's, and more noble, too, and—"

"Hold your tongue! You should have thought of that noble family before you started behaving so common. I'm your master as long as you're on this vessel, and I'll hear no more lady this-and-that, or I'll dangle you from the yard-arm myself. Do you understand me, woman?"

He glowered at her from beneath his brows until, reluctantly, Dianna nodded.

"Good." Welles cleared his throat, drumming his fingers on his crossed arms as a slow, knowing smile crept across his face. "Now, pretty lady, as to what I'm intending."

Chapter Three

Dianna braced herself for the demand that she felt sure would come.

"You don't deserve it, not for a moment," continued Welles, "but on my ship you'll have one last chance to set your life to rights. I'll put you among honest people who know nothing of you or your sins, and you'll be like any other poor lass out to make her way through indentures, though, to be sure, you'll work off your passage when I sell your papers in Saybrook."

"And what..." asked Dianna slowly, "...what will you expect in return?"

"Only that you behave like a decent woman on my ship and keep yourself clear of my men."

Even to Dianna, the proposal seemed odd, and she peered at him closely, waiting for the catch. It was very much to her advantage, and none to Captain Welles's, and yet she had the distinct feeling he was trying to coax her into agreement.

He laughed again, this time with a false heartiness, and nervously drew his hand across his upper lip. "I warrant I'm just soft-hearted and loath to see a little mite like you suffer. You'd likely not last through the crossing on one of the ships bound for the plantations in the spring. Worse than slavers for disease and dying, they are. But *Prosperity* here, she's true to her name."

There were little beads of sweat on his upper lip as he once again wiped his hand above his mouth. He's lying, Dianna realized with surprise, lying and afraid he'll get caught.

Welles glanced past Dianna to the cabin's door. "Look here, girl, I haven't all day. Truth is, *Prosperity*'s owner is a God-fearing man and wouldn't take well to a convict wench on board. You swear to act proper, and I'll see you're treated well enough."

The truth perhaps, decided Dianna, but only part of it. "It's my uncle, isn't it," she said softly. "Sir Henry Ashe. He has paid you very well to take me away, hasn't he?"

Beneath his weather-worn skin, Welles flushed and Dianna had her answer, just as she knew it didn't matter. Her life here in England was over, and had been, if she were honest, since her father's death. If she were honest, too, she would admit that the opportunity Captain Welles was offering her was not so very bad. She would be done with prison and beyond the groping reach of Sir Henry Ashe. Besides Captain Welles, no one would ever know she had been a convict.

She lifted her head high and bravely met Welles's eyes. He had accepted money from her uncle, but he had neither abused nor robbed her nor, as Potter had suggested, had he simply claimed the money and tossed her overboard.

"Please, would you tell me, Captain Welles," she said. "Is it hard work, this planting and harvesting of tobacco?"

"Tobacco! Nay, girl, I told you before. *Prosperity*'s no convict ship, and she doesn't traffic with the southern colonies. She's a Yankee ship to the heart of her timbers, and you should thank your maker she is. You won't break your back pulling tobacco leaves where we're headed! We're bound for New England, the prettiest, finest country under heaven."

"To New England, then," said Dianna defiantly. "And may I never see the old one again!"

"Cap'n's respects, sir," said the boy, "but we're passing the last landfall, if you've a mind to see it."

"Very well, Isaac, tell the captain I'll be topside directly." Carefully Kit sanded and blotted the ledger before closing it. He had worked without stopping since before dawn, striving to settle the last loose bits of his London business while the details were still fresh in his mind. The sun was high overhead now, and a break would do him good. "The last of England," some sentimental fool would feel bound to say to him, and though Kit shared no such attachments, the dark strip on the horizon would be the last land he would see for weeks, maybe months, and he'd do well to look his fill while he could.

He plucked his hat from the narrow bunk and, with a sigh, glanced around his tiny quarters. The bunk, a folding, triangular table, a mended chair and his trunk

were all the cabin's meager furnishings, yet Kit still
had the sensation of squeezing his outsized frame into
a child's playhouse. He thought again, longingly, of
the captain's cabin and the seven-foot-long bunk tai-
lored to fit his brother. By rights, Kit could have
claimed it in Jonathan's place—he was, after all, the
vessel's owner, if not the captain—but in a moment of
rash generosity, he'd chosen the first mate's cabin instead, and it was too late to switch now. Besides, after
the mess he'd made of this voyage, he didn't deserve
any rewards.

It wasn't that he'd failed to turn a profit, for the
ledgers showed he was every bit as sharp a trader as
Jonathan. But in the process he'd managed to destroy
the carefully built relationship with one of London's
most powerful merchants and abruptly ended their
best market for Sparhawk timber.

Even now he wasn't exactly certain how he'd become so embroiled in the personal affairs of Sir Henry
Ashe. It had been bad enough to stumble into the
quarrel between the man and his mistress, and worse
still to have to testify against the girl in that circus of
a courtroom. Although Kit had told only the truth, no
more, no less, the lawyers had twisted his words to
serve Sir Henry's case. No wonder the dark-haired girl
had blamed him for her own misfortune. She had listened in silence to his testimony, denying nothing, but
the look that flashed from her silvery eyes might have
scalded him with hatred and reproach.

No, not a girl, but a lady, and an elegant one, too.
Lady Dianna Nerissa de Vere Grey. With her face and
throat ivory pale above the black silk bombazine of

her gown, she had stood as proud as a queen in the defendant's box, and as the lawyers had accused her of every sort of debauchery, Kit had found it almost impossible to reconcile this self-possessed noblewoman with the frightened girl who had wept in his arms. A practiced performance, that was all it had been, and now Kit felt thoroughly disgusted with her—and with himself, which was worse—for believing it.

The disgust hadn't lessened when Sir Henry congratulated Kit on his useful testimony and gleefully expressed his hope to see his niece on the gallows. But when the man offered to show his appreciation by completing the Sparhawks' return cargo without charge, Kit's temper had boiled over. He had first wished Sir Henry to the devil, and then, while the baronet had sputtered indignantly, Kit had struck the man's fleshy jaw so hard that Sir Henry might still be lying glassy-eyed in the muddy street. No, thought Kit sourly, there would be no further business between the Sparhawk brothers and Sir Henry Ashe.

On deck, an icy wind whipped off the Channel. With his hands in his coat pockets, Kit watched with satisfaction as the ship raced across the dark green water, dancing neatly through the whitecaps. At this rate, they'd be home in no time. He pulled his hat down lower on his head and hunched his shoulders as he made his way into the wind, back to where Abraham Welles stood by the wheel.

"A fair morning and a stout breeze at our tails," said the older man cheerfully. "What more could a man want? I'll have you back among your blessed trees before you know it.''

Kit grinned. After the stuffy little cabin, the wind felt good on his face and in his lungs. "I'd wager by now my brother's just as eager to back on *his* blessed ocean. He hasn't been this landlocked since he hopped off our mother's lap and toddled off to sea.''

"Aye, he's part fish, that lad. Though we likely could 'ave made a shipmaster out of you, too, if you'd a mind to try.'' Welles shifted his clay pipe from one side of his mouth to the other, and his expression grew serious. "Have you heard more of him, Kit?''

"Nay, just that first letter from Dr. Manning, and that was only a fortnight after we'd sailed. Too soon to know anything for certain. Months ago, now.'' Kit frowned, his green eyes clouding as his thoughts turned to his brother. Two days before the *Prosperity* had left Portsmouth, a snapped cable had sent his brother tumbling twenty feet to the deck. His right leg had borne the brunt of the fall, an ugly, jagged fracture splintering bone and tearing into muscle. It was the kind of injury that could easily turn putrid and cost a man first his leg, then his life. That fear had haunted Kit in the months since he'd left. Again and again he'd prayed for his brother. Please, God, not Jonathan, too!

Welles touched Kit lightly on the shoulder. "Your brother's a strong man and too full of spark and rum to let a little fall best him. You'll find him hobbled, mayhap, but well enough.''

Kit forced himself to smile. "Thank you, Abraham, for both of us. Jonathan couldn't have sailed the *Prosperity* better himself."

"'Twas nothing I wouldn't do again for you boys, for your father's sake, and I 'spect you know it." Embarrassed, Welles cleared his throat gruffly and squinted up at the sails. Kit, too, looked away, to the bow. For the first time he noticed a small group of people clustered along the rail, three men, and women and children, too.

"Ah, Kit, those are the passengers I told you of," said Welles, noting Kit's interest. "Likely having second thoughts about leaving home, from the looks of them."

The little group huddled against the wind as they stared back at the last glimpse of their homeland, and Kit felt a surge of sympathy for them. "Immigrants, are they?"

"Aye, and so desperate for passage they offered me double the fare. One of the women's with child, and they want to be settled before her time. When Sir Henry pulled out his cargo that way—"

Kit's tone turned chilly as the wind. "That could not be helped, Abraham."

"I'm not saying it could, Kit, am I? Nay, it just seemed wiser to take a few passengers 'tween decks than leave the space empty."

"I told you before that the decision was a good one, Abraham. You don't have to justify it to me again."

"They won't be any bother to you, Kit, none at all. They'll keep to themselves. They're only on deck now to say farewell, then they'll go back down. Why, you'll scarcely know they're on board!''

Kit listened curiously. This was at least the fourth time Welles had explained about the passengers, and Kit wondered if perhaps his father's old friend had accepted that offer of a double fare and kept the difference himself. Not that Kit particularly cared—Welles had done him an enormous favor by replacing Jonathan as captain on such short notice—but Kit hoped that he wouldn't have to hear about these miserable immigrants for the entire voyage home.

''More women than men, I see,'' said Kit, hoping at least for a different perspective on the same wearisome topic. ''Any comely daughters to ease my journey?''

''Two girls of an interesting age, but you keep those thoughts to yourself, Christopher Sparhawk! I swore to their father that this was an honest, Christian ship and his daughters' virtue would be safe enough. So you leave them be, mind, and the wives, too.''

Kit laughed. ''Lord, Abraham, you make me out to be a threat to all womankind!''

Welles studied him narrowly, working the pipestem in his teeth. ''You know what I mean. You're too handsome for your own good, you and Jonathan both. The pair of you have the mamas lined up from Falmouth to New Haven, hoping to get a good shot at landing one or the other!''

''It's not the mothers I fancy, Abraham.''

''Young or old, you leave them all a-sighing and swooning.'' Welles shook his head. ''Now I've heard Sam Lindsey's youngest girl has set her cap for you.''

"Constance? Oh, aye, I suppose she has, like her sisters before her." Kit tried to remember the girl: yellow hair, or maybe it was red. He'd done no more than dance with her twice at a party last summer, and now the gossip already had them linked. "A pretty enough little poppet. I'm bringing her the ribands she begged from London, but if it's a husband she's after, she'd best look elsewhere."

"Pray her father thinks the same."

"Save your warnings, Abraham. I'm always careful with the maids, no matter how they tempt me. I'll be thirty-three years a bachelor come next spring, and I know well how to keep my neck from that particular noose."

"Truth is, Kit, you're married already, to Plumstead and the mills and trading posts and warehouses and whatever else you've built. That's well and good, I warrant, excepting I don't know how a sawmill's going to keep you warm on a January night the way a wife can."

Kit shrugged. "The farm and the rest give me back double what I give to them, which can't be said of most wives. Hester keeps my house and sets the best table in the colony, and the nieces and nephews my sisters seem so fond of producing are children enough for me." He couldn't resist grinning wickedly at the older man. "As for warming my bed, the world's full of loving, lonely widows."

Welles snorted. "You're bad as your father was before your mother caught him, sneaking around kitchen doors like some old rogue tomcat!"

But Kit only half heard him. Now that England had slipped below the horizon, the little group of passengers was beginning to abandon the post by the rail, and the men and women were carefully feeling their way across the rolling deck to the companionway. Finally only one woman remained. Although her face was hidden by the hood of her black cloak, Kit knew at once she was different from the others. She alone looked westward, her gaze intent not on what she was leaving, but on what lay ahead. Her small figure stood braced against the wind as her cloak and skirts swirled about her legs, and there was something oddly touching about how bravely she turned to meet the unknown. One of the daughters, he guessed. No matter what Abraham had promised, she might be worth seeking out. He liked spirited women, and this one, Kit felt sure from her posture alone, would have spirit to spare.

She turned her face upward, to the sky, and the wind caught her hood and whipped it back. Now Kit could see her clearly, her cheeks rosy from the wind and her lips slightly parted, and the way her dark hair, shining with copper streaks in the bright sunlight, swirled around her shoulders. He stared at her there at the rail and swore, violently, under his breath. So this was the reason why Abraham had been so anxious to keep him away from the immigrants.

Immigrants, hell. The woman was a convict.

Chapter Four

Dianna remained at the rail long after the others had left. She had spent the first three days of the voyage either retching into a bucket or curled miserably on an ancient, wool-stuffed mattress. But this morning, she had finally begun to become accustomed to the ship's motion, and the wind and spindrift on her face made her feel almost like herself again. She had never been on the open sea before, and she found the wildness of the ocean and sky exhilarating and limitless. For the first time in her life she felt truly free—free of the past and the present, and free of the responsibilities of being Lady Dianna Grey. Lost in her thoughts, she was oblivious to the curious interest of the seamen working around her, and oblivious, too, to the heated words between the captain and the *Prosperity*'s owner near the wheel. Not until her fingers and nose were numb from the cold did Dianna reluctantly turn away from the ocean and head back down the companionway.

The space she shared with the other passengers was nothing more than the orlop deck usually reserved for cargo. By hanging quilts and lashing their trunks to the bulkheads, the women had managed to divide the area for the three families travelling together.

"Ah, there now, I told ye th' wind would bring th' color back to your cheeks!" declared Mary Penhallow as Dianna slowly made her way through the clutter toward the older woman. From the first day, Mary had adopted Dianna into her own large family. She had been the one who held Dianna when she'd been seasick, and dosed her with peppermint oil to ease the quaking in her stomach. Plump and pink-cheeked and always slightly out of breath, Mary reminded Dianna of the nurse she'd had as a baby, and she couldn't help but warm to her.

But although Dianna's mattress was now a part of the Penhallows' circle, she still felt shy around them. She had no experience with the boisterous give and take of a large family, and she could not quite sort out the six younger children. But the eldest daughter offered no such problems. Eunice Penhallow had latched on to her with the instant devotion of a shy, dreamy fourteen-year-old, who found Dianna just old enough to be fascinating, but not so old as to be lumped among her mother's friends.

Even now the girl rushed forward eagerly to greet Dianna. "I'd have stayed with ye, Dianna, but Mam said it weren't proper to be so long before th' sailors."

"Nay, child, ye put th' words crossways," scolded her mother. "I said 'twasn't proper for ye to be ogling th' sailor-men, not t'other way 'round. Come sit by me, ye silly goose, and leave Dianna to settle herself."

Eunice tossed her head smugly. "Nay, Mam, 'tweren't no common sailor caught my eye, but Master Sparhawk, what owns this very ship. Isaac says that where we're bound he owns farms an' a great manor house an' acres an' acres o' land that jus' sits fallow, he's so much of it!"

Dianna whipped around. "What is the man's name?"

"Christopher Sparhawk." Eunice's eyes grew dreamy. "An' a more comely gentleman never lived! His smile alone would fetch you, Dianna, an' th' span o' his shoulders, oh, lud!"

"Christopher Sparhawk!" Dianna wailed. "By all that is holy, how could I land on the same wretched ship with that—that rogue!"

"Ye know the gentleman then, miss?" asked Mary curiously. "There could be more than one man by th' name."

"A great, blond, green-eyed ox who begs you to trust him even as he lies? The worst kind of colonial oaf, so long among the savages that he can hardly speak the Queen's English?"

"Aye, Master Sparhawk is a large gentleman, and very fair," answered Mary cautiously. "But for lying and th' rest, I cannot say. Captain Welles spoke most winningly of Master Sparhawk as a Christian gentleman."

"What else could he say when he owes the man his livelihood? A scoundrel of the first order, that's your fine Master Sparhawk!" Just in time, Dianna stopped, in her frustration nearly forgetting that the Penhallows knew nothing of her trial. Angrily she pounded her fists across her knee. Once again she'd been the foolish, trusting innocent. How Sir Henry and Christopher Sparhawk, and likely Captain Welles, too, must have laughed at her naïveté!

The boy, Isaac, came clattering down the companionway. "Dianna Grey, yer wanted for'ard!"

Dianna stood, her hands on her hips. "Oh, I am, am I? Dare I ask by whom?"

"Master Sparhawk himself, that's *whom,*" said the boy scornfully, "an' you'd best move yer tail, for he be in a righteous temper!"

Mary laid her hand gently on Dianna's arm. "Go with th' lad, miss. Whatever th' quarrel, yer pride's not worth the sorrow ye could bring t' us all if ye cross Master Sparhawk."

"Oh, yes, I'll go to lordly Master Sparhawk," Dianna said as she gathered up her skirts to climb the narrow steps, "though when I'm done, he might well wish I hadn't."

Muttering crossly to herself, Dianna followed the boy aft to where the *Prosperity*'s few cabins were. Without thinking she ran her palms across her hair to smooth it before she caught herself in the gesture and pulled her hands away. What did she care how she looked before a man like Christopher Sparhawk? She tipped her head forward and with angry fingers tousled and ruffled her hair and then tossed it back, satisfied that now he wouldn't think she'd primped for him.

They stopped before a narrow louvered door. Isaac knocked twice, shoved the door open for Dianna and then abandoned her at the doorway. Tentatively she peeked inside. The cabin was much smaller than she expected, low and cramped, and when Christopher Sparhawk rose from the single chair, he seemed to fill it.

Lord, how had she forgotten the man's size, his height and the breadth of his shoulders? Yet it was more than that that made the tiny space seem smaller: there was an air about him of strength and confidence that would have filled a ballroom. Although he was dressed like a gentleman, his skin was burnished dark as a common laborer's, and his hands were worn like workman's hands, the long, tapered fingers scarred and callused. Instead of a wig, he wore his own hair, dark near his jaw, but streaked to pale gold near the crown. Around his eyes and mouth the sun had etched fine, pale lines that would, she suspected, crinkle with amusement when he laughed.

But there was no laughter in his eyes now. "So it is you," he said coldly, with no further greeting. "Come in, then, and close the door. I don't want what's said between us becoming gossip for the seamen's supper."

Dianna drew herself up sharply, refusing to be intimidated by his rudeness. "Why do you wish to see me? So you can laugh or gloat at my change of fortune? Was that part of the bargain you struck with my uncle? You are a merchant, I'm told, so perhaps such transactions are common to you." She couldn't resist letting her gaze sweep past him, around the cabin. "A merchant, yes, but not a very successful one, if these are the accommodations you can buy yourself."

For a long moment Kit stared at her in silence. She stood as straight and tall as such a diminutive creature could, her whole person radiating the same pride and defiance as she had during her trial. But she was much changed from the elegant lady in the defendant's box. Her silk bombazine gown was crushed and salt-stained. Gone were the cuffs and collar of Alençon lace, and gone, too, were the dangling earbobs of pearls and onyx, and the jeweled rings that had decorated half her fingers. The wind off the Channel had brought a rosy color to her cheeks, and her hair was wild and loose, tumbling down over her shoulders and breasts as though she'd just risen from her bed. It was easy now for Kit to recall her as she had been that first night, and the memory of how neatly she'd played him for a fool returned as well.

"Oh, your tongue's tart enough now, isn't it, when there's nothing to be gained by honeyed words," he said softly. "The only transaction that's brought you here is between you and your dear uncle."

"Why should I believe you? I know Sir Henry paid Captain Welles to take me on board. Why should you be any different?"

"Because I *am* different." He remembered how Welles had sputtered and squirmed when confronted about this one special passenger. "Likely more different than any man you've ever known."

His arrogance infuriated her, all the more since he was right: she hadn't ever known a man like him. His features were hard and lean, his nose and cheekbones prominent, and there was none of the indolence about him that Dianna remembered from her father's friends. "Do you think I would have willingly come aboard this ship if I'd know you were here, too?"

"Perhaps the shackles and a Bridewell guard colored your choice." Welles had told him how she'd come stumbling into the cabin, her face white with pain and her ankles torn and bleeding from the irons. Kit caught himself wondering if the wounds had healed yet, and what the curve of her ankles must be like. "Either one of us is lying, or else Sir Henry Ashe has played us both for fools."

"You lied readily enough under oath!"

"I don't lie, my girl, not under oath, and not for the likes of you." Kit wanted to grab her by the shoulders, to shake some sense into her foolish, overbred head, but he remembered too well how soft her body was and how it had addled his judgment before. He wouldn't let it happen again, and he clasped his hands behind his back to be sure. "I told the court exactly what you told me, that you had killed your uncle."

"I struck my uncle in my own defense, not to kill him. And I am not your girl." Dianna forgot her promise to Captain Welles. "I'm Lady Dianna—"

But Kit cut her off. "You are Dianna Grey, spinster, no more. I understand Welles made that quite clear. Or do you prefer Dianna Grey, wanton? Dianna Grey, murderess? Dianna Grey, actress? There, I think that's the one I like best."

Dianna winced. His words hurt her so effortlessly. *Spinster, wanton, murderess, actress...* Dianna thought of the Penhallows, of Mary and Eunice and the children. She would lose their friendship in an instant if they found out about Sir Henry and the trial.

"Captain Welles promised that no one else would know."

Kit shrugged. "Why do you care? You've broken your part of the agreement by insisting on your title."

"But I haven't, not with anyone else, anyway." Her dream of a new beginning was crumbling before it had even begun, and all because of one selfish man. She could sense him watching her with those green eyes, cat's eyes, waiting for her reaction. What does it matter to him, she wondered desperately. Why should he care? "I swear the other passengers know nothing of who I am, and I'd—I'd rather they didn't."

She raised her chin a little higher, and for the first time Kit noticed the cleft that divided it neatly in two. Her face was not conventionally pretty. Her aristocratic nose was a shade too long, her mouth too full to be the fashionable rosebud. But there was a sensuality to her features that attracted him more strongly than he wanted to admit. In spite of his intentions, his irritation with finding her on board was quickly changing to something a good deal more enjoyable.

"No matter how far you run, my girl," he said softly, "you won't leave the past behind."

"Then what will you do with me?" she asked bitterly. "Pitch me over the side? Aren't you afraid I'll defile the whole ocean as well as your sainted ship?"

He cocked one eyebrow in surprise at the bleakness of her tone. "Nay, there must be some better use for you than that, isn't there?"

He had meant it as teasing, a way to coax the bitterness from her. But Dianna heard only the bare words. Her uncle had said the same things to her, and she knew what they had meant, just as now, she understood why she had been brought to Christopher Sparhawk's ship. The man wanted her—no, expected her to be his whore for the voyage. She felt her cheeks burn with shame, and automatically she glanced at the bunk behind him. Lord, a man of his size could kill her! Her mouth went dry, and she bit her lower lip to fight back the tears as she looked down, unable to meet his gaze.

Kit in turn could not take his eyes from her. The way she'd blushed so prettily as she'd looked at the bunk, her little white teeth nibbling on her lip as she'd glanced up at him through her lashes—God's blood, she'd have to have her invitation engraved to spell it out any clearer!

"Dianna, lass," he murmured, low and dark, as he reached out gently to stroke her hair. But when he touched her, she gasped and turned her face full toward him. It was not the tears in her eyes that stopped him. It was the fear. She was so clearly terrified of him that his hand drew back at once as if it had been burned. Awkwardly he jammed both hands in his coat pockets, wondering what the devil had gone wrong.

Dianna saw how he pulled away and relief washed over her. But mixed with the relief was a kind of chagrin, too. She had saved herself by crying, and though she hadn't done it intentionally, she felt no better than some blubbering milk-maid cornered by the master. Weak and cowardly, that's how she'd acted. What had happened to her pride?

She squared her shoulders and sniffed back the tears, fumbling for her handkerchief. "I'll have you know," she said with as much dignity as she could muster, "that I don't usually do this."

He narrowed his eyes at her suspiciously. "Don't do what?"

"Why, cry, of course." She sniffled again, loudly, and without comment he handed his own handkerchief, an enormous square of bleached homespun. "Thank you. I'm sure I don't know what happened to my own, but I'm quite short of linen for a journey of this sort."

"Indeed," he said dryly. "Not what you're accustomed to?"

"Faith, no! When Father and I travelled to Paris last spring, we had four trunks between us, and that didn't count what we bought there. You should have seen the long faces on the porters when they saw all the baggage on top of the coach!" She began to laugh at the memory, until she realized Kit wasn't laughing with her.

He wasn't even smiling. For an instant she dared to meet his gaze and the intensity of those half-closed cat's eyes. Their expression baffled her. She saw none of the hostility that her uncle had shown when she'd refused his advances, no threats, but the question she found instead was one for which she had no answer. Quickly she looked away, lower, to the front of his shirt. His neckcloth was loose, his waistcoat partly unbuttoned, and his shirt hung open at the throat in a deep V.

She had never stood so near to a man other than her father, and curiosity unwittingly made her bold. Intrigued, she stared at the tanned triangle and the pattern of the dark curls upon it. Her eyes wandered farther, following the horsetail braid down the front of his waistcoat, across a belly that was flat and lean. Lower still, his hips seemed surprisingly narrow for the breadth of his shoulders, while his breeches were cut so snugly that Dianna looked hastily away. The breeches were tucked into tall leather boots, the leather worn and comfortable from long use, and his feet, like the rest of him, seemed enormous. She raised her gaze, stopping short again of his chin. At the base of his throat she could see the measured beat of his pulse, and wondered if it matched the quickening rate of her own.

She was no longer frightened, though even in her innocence she knew she had more reason to be now than before. Still, she stood before him and could not bring herself to meet his eyes. Instead her own gaze shifted sideways, past the row of polished coat buttons, across the expanse of his chest and shoulders. With a little shiver, she remembered how his arms had felt around her that night at her uncle's house, how he'd held her gently, like a fragile piece of porcelain, yet how aware she'd been of his strength.

For Kit, her eyes roamed over him with the intensity and the intimacy of a caress, and he wondered how she'd react if once again she looked lower and discovered the effect she'd had on him already. My God, what would happen when she actually touched him? He wanted to catch her and take her now, fiercely, while the desire ran hot in his blood. A woman this brazen would not expect to be wooed, nor deserve to be, either.

· "What shall we do with you, eh, Dianna?" His question came from deep in his chest, almost a growl.

She swallowed, "That, Master Sparhawk, is—"

"Kit. Call me Kit, Dianna."

"That's—that's a decision you'll make, not I," she answered in an odd, throaty voice that refused to sound like her own. What is wrong with me, she thought uneasily. She felt giddy, almost light-headed. "Whether I like it or not, you own this ship, and I am only an unwilling passenger."

He didn't answer, and her voice slipped even lower, to scarcely more than a whisper. "That is the way of it, isn't it . . . Kit?"

He heard the promise in her voice, and almost groaned aloud at the eager way her lips were parted, beckoning to him. The sound of his name on her tongue was heady magic. He couldn't remember the last time he'd wanted a woman this badly.

But the tears that still glistened like tiny diamonds in her lashes stopped him. She kept changing like quicksilver, by turns coyly shy, then seductive. She was playing with him, reeling him in as neatly as a fat, open-mouthed trout. Well, he'd be damned if he took her bait. If he could get his wits out of his breeches and back into his head, he'd realize there were too many things about the girl that promised trouble. She was a convicted felon for one. She was also the niece of one of the most debauched noblemen in England, and she'd already made a fair start on a similar reputation herself. She might even try to kill him, too, the way she had her uncle; maybe Sir Henry himself had put her up to it. At the very least he might end up with a case of the French pox.

Kit frowned and shook his head, almost as if he were arguing with himself, and for the first time since she had entered the cabin, he looked away from her. Slowly Dianna felt her heart begin to quiet, and the breath return to her lungs. Strangely, too, she felt an odd sense of regret that she couldn't put into words.

"Because Welles is the *Prosperity*'s master, I'll honor your agreement with him," Kit said carefully, looking somewhere over her head. "You behave yourself, and you'll be treated as decently as any woman on board. God knows you don't deserve it, and I don't like it, but I'll honor it just the same."

With a sigh, he dropped heavily into the cabin's one chair. He stretched his legs out before him, and, with his elbows on the chair's arms, touched his fingertips together and pressed them lightly to his lips.

"You might," he said at last, "thank me."

"For what, offering to treat me decently?" She knew that was not what he meant, not really, but she gambled that he wouldn't correct her. "No, I don't think I shall thank you for that. May I return to my quarters, Master Sparhawk?"

So he was once again Master Sparhawk. Kit scowled and bent his head deeper against the arch of his fingers. "Aye, go." Damn her nose-in-the-air politeness! She made him feel as if he'd been the one dismissed, not the other way around. "No, one moment, stay."

She faced him again, waiting, and without any real reason to call her back, he asked the first question that came to his mind. "In the court, they said you wore mourning only as a sham to sway the judge to pity. Yet still you dress yourself in black. Why?"

She hadn't heard that before, and she stiffened at the implication. "My father was killed while hunting four months ago. It is for his memory alone I wear mourning."

"And your mother?"

"She died birthing me. May I go now?"

He should have said something to her then, for he knew too well the pain of parents lost. Instead he merely nodded and watched her go.

But at the door she paused, her hands balled in tight fists at her sides. "Whatever else my uncle told you about me, about my—my being his mistress, I would have you know he lied. He lied!"

She saw the disbelief on Kit's face and fled before he could see the disappointment show on her own. He despised her, that was clear, and he had accepted every foul word Sir Henry had said against her. And what was that to her? He was a liar, a rogue, the over-sized colonial ox responsible for her conviction. Why, she'd almost fainted from being shut in the same cabin with him! So why, then, did it matter so much that he believe her?

She slammed the door after her, and Kit heard her heels echo on the deck as she ran toward the forward companionway. Why the devil did she have to say that about her uncle? The more the chit denied her past, the worse he decided it likely was. He swore to himself and kicked the bulkhead. He had no choice but to avoid her for the rest of the voyage. Two months, at most three. Not so very long.

He remembered how her silvery eyes had roamed so freely over his body, and he swore again. He knew he had to leave her alone. And he knew, just as surely, that he probably wouldn't.

Chapter Five

Carefully, Dianna opened her hand and stared down at the hard half-biscuit that would be her supper and her dinner, as well. For the past four weeks, since the end of the fresh food, ship's biscuit had been all any of them between decks were given to eat, and even that had dwindled from three biscuits a day to one. The slow starving worsened each day, gnawing mercilessly at both strength and will.

Sitting on the deck beside Dianna, Mary Penhallow cradled her youngest son in her lap. The dry rattle of the boy's breathing shook his wasted little body, and he was too weak now to resist the fever that unnaturally brightened his cheeks. The arc of light from the swinging lantern overhead caught the dread in Mary's face, and Dianna looked away.

The sailor who brought the biscuits and water each morning growled that they should expect no better on a winter crossing, but Dianna didn't believe him, not with his jowls and fat belly. But the Penhallows and the others did not agree with her. The *Prosperity* was a Christian vessel, they argued doggedly, the captain a good man, a gentleman who had promised to treat them well, and to question him would only cause trouble.

The sick boy cried out fretfully. As Mary tried to comfort him, something inside of Dianna at last rebelled. Abruptly she shoved the dry biscuit back into her pocket and rose, steadying herself against the ship's rocking, and hurried toward the companionway. She could no longer sit and do nothing. Somewhere in the ship there was still plenty to eat, and she meant to find it.

Kit pushed his chair back from the captain's table and let his head drop back on his shoulders. He was past exhaustion, but even the hot stew and Abraham's rum could not make the tension in his body fade. To fight his boredom and restlessness, he'd chosen to work the same watches as the crew, and it was hard work, made harder by the winter storms that haunted the North Atlantic. Kit would not soon forget this last one, a blizzard that had shrouded the deck in white and treacherously coated every line with ice. For fourteen hours they had struggled to keep the *Prosperity* from destroying herself in the shrieking wind and snow.

Despite his inexperience, Kit was strong and agile, and that was what had mattered most. Another man on the foremast had not been so lucky. One moment Caleb Tucker had been beside Kit, reefing the sternsheets, and then the next he was gone. Kit wished he could forget the memory of Caleb's startled face as he'd lost his footing. And Caleb still scarce a bridegroom when they'd left New London, his pretty wife—widow, now—Patience, newly with child. Although he'd make sure Patience never wanted for anything, the old fear ate at Kit again. Why had Caleb died, and why had he, Kit, been spared?

"By my reckoning, Kit, we'll make New London in less than a week," said Abraham with satisfaction as he lit his pipe with a wisp from the candle. "Your *Prosperity*'s a sweet sailer, no mistake."

"She's Jonathan's, not mine," said Kit automatically. It bothered Kit that Abraham had made this assumption about his brother before, just as it bothered him that the captain seemed so unaffected by Caleb's death. But then Kit had learned more than he wished about his father's old friend on this voyage. Abraham was a superb mariner, but as a companion, he was far less satisfactory. "I may be the *Prosperity*'s owner on paper, but she's all Jonathan's in every other way."

Abraham sucked on his pipestem. "About Jonathan, Kit. I'm not wishing ill to the lad, but if he's still not well-mended, I'd be willing to take on as captain for you again."

"There'll be no need," said Kit quickly. "I'm certain Jonathan's fine." If Kit said it often enough, maybe he'd come to believe it, too.

"There now, Kit, I told you you'd be taking it wrong." Suddenly Abraham scowled and laid down his pipe. The rapping on the cabin door was sharp and insistent. "In with you, then, if you be in such an infernal hurry!"

It was the heady fragrance of the stew that struck Dianna first, the sweet smell of onions and, oh, could that really be chicken? She inhaled convulsively, gulping at the air as if it alone could end her hunger.

"Don't stand there a-gapin', girl," said Abraham irritably. "If you've something to say, then say it and be gone. You don't have no place here anyways."

With a little shake, Dianna drew her attention away from the table and boldly confronted the captain. "You don't give your passengers the food they've paid for."

Abraham snorted. "No French pasties and kick-shaws, y'mean! What would a spoiled female like yourself know about seagoing fare?"

"I know that you're letting them starve so you can fill your purse with the difference! There's half of them sick already, some close to death, and the children—oh, the children . . ." She faltered, thinking of little Benjamin Penhallow.

Abraham struck his palm sharply on the table. "If things be so bad, why don't one of the menfolk come to me, eh? Why did they send a little baggage like you t'do their begging?"

"They don't know I'm here. They don't believe you'd try to cheat them or that there's more in your stores than one mealy biscuit apiece each day!"

"One biscuit apiece?" asked Kit incredulously. There should still be plenty for the passengers to eat. "One biscuit a day?"

Dianna tried to answer him evenly. Why hadn't she noticed him there before, sprawled in the chair at the end of the table? "Aye, one a day, and that often as not ripe with weevils."

"She's daft, Kit, a troublemaker," said Abraham quickly. "You've told me that yourself."

But Kit wasn't listening. "Leave us, Abraham," he ordered. "Now."

Crumbling, Abraham shrugged on his coat and left the cabin. If the captain cared at all for his reputation, thought Kit grimly, he'd be off to find those missing provisions, and fast.

With a sigh, Kit turned his attention to Dianna. He had intended to ask her more about the conditions between decks, but now that he really looked at her, he knew she had not exaggerated. Hunger had hollowed her cheeks, and her black gown hung loosely from her shoulders. He'd been so intent on avoiding her that he'd forgotten the other nineteen passengers in his ship. God only knew what else that avaricious bastard Welles had done to them, and it was Kit's fault for letting it happen. The girl had mentioned children, sick children. Wasn't his conscience burdened enough already? Angrily he swore beneath his breath.

Dianna watched him warily in return. Kit looked well-fed, true, but his eyes were red-rimmed, and beneath a ragged growth of dark beard, the lines around his mouth were drawn deeper than before. She was no longer afraid of him—if the man had left her alone this past eight weeks, she doubted he'd be interested in her now.

Curiously, she was almost sorry. Throughout the long misery of the crossing, she had clung to an image of Kit Sparhawk that likely didn't exist. Instead of his scorn and betrayal, she remembered his kindness when he'd come to her defense and how gently he'd held her. And more. She remembered the strange warmth she'd felt when he'd told her—or dared her?—to call him by his given name; how his voice alone had made her tremble. It was all pure foolishness, she reminded herself sternly. Yet, once again in his presence, she felt agitated and unsure, and she wished Captain Welles had stayed.

"I hope you enjoyed your meal," she said pointedly, glancing at the empty dishes. "I trust Captain Welles has gone to share your bounty with the others."

"He'll damned well do what I tell him to!" thundered Kit with a fierceness Dianna hadn't expected, and her own anger flared in response.

"So it's you who decides who goes hungry, is it?" She stepped closer to stand defiantly before his chair, her hands on her hips. "But then, Captain Welles would have nothing to gain from letting others suffer, while you could claim the profit."

Kit did not bother to correct her. Though she could not be more wrong about Welles, Kit doubted she'd listen to the truth from him.

"Why didn't you come to me sooner?" he demanded instead.

In confusion, Dianna's thoughts flew back to the last time they'd been together, in the little cabin, and how he'd rejected her. "I did not seem to find your favor, Master Sparhawk," she answered stiffly.

"God's blood, I meant come if you'd found fault with your quarters!"

Dianna's cheeks flamed with embarrassment and shame. Of course, he hadn't meant *her*. There was no graceful way to recover, so instead she rushed on. "I came to Captain Welles because I believed he could help. I did not know you would be here, or I would not have knocked. I am, you see, not accustomed to dealing with men who are not gentlemen."

His green eyes narrowed, and his response was washed with sarcasm. "Then tell me, my lady, how a gentleman would address these particular circumstances. A fine fellow of breeding and fashion. Your uncle, say."

Dianna's dark eyebrows drew sharply together. "I do not see—"

"Oh, aye, I think you do," he said softly, watching the quickening beat of her pulse at her throat. He was intentionally baiting her, challenging her, though he wasn't sure why. In a week he would be back in New London, and there would be any number of women, beautiful, uncomplicated women, to welcome him home. But, strangely, he didn't care. Dianna Grey was arrogant and corrupt, and currently quite filthy, yet he couldn't deny the excitement he'd felt when he'd seen her in the doorway. She'd plagued his thoughts, awake and asleep, ever since they'd cleared London, and he didn't like it.

She didn't flinch beneath his scrutiny, and that irritated him, too. She was too proud by half, this one. She looked close to fainting from hunger, yet not once had she asked for food for herself. Although her gown was scarcely more than rags now, she still acted the grand lady, dismissing him as if he wasn't worth her notice. Maybe that was why he was goading her now, trying to make her as angry with him as he was with her. Slowly he rose from the chair, using his full height to compel her to look up at him.

"Now tell me true, my lady," he continued with deceptive calm. "A gentleman like Sir Henry wouldn't give a crooked farthing for that sorry bunch of pilgrims between decks, and I'm surprised, my lady, that you've become their champion. Mayhap you've a favorite among the good farmers? I recall now your uncle wasn't too particular in his pleasures either, was he?"

Dianna gasped. "You have no right to speak to me like that—no right at all! The Penhallows and the others welcomed me and accepted me with kindness and without question. Not like you! You can't forget the tattle and the slander, and then you dare to stand in judgment of me for sins I've never committed! Why can't you and all the others understand! I am *not* like my uncle!"

The hint of a smile seemed to play around the corners of his mouth. "There is, my lady, one way to tell if you are, isn't there?"

Before she realized what was happening, he caught her by her arms and lowered his face swiftly to meet hers. She pushed against his chest, struggling to free herself, but his lips were already on hers and he was kissing her. The more she fought, the more insistent he became, his mouth slashing boldly across hers. She felt the rough stubble of beard across her cheek and the surprising softness of his lips as they pressed against hers. She tried to twist away and began to protest, but he captured her open mouth. The only other man who had kissed her had been her uncle, and this was nothing like that awful experience.

This was different, very different. Dianna was unprepared for the masculine taste of him and for the sinuous dance of his tongue against hers as he coaxed a response from her that she had not known was hers to give. A curious languor swept through her body. Tentatively her hands circled around his neck for support, her fingers tangling in the thick mane of his hair. His arms tightened around her and he lifted her upward and closer against him until her feet were off the deck. She was floating weightless on a sea of new sensations, and she had no idea where it would end.

The reality of kissing Dianna was unlike anything Kit had imagined. She was smaller than he remembered, a tiny bit of a thing who'd had little enough flesh to spare before the voyage's hardships and now seemed swallowed up in his embrace. But there was nothing slight about her ardor. From the first moment their lips met, he realized she was different. There was fire there, to be sure, and a promise of more. Yet there was an unexpected wistfulness, almost an uncertainty to her response, as well, that captivated him. He tried to remind himself that this guilessness was only part of her acting, but still the kiss he'd begun in anger deepened into something else.

Or maybe it hadn't been anger at all. Maybe it was just because Caleb Tucker was dead and Dianna Grey was alive, wonderfully, gloriously alive, and able to make Kit feel that way, too. His lips traced along her jaw to the special soft place beneath her ear, and she rewarded him with a little gasp of startled pleasure.

It was that same little gasp that finally roused Dianna's numbed conscience. Why was she letting him do this to her? She heard the ragged catch in her own breathing as he whispered her name, and she closed her eyes tight against the miserable truth. He had kissed her and held her, and she had scarcely fought him at all. Rather, she had enjoyed it, and worse yet, she had freely kissed him back. Kit was right. She *was* as wanton as Sir Henry had always claimed. She tried to remember why she'd come here at all. *Remember Mary Penhallow and Benjamin and mealy biscuit with weevils.*

She twisted in his arms, trying to pull free. "You will give them food now, won't you?" she asked unsteadily.

"Hush, sweeting, now's not the time or place for chatter." Gently his lips feathered down her throat and she shivered in spite of her intentions.

"Nay, mind me." Resolutely she placed her palms against his shoulders and shoved as she tried to make her voice stern. "I want you to swear, Master Sparhawk, that you will grant your passengers the food they're owed."

"'Master Sparhawk', is it again? You kiss me like the devil's in your blood, and then it's Master Sparhawk?" Unceremoniously Kit released her, and she slipped clumsily down his body. She backed away slowly, rubbing her arms where he'd held her. The unconscious gesture jabbed at Kit's pride almost as much as her words. He felt perversely disappointed, even as he realized once again she'd bettered him. His own desire had been all too genuine. He clenched his hands behind his back and stared coldly down at her. "Pray, tell me, Dianna, are you bargaining with me?"

Dianna swallowed. There was no sign of affection in that handsome, stone-hard face. Part of her wished that he hadn't been willing to set her aside quite so easily, but his callousness also served to steady her nerve. "You are a merchant, a trader," she said disdainfully, managing a small, careless shrug. "If such terms are those you understand, then aye, we shall bargain."

Kit wondered if she would have given herself to Welles if the man had been here alone. Maybe, on another night, she already had. "A simple transaction, then, between us alone?"

Dianna nodded, though her thoughts were full of uncertainty. She had nothing to trade beyond what she wore, and he knew it. What she had asked was not complicated. Why was he bent on making it so?

His jaw tightened, his green eyes as cold as the winter sea around them. "Where I am from, my lady," he said contemptuously, "there is a word for women who would sell themselves for favors. And it's a great deal worse than being called 'merchant'."

Dianna gasped. "You're a vile, hateful rogue, a despicable snake, a—a— Oh, damn you!" She slapped him as hard as she could, so hard that her wrist stung. "I hate you and wish I'd never, ever met you!"

"And I'd say the same about you, madam!" The mark of her hand burned red on Kit's cheek, and it was all he could do to control his temper. He was tired of her everlasting games, and he refused to play them any longer. He stalked to the cabin door and jerked it open. "There, go! We have no more than a week before we reach land. If you don't wish me to throttle you before then, you will keep to your quarters and out of my sight!"

Dianna was too angry to reply, and with a little roar of frustration, she stamped her foot. She had failed miserably, and she hated to return to the others empty-handed, with no promise of relief to come. Then her gaze caught the tureen that was still half-filled with stew. She grabbed it with both hands and, cradling it to her chest, she raced past Kit and down the companionway.

Dumbstruck, Kit watched her scurry away with her prize. He slammed the door and walked back to the table, staring down at the damp, steamed circle left on the wood by the tureen and considering the maddening contradictions of Dianna Grey.

The morning the *Prosperity* finally reached Saybrook was cold and clear, the sky whipped to a brilliant blue by an icy March wind. As the word spread that their journey was almost over, the passengers rushed to the deck, eager for this first sight of their new homeland. But while everyone around her at the rail chattered excitedly, Dianna's spirits plummeted as the ship rounded Lynde Point and the town itself came into view.

No, she decided, *town* was too grand a word for the forlorn assortment of buildings strung along the waterfront. Houses and businesses alike had a raw, unfinished look, their unpainted clapboard or shingled sides weathered to a silvery gray, their proportions squat and mean. No trees softened their harshness, only mud and dirty snow and wisps of smoke that the wind tore from the chimneys.

Dianna twisted her hands in the worn remains of her cloak and tried to picture herself in such a setting. As a lady, she was both educated and accomplished. She could read and write and cipher, play on the spinet and sing, speak French and a little Italian. But none of that would matter unless the buyer of her indenture was genteel as well, and Saybrook, to her eyes, did not have the look of a genteel place.

She glanced back to where Captain Welles stood by the wheel, and at once felt reassured. He was a good man, if plain-spoken, one she could trust. He had treated her civilly since the moment he'd had the shackles removed, and he had risked the displeasure of his employer to bring the passengers food. He had promised to find her a decent place, and she was confident he would, and she thanked God once again that her future did not depend on a man as unpredictable as Kit Sparhawk.

News of the *Prosperity*'s safe return had raced through Saybrook, and already a crowd was gathering—wives and mothers with new babies, children hopping with excitement, friends and neighbors calling greetings across the water, their words frozen into clouds in the cold air. As soon as the ship bumped alongside the uneven cob dock, the welcomers swarmed on board, the joyful reunions began in earnest. The happiness was infectious, and Dianna couldn't help grinning herself. She had come this far without harm. What worse could lie ahead?

Across the heads of the jostling crowd, she spotted Kit, hatless, his long hair blowing wildly in the wind. Against her will something inside her gave a little lurch. He was laughing, his flashing smile brilliant with the pleasure of homecoming. But his eyes seemed joyless as he scanned the faces around him, and curiously Dianna wondered whose he sought. Then abruptly his grin vanished and his expression grew solemn. Effortlessly he dropped over the side and hurried to meet a young woman with auburn hair who blushed shyly as Kit took both her hands in his. She was pretty, noted Dianna miserably, very pretty, indeed and even the heavy cloak she wore was unable to disguise her obvious pregnancy. Seven months the *Prosperity* had been away, but time enough.

"Ah, so he's found Patience Tucker already," said a sailor softly to his wife. "Poor lass! 'Tis well she'll have Master Sparhawk to watch after her now."

"Not before the young ones, mind," murmured his wife, cocking her head toward the two boys who tugged excitedly at their father's coat. "They'll learn such things soon enough."

The chill that passed through Dianna had nothing to do with the wind. Too well she remembered the scandal when one of her friends had let herself be seduced by a handsome favorite of the Queen's, an earl he was. He'd gotten the girl with child, killed the girl's brother in a duel, and then Dianna's friend had drowned herself. The earl, along with the rest of London society, had merely shrugged it all away as unfortunate unpleasantness and been back again at court the next week as if nothing had happened.

So Kit Sparhawk was kinder than that, but still there seemed no likelihood of him wedding the girl. Perhaps he, too, was already married to another. Dianna watched the pair walk slowly away, her arm in his for support.

Dianna shivered, all pleasure in the morning now gone. What would have become of her if she, too, carried Kit's child? She'd come so close, so dangerously close, to lying with him, Lord help her! She had been weak and Kit had been strong, and his kiss and touch had brought a fire to her blood that she hadn't known existed. She had been willing. He had been the one to stop. Again she heard her uncle's taunting voice and his bitter accusations. New England or old, some things would never change.

For the next week, Dianna continued to live on the *Prosperity,* waiting while Captain Welles sought a buyer for her indenture. From the way he avoided her, she suspected this had not proved as easy as he'd hoped, and she hated not knowing what would come next. But steadfastly she ordered herself not to worry and tried to fight back the insecurity that gnawed at her. She still had the company of the Penhallows, who also remained on board. Soon they would begin their journey westward, by wagon, to their new land.

It was late one afternoon when Dianna and Eunice stood together on the deck, idly tossing biscuit crumbs to make the gulls wheel and dive. Dianna had been careful to choose the larboard side, away from the dock, and away from Kit, who was supervising the men unloading the hold. Every so often she could hear his laughter over Eunice's chatter, and her back would stiffen with irritation. What cause did he have to be so merry? If he was the fine gentleman he pretended to be, he wouldn't be here carousing with common sailors. Why didn't he just go away, so she could forget she'd ever seen him? Crossly she bounced a bread crust off a gull's head, wishing it were Kit's instead.

Suddenly a great clattering on the dock scattered all the gulls into noisy flight, and every man raced across to the starboard side, cheering and waving. Excitedly Eunice hurried to join them, and with an impatient sigh, Dianna followed.

"Oh, lud, ye know who it must be, don't ye, Dianna?" exclaimed Eunice, her eyes round with wonder. "It must be Cap'n Jonathan Sparhawk hisself, what everyone feared were dead!"

Dianna stared down at the man on the back of the black stallion, calling out to the crewmen as he swung his three-cornered hat over his head. He wore a scarlet coat laced with gold, the polished buttons winking in the late afternoon light, and his neckcloth fluttered over his shoulder as he expertly brought the horse to a halt at the water's edge. His clumsiness as he dismounted surprised Dianna, until she saw how he favored his right leg as it touched the ground, and the brass-headed cane he untied from his saddle.

And even if Kit had not leaped at him at once, nearly knocking him sideways with the fierceness of his greeting, Dianna would have known they were brothers. They were too much alike not to be, both pounding each other delightedly on the back, grinning and howling like madmen. Jonathan stood a shade shorter and his hair was black as the stallion's coat, but he had the same green eyes as Kit, the same powerful build and easy physical confidence. And, decided Dianna instantly, he had the same damnable charm.

"What a sight they be," Eunice said with a sigh, "each one handsomer than th' other! To think there be two such, oh!"

"And twice the trouble to bedevil womankind," said Dianna tartly. Yet her eyes still lingered on the brothers, just as Jonathan, over the first flush of reunion with Kit, had instinctively turned to find the two young women watching from the rail.

"By all that's holy, Kit, you've women in my sweet *Prosperity!*" he exclaimed with relish. "Delectable ones, too, from the look of them. And here I pitied you old Abraham's company!"

Kit scowled and made a disgusted noise deep in his throat. "The one's a silly little maid with her whole clacking family behind her, but the other's worse trouble by far." Briefly he recounted Dianna's past, carefully omitting himself.

"A rogue gentlewoman!" Jonathan's eyebrows rose suggestively. "She's still a plump enough little chick with that cloud of golden hair."

"Nay, Jon," said Kit too quickly. "It's the beauty, the dark-haired one."

Jonathan scratched his jaw, considering. He had spent enough nights wenching side by side with his brother to know the scrawny little creature with the thatch of eyebrows was not to Kit's usual taste, nor had his explanation rung quite true. "So Abraham expects to get ten guineas for her. She doesn't look worth half that to me, but I'll buy her for you if you wish." He grinned wolfishly. "For those cold nights at Plumstead."

"Toss your gold in the river before you spend it on her!" exclaimed Kit, appalled at the idea. "I'd not have the little baggage within twenty miles of Plumstead!"

Kit saw the gleam in his brother's eye and realized he'd tipped his hand. Blast the girl for showing her face to Jonathan! Tonight, in some tavern, he'd likely spill the whole sorry tale, and Jonathan, the cocksure little whelp, would just as likely gloat and taunt him for being an old, worn-out fool.

But then he recalled how close he'd come to losing Jonathan's taunts forever. For the first time, Kit noticed how heavily his brother leaned on his cane, the strain on the edge of his smile, and he realized just how much pain Jonathan's bravura entrance on horseback had cost him. He swung his arm around Jonathan's shoulder, offering support, and was both surprised and concerned by how readily his brother leaned into him.

"Come along, Jon," he said gruffly. "We've much to say, you and I, and there's far warmer places to say it."

But first Jonathan looked back to the ship, and, with a grand flourish, doffed his hat to the two girls. "Ten guineas," he said slyly to Kit, "and she's all yours. Call her my gift to you."

Eunice giggled into her hand at the attention, but Dianna wished it had been Kit, not his brother, who had turned back. With Jonathan Sparhawk now here to oversee the *Prosperity,* there would be no need for Kit to remain. This, then, could be the last she ever saw of him....

"Dianna Grey!" Captain Welles's voice was sharp, and Dianna guiltily wondered how many times he'd called her before she noticed. "Come, girl, I haven't all day."

There was a stranger beside the captain, and the frank appraisal the man gave Dianna made her blush. He wore a large-brimmed hat with a beaded band, a long black coat like a parson's and greasy leather leggings. He was not tall, but stocky, his legs bowed outward, and although his hair was wispy and white, Dianna could not guess his age. The bones of his face seemed to almost jut through his leathery skin, and Dianna feared the man himself would be equally sharp, with no softness or gentleness, no humor in him anywhere.

"Stop gawking like a lackwit, girl," growled Captain Welles impatiently. "You won't favor yourself keeping your new master a-waiting."

Chapter Six

Dianna sat on the deck of the sloop *Tiger,* her back braced against the hatch cover and sheltered from the wind. She had been there since they had left Saybrook that morning, preferring the open air to the small, stuffy cabin below and the seemingly endless dice game her new master had begun with the two other passengers. Every so often she heard Asa Wing's voice rise above the others, and she wondered if he had won or lost.

The only thing she now knew of the man was that he liked gaming; he had volunteered nothing else about himself or their destination. She didn't even know why he had bought her indenture in the first place. He was clearly not accustomed to servants, nor did he seem interested in her in the lustful way her uncle had been. In fact, he really didn't seem interested in her at all.

She rested her head on her arms. She hated the feeling of helplessness, the way a total stranger now controlled her life for the next seven years. *Seven years!* She would be thirty then, an ancient crone, too old by far for any husband. When her father had lived, he had been family enough, but after two months with the Penhallows, she imagined herself more and more with a home of her own and babies and a husband that, to her dismay, always looked like Kit Sparhawk.

She sighed and brushed her hair back from her face. She had never been in love, but she realized how close she'd come to it with Kit. She tried hard to forget his unpredictable kindness and his smile and the way his kiss had left her breathless and eager, and tried to remember instead how he always believed the worst of her, how he'd played along with her uncle, and how he'd tried to starve them all on the *Prosperity*. And, too, she couldn't forget the auburn-haired girl who'd met him at Saybrook.

No, it was better like this, better to never see Kit again. There were other men as handsome in the world, and others who might come to love and cherish her in a way Kit Sparhawk never would.

She stared out over the water. The river had grown narrower, and shallower, too. The rippled surface had changed from green to silver, and the tang of the ocean faded as salt water gave way to fresh. The landscape was changing as well. First the town had been replaced by neat farms, barns and houses centered in snow-dappled fields. Then had come the wild meadows, where big trees had long ago been cut for timber and firewood and where new saplings grew brave and leggy among the stumps. But now, as the sun dropped low, there seemed nothing but old snow and rocks and trees, endless trees, their dark boughs hanging over the river and brushing against the sloop's mast.

"Here, girl, you'd best eat." Startled, Dianna looked up as Asa squatted beside her and handed her a chunk of the coarse bread he was eating. He wore soft-soled shoes, sewn of leather, that had made his footsteps silent, and the ease with which he could appear without warning unsettled her.

Chewing, he flipped up one corner of her cloak and fingered the fur lining. "What d'ye Londoners pay for a cloak like this?"

"I don't recall exactly," said Dianna. "Seven, perhaps eight guineas. My father bought it for me."

Asa grunted with disbelief. "Mighty dear for rabbit."

"Nay, it's beaver. Madame du Paigne would not have sold rabbit in her shop."

"Nay, girl, 'tis rabbit," he countered amiably, unimpressed by Madame du Paigne or her shop. "Oh, it's been dyed an' clipped to look fair, but them pelts grew up by hoppin', not swimmin'."

He uncorked a small earthenware jug and tipped it back. When he was finished drinking, he sighed contentedly, wiped the jug's neck with his thumb and offered the jug to Dianna. She shook her head, but decided instead to take advantage of his good humor. He must, she thought, have been the winner in the game below.

"Where are we bound?" she asked.

"Wickhamton."

He might have said the moon for all that meant to her. "Is that where you live?"

"Near enough. Though the house be Mercy's now."

"Is Mercy your wife?"

"Nay. *That* needle-tongued article left so long past I disremember her face. But I miss our lad," he said sadly. "Aye, Tom I miss."

He recorked the jug and pointed ahead to where the river curved. High on the spit of land stood a square log building. "We'll sleep at Brockton's ordinary this night."

There was no dock, and Dianna wondered if she'd be expected to wade ashore through the icy water, or worse yet, be carried. As the sloop hove too close to the bank, one of the crewmen swung a long, thin board from the sloop's side to the riverbank to serve as a gangplank. Asa went first, and quickly Dianna followed—too quickly. To her surprise, the plank still bounced up and down from the weight of his footsteps, tossing her upward. Instinctively she outstretched her arms for balance like a ropewalker and kept her eyes straight ahead. When she reached the shore, the sailors laughed raucously behind her, and she knew then they'd expected her to tumble off. So much for *their* fun, she thought crossly, and trotted after Asa.

She had not realized how cold she'd become until she stepped inside the ordinary and felt the welcoming warmth from the hearth. There was only the one room, the walls unpeeled logs and the floor packed earth. Five men, dressed piecemeal much like Asa, sprawled on benches around a trestle table, eating and drinking with their hats still on. Before the hearth, a haughty black woman with notched earlobes stirred her kettles, and a man leaned against the wall, smok-

ing a Dutch clay pipe. Every last one of them turned
to stare at Dianna.

"Ye be a mite old to start up with a trollop, Wing,"
said the man with the pipe, speaking what the others
were all thinking. "How'd you coax her t'come with
yer sorry old carcass?"

Asa rested his hand on Dianna's shoulder. "Keep
yer foul thoughts to yerself, Brockton. This be a lady,
not a trollop, and she's come to help me wit' Mercy.
Stay close to me, Annie," he said stoutly, "and these
rogues will show ye no mischief."

It was the first time anyone had shortened Dianna's name to Annie and the first time Asa had called
her anything more than "girl." Dianna stared up at
him in wonder. He was defending her honor. There
was no other way of looking at it. He believed her a
lady, and even here in this rough inn in the wilderness, he was insisting on her being treated like one.
The questions of what her tasks would be or who
Mercy was, seemed suddenly insignificant. She would
have her new start after all. Asa's unexpected gesture
warmed her more than the fire, and she couldn't help
smiling shyly as she slid onto the bench beside him for
supper.

They ate beans steeped in molasses and laced with
salt pork, and drank cider that was thick and sweet.
When at last the wooden trenchers were cleared away
and the table and benches pushed back, each man
wrapped himself in his blanket or coat and lay down
on the dirt floor. Reluctantly Dianna joined them,
doubting she'd sleep at all among the snoring and
wheezing bodies.

But almost at once the black woman was shaking her awake, and Dianna gulped down her breakfast as she hurried to meet Asa. She found him by the river, loading his bundled belongings into a long, bark canoe. With him was a wiry young man with waist-length hair like cornsilk and pale eyes that were oddly blank.

"We'll make our own course from here," explained Asa. "I've stops to make along the way, but we should reach Wickhamton in three days' time. This 'ere be Jeremiah, and he'll paddle stern."

The pale young man stared at Dianna, but did not return her smile, and inwardly she shivered at the emptiness of his expression.

"Y'must not mind Jeremiah," said Asa. "He's not full right with his thoughts. When he was a lad, the Abenakis took him captive. Six years he lived with 'em, until his people finally paid the ransom. More red than white he was by then, an' kind of daft in th' head. But he's good with a paddle an' don't talk overmuch."

"How terrible," murmured Dianna, but she still found Jeremiah's staring eyes disturbing. "Thank God the Indians are gone now."

Asa snorted. "That's what ye Londoners may believe, but here, we know otherwise. Oh, Indians don't go in fer showin' their faces unless they've a reason, an' these days, they've kept to themselves, mostly, 'cepting for all that trouble at Deerfield, of course. Sorry sad business, that. But there be good Indians an' bad, same as white folk, an' if I knew for certain what riled 'em, I'd be sittin' in Boston with the other peri-wig-lords.''

''Are there Indians at Wickhamton?''

Asa shrugged nonchalantly. ''Nay, not t'bring ye any grief. I'd worry on other things afore Indians, like bears an' snakes an' wildcats an' such.'' He fastened the last bundle in place with rawhide straps. ''Now get ye in, Mistress Annie, else we stand here a-jawin' 'til midsummer.''

Not at all reassured, Dianna climbed into the center of the canoe. Of course, she'd read about Indi-ans—Asa was right about Londoners loving every thrilling story about dangerous savages in the wilder-ness, especially those vanquished by true-hearted Englishmen—but she hadn't dreamed they'd be part of her new home, any more than she'd considered the string of wild animals he'd named. Now behind every tree or rock, she was convinced she saw an Indian lurking, or a bear at the very least, and she was re-lieved when Jeremiah shoved the canoe into the water and they floated gently into the river.

As Asa promised, they reached their destination after three days of travelling. At nightfall, they pulled the canoe onto the bank as they had the two previous nights, but this time Asa and Dianna left Jeremiah behind and headed off into the woods. After months of inactivity, Dianna was in no condition to keep pace with Asa, and even though he willingly paused for her to rest, she was out of breath and the stitch in her side refused to go away. Although it was April, snow still covered most of the ground and ice soon packed into

Dianna's shoes until her feet were numb from the cold. She had no idea how long or how far they trudged through the moonlit forest, and it seemed as if they had crisscrossed the same piece of ground over and over. She was close to weeping from cold and weariness when Asa stopped and pointed to a clearing ahead.

"We're here at last, Annie," he said happily. "You'll take to little Mercy, I know it. Ye both be cut from th' same cloth."

Yet even by moonlight, the house in the clearing was not what Dianna had expected. It was small, very small, with a peaked roof that slanted lower over the back. The clapboarding was unpainted and worn dark, and the windows were tiny casements of oiled paper, not glass. There were no shutters or trimmings, no decoration at all beyond a crude border of nailheads hammered into the massive plank door.

Eagerly Asa hurried to the house, and pulled open the rope latch. "Mercy, child, come and give yer old grandfer a kiss!" he called. "I'm happy ye not be abed yet, for I've someone for ye to meet, someone t'help ye wit' the house."

"But I don't need any help, Grandfer!" cried a small, anguished voice. The only light in the room came from the last embers of the hearth fire, and by it Dianna could finally make out Mercy herself. She had plump cheeks and a turned-up nose and dark hair that straggled from beneath her linen cap. A knitted woolen tippet was tied over her shoulders and around her narrow waist, and her hands, in fingerless mitts, twisted nervously in her apron. She looked to be six, perhaps seven, and Dianna was shocked that a child so young had been left alone. No wonder she seemed frightened! "If you'd only let me stay at Plumstead—"

"Nay, Mercy, an' that's an end to it!" said Asa sharply, and his granddaughter's shoulders sagged unhappily. Huddled in the half-light, she looked as lonely and forlorn as Dianna had often felt herself, and her heart went out to the waifish child.

"Mercy, my name is Dianna, Dianna Grey," she said softly, holding her hand out in greeting. "I hope we might be friends, you and I—"

But Mercy cut her off, shaking her head fiercely. "Nay, I want none of ye, mind?" Her words strangled on the sob in her throat. "None of ye at all!" With her head down, she bolted past them and out the door.

Dianna called her name and began to follow, but Asa held her back and gently closed the door instead. "She'll be back in her own time. She'll be off to weep among th' beasts in th' barn, an' she'll come to no harm." Sighing, he prodded fresh life into the dying fire and sat heavily on the three-legged stool Mercy had fled.

"But where are her parents? Surely a girl her age—"

"Dead, the pair o' them, not twelve months past, of a putrid quinsey," said Asa. "My lad, Tom, an' his wife, Lucy. Poor Mercy! She cannot accept it as God's will that she be spared an' her parents taken, an' she grieves more than is right for a young one. Y'see now why she needs ye."

No wonder she had felt a bond to the girl, thought Dianna sadly. "And this place she spoke of, Plumstead . . . ?"

"Ah, that be the colonel's great fine house." Asa's voice hardened. "Like a lord he be in these parts, that man, an' because my Tom called him friend, he strives to take Mercy from me. Claims he could do better by the girl. Well, that may be, but Mercy's all th' blood kin I've left in this world, an' kin should stay wit' kin, t'my mind."

Dianna rubbed her arms and stared at the closed door. "Are you sure we shouldn't go after her? It's a cold night."

Asa shook his head. "Nay, it's best to let her sort it out herself. She'll come in when she be ready." He rose stiffly from the stool. "Now I'll show ye where you're t'sleep, up here in the loft."

But tired as she was, Dianna did not sleep until she heard Mercy come inside. Quietly the girl refastened the latch and, creeping past her snoring grandfather, joined Dianna in the overhead loft. From her breathing, Dianna was certain the girl did not sleep, either, but she respected her silence and the privacy of her grief. Cut from the same cloth they most definitely were.

Chapter Seven

Dianna intended to rise early the next morning and have breakfast waiting on the table for Asa and Mercy. But the sun was well up by the time she awoke, and ruefully she realized the other two were already gone from the house. After three months of sleeping on floors or decks, one night in a bed, albeit one with rope springs and a mattress stuffed with rustling corn husks, had reduced her to a lazy sluggard.

She washed quickly in a bucket of water by the ladder, hoping that Asa hadn't brought it especially from the well for her, and neatly braided her hair the way Eunice had taught her on the *Prosperity*. Then came the question of what to wear. With her London gown little more than rags, Asa had told her to take what she needed from the chest of clothing in the loft. First came a bleached linen shift, the soft, clean fabric almost unbelievably luxurious against her skin. Over that she put a dark red kersey skirt and a bodice of blue linsey-woolsey. She fumbled awkwardly to thread and tie the laces behind her back and cursed the lifetime of pampering lady's maids that had made her embarrassingly clumsy at dressing herself. Finally she tied on an apron and backed down the loft's ladder to the one large room below that served as kitchen, keeping room and parlor.

Hands on her hips, she surveyed her new domain and considered where to begin with breakfast. That she had absolutely no experience cooking did not faze her; it could not be so very difficult, given some of the thick-witted cooks she'd met in her father's houses. She decided to try eggs. All men liked eggs for breakfast, and there was a large basket of them on the table. But first she must build up the fire, and she went outdoors in search of firewood.

The woodpile was not far from the house, and for good measure she chose the largest log from the top, staggering with it in her arms as she returned to the house. At the doorway she spotted Mercy, trudging from the barn with a bucket of milk.

"Good morning!" called Dianna cheerfully. "It's a fine day, isn't it?"

Stunned, Mercy's face went white as she studied Dianna from head to foot. "You're not my mother," she said as she backed away, the milk sloshing from the bucket over her clogs. "Ye may take her place and her clothes, but you're not her and ye never will be!"

"Mercy, wait, please!" But Mercy had already retreated to the cowshed, leaving a trail of spilt milk on the bare ground. Of course, the girl would be upset to see her dressed like her mother; Dianna blamed herself for not being more considerate. After breakfast she would go and set things right with Mercy. With a sigh, she dropped the snow-covered log onto the banked embers of last night's fire, prodded the ashes for a spark and turned her attention to the eggs.

With both hands she lifted a heavy iron skillet onto the table and cracked an egg on the side. The eggshell burst with the impact, and its contents splattered down Dianna's clean apron and onto the floor, white and yolk slipping between the floorboards. The next egg made it into the skillet, but so did its broken shell, and the next three fared no better. As carefully as Dianna tried to pick out the bits of shell, the pieces only slid farther from her fingers into the slippery mess in the skillet. She frowned, concentrating, and not until her eyes stung and she was coughing did she realize the house was filled with smoke. The fire, something was wrong with the fire, and she turned toward where she thought it was. But there was only more smoke, thick and acrid and blinding her, choking her. Panicking, she tripped and stumbled to her knees and groped across the floor.

Then suddenly she felt an arm circling her waist and pulling her from the smoke, a masculine arm that, even as she coughed, she knew was too strong and muscled to belong to Asa. The man was carrying her now, out the door and to the fresh air, murmuring odd bits of nonsense to comfort her. He propped her up against the well as she struggled to get her breath.

Then Kit Sparhawk sat back on his heels and swore, long and colorfully, at the woman he thought he'd never see again. She was garbed simply now, like any decent Yankee goodwife, though covered with soot and her eyes red-rimmed from the smoke. But even before he'd seen her face he had recognized her at once from the way her small body had filled his arms, and the dismay he'd felt had been tempered by a fierce joy at finding her again—a joy that angered him for being both unreasonable and irrational.

Coughing, Dianna could only stare at him in return with equal dismay. She had believed him left behind with the *Prosperity* in Saybrook, yet here he was, every bit as handsome as she remembered, and every bit as angry with her, too. He was, she decided, dressed quite outlandishly. Gone was his English gentleman's suit. In its place was a coarse linen hunting shirt, the yoke and collar elaborately fringed to emphasize the width of his shoulders, and a bright woven sash knotted around his waist. He wore deerskin leggings, not breeches, the soft leather straining across the muscles in his thighs as he knelt, and on his bare feet were moccasins. A curved powder horn with pewter tips swung from his neck, along with a fringed leather bag for rifle balls, and tucked into his sash was a long knife with a stag-horn hilt. Yet it all suited him, and with his long, sun-streaked hair and his cat's green eyes, he looked like a savage himself.

"Dianna Grey," he said at last. "What in God's holy name are you doing here?"

Dianna's lungs were still too choked to reply, but Mercy, standing close to Kit, was quick to answer for her. "Grandfer says she's to watch o'er me, but I ask ye, who's to watch o'er her? She don't even know wet wood from dry, nor split from a blessed log. Faith, she near smoked us like a very ham in our own house!"

Humiliated, Dianna saw the wretched log still smoking beside the door where Kit had tossed it, and she prayed he hadn't seen the mess she'd made of the eggs, as well.

Kit stood, wiping the soot from his hands with a red handkerchief. "You'd best come back with me. I can't leave you here, not until your house has a chance to air. Asa will guess where you are." He smoothed his hair back from his brow, and settling a broad-brimmed beaver hat on his head, he gazed contemptuously at Dianna. "Are you well enough to ride?"

Dianna nodded. She should thank him for rescuing her, but the words stuck stubbornly in her throat. If he'd known it was she in the house, he probably wouldn't have bothered. "How should I know the log would smoke?"

"Because any child in these parts should, and would, or risk killing himself with stupidity like you very nearly did." He clicked his tongue, and a black stallion like the one Dianna had seen his brother ride into Saybrook came to him and nuzzled his shoulder affectionately. He had been hunting; his rifle and three dead partridges hung from the saddle. "Though ladies, I suppose, do not dirty their hands with such tasks."

"Lady!" exclaimed Mercy, her turned-up nose turned even higher. "She looks like no lady I've ever seen!"

"Oh, aye, Mercy Wing, and you've seen so many to judge," said Kit dryly. "Don't be fooled by how she looks now. She's more things than you've ever dreamed."

Mercy frowned and sucked in her lower lip, considering. "How d'ye know her, Kit?"

"I know Master Sparhawk from London," answered Dianna, tired of being discussed as if she wasn't there. "And don't be impertinent, Mercy. He's your elder, and you call him Master Sparhawk."

Mercy's frown deepened. "Kit's my friend," she said stubbornly, "and I'll call him Kit."

"Dianna's right, Mercy," said Kit, laughing. He caught the little girl's hands and lifted her, giggling, high into the air. With each word he pretended to drop her, and she shrieked with delighted excitement. "You're the most impertinent little baggage in this entire colony, and you'll never be a lady yourself until you learn some manners! Now up with you!"

Lightly, he boosted the girl up onto the horse and turned expectantly to Dianna.

"Where will you ride?" she demanded crossly. The silly play between the two had made her feel even more like an outsider.

"Why, on Thunder, of course. He'll scarce notice a mite like you in front of me." Slowly he smiled, smug and superior. "Unless you're afraid."

Exasperated, Dianna stepped closer to him, her hands on her hips. "By now, Master Sparhawk, you should well know I am not afraid of you or anything to do with you. But I don't see what good will come of traipsing off with you God knows where just because you wish it."

Kit toyed with the reins in his hands, and ever so slightly, his smile widened. "Mercy wants to come with me. She's had no breakfast and knows she'll eat well at my house. You are, nominally at least, her caretaker. You can come with her and with me, or you can remain here and answer to Asa as to why you abandoned your charge.''

Dianna hated to admit that Kit was right, though, of course, damn him, he was. She had already turned the house into a smoky disaster. What would Asa think if she let his granddaughter run off without her, as well? In frustration she stamped her foot. "Well, then, let's be off. I've no— *Oh!*''

With his hands on her waist, Kit picked her up as easily as a doll and sat her on the horse behind Mercy. In another moment he had swung himself into the saddle, and with his arms circling around them both, he urged the big horse forward. Dianna fell back against Kit's chest; there was no way to avoid it. Despite the layers of clothing between them, she was aware of the warmth of his body touching hers, the strength of his thighs beneath her own as he guided the horse. Sternly she reminded herself that Mercy was her responsibility, and she clasped her arms around the little girl's waist for safekeeping. Better to think of Mercy than of how her own body seemed determined to slide against Kit's. Lord help her, how far *was* his house?

But for Kit, who knew the distance was short, the ride seemed interminable. He was all too aware of the soft curve of her hip and bottom pressed against him, and her wriggling as she tried to ease away from him only made matters worse. He recalled how sweet her mouth had been to kiss and how passionately she had responded to him, and he almost groaned aloud at the memory. Beneath his nose her hair smelled smoky, plaited into a thick, tight braid. How he'd like to set

it free and bury his face in the silkiness as he kissed her
lips, her throat, her breasts—

"There be Plumstead now!" cried Mercy excitedly.

Sitting high on the crest of a hill, the house itself was
old-fashioned by English standards, a bit rough-hewn
in its lines, with sharply peaked gables and diamond-
paned windows. The second story overhung the first,
and elaborately carved pendants hung at the corners
like giant water drops. From the center of the shingled roof rose a massive chimney, shaped and angled
like a castle's tower, the pink brick in contrast to the
dark, weathered clapboarding below. But in this setting, on land so recently claimed from the forest, the
house seemed exactly right. Dianna could imagine it
in the summer, when the hill that rolled down to the
small river would be green and the two huge beech
trees would shade the twin benches by the front doorway. Plumstead: Kit Sparhawk's home, and the home
of the man who wished to steal Mercy away from her
grandfather.

"Follow the child," Kit said to Dianna as Mercy
scrambled off the horse and raced for the back door.
"She knows today's baking day, and she'll lead you
straight to Hester and the sweetbuns."

Self-consciously Dianna untangled herself from Kit
and slid off the horse before he could help her. She
began toward the house, then paused. "Why do you
wish to take Mercy from Asa?" she asked curiously.
"That you are fond of the girl is clear, but he is her
grandfather and he loves her."

She was startled by how quickly Kit's expression
grew hard as flint. "You have been among us but one

day," he said sharply. "Don't be so quick to judge matters you can't understand." He jerked the horse's head toward the barn and left her alone and puzzled.

"Welcome to Plumstead, mistress!" called a merry female voice, and in the kitchen doorway stood a tall, angular woman wiping her hands in her apron, squinting into the sun as she smiled at Dianna. "I'm Hester, Hester Holcomb, an' y'must be Asa's new servant, Dianna! Mercy's already told me ye had a smidge o' trouble with th' hearth. No matter, I say. Ever'one's different. Ye best come get yerself tidied, now, an' have some tea an' cookies."

Shyly, Dianna followed Hester into the house. The Plumstead kitchen was huge, running almost the entire length of the house, and the plaster above the wainscotting was painted golden yellow. Iron skillets and kettles, marsh-willow baskets and bundles of dried herbs hung from the rafters overhead. Three dozen loaves of new bread were laid out to cool on the long table, and the sweet fragrance of baking filled the room. There was no sign of Mercy, and in a way, Dianna was glad. Responsibility or no, she'd had quite enough of the girl this morning.

She watched as Hester deftly used a long-handled peel to shove a pan of cookies into the oven behind the hearth. "Are you Master Sparhawk's cook?"

"His cook, his housekeeper, his laundress, his chambermaid an' whatever else he needs." Hester swung the iron door of the oven shut. "With only Kit, Plumstead don't need more'n me. Not like th' days when there were six Sparhawk children, all runnin' wild an' underfoot."

"Is that why he likes having Mercy here?"

"I warrant so, aye." The woman looked away, and her answer had a forced heartiness that made Dianna wonder what she hid.

"Will Kit—I mean, Master Sparhawk—eat all this himself?"

Hester laughed. "Nay, 'tis just for th' dinners for th' farm workers. Kit believes a man gives better work when his belly's full. He be a good master that way, better'n most. But tell me of London! It's been forty years since I left, an' neither Jonathan nor Kit be much for recalling how th' ladies be dressin' their hair."

Dianna perched on the edge of a tall stool and scrubbed at her face with a towel. "Of course, I can tell you such things, if you wish, Hester, but this morning I'd rather speak of useful things—all the things I can't do and you can."

Now that she'd begun, the words tumbled out, and she balled the towel up in her fist. "I can't cook or bake or make a fire or *anything!* I don't even know how to get water from the well! Mercy's right. She'd be better off looking after me, for all the good I can do her!"

"Ah, now, 'tis only because you've never had t'make do, not because y'can't." Hester patted her shoulder, leaving a floury white handprint on Dianna's sooty bodice. "Ye be clever enough. I can see that. Y'only need someone t'show ye how."

"Then, please, please, I beg you, Hester, teach me how!" cried Dianna eagerly. "Teach me now, this morning, how to cook and keep a house and—"

Hester laughed again, deep in her chest. "Oh, lass, I'll be needing more'n a morning to learn you all that! I'll send ye home today with enough t'keep Mercy an' Asa from complaining. Tomorrow's the Sabbath, an' no work's done, but ye come back with Mercy on Monday, an' I'll begin your schooling proper. We'll make a huswife from ye yet!"

But Dianna's enthusiasm faded. "I'm sorry, Hester, but I don't believe your master would want me back in his home. He—he doesn't care for me."

Hester rolled her eyes. "I'd like t'see the time when Kit Sparhawk turns a pretty young lass like ye out o' Plumstead!"

"Nay, truly, he hates me. I sailed from England on the *Prosperity*—"

"On the *Prosperity!* Don't mark a single word Kit said on *that* ill-starred venture!" exclaimed Hester warmly. "Why, ye be lucky ye weren't starved down t'your bones by that old skinflint Welles, th' devil claim his greedy soul! Fancy him trying t'blame it on Kit, too, as if the Sparhawks haven't always been known for their charity t'others! Keeping back food from children—why, that near broke Kit's heart, he's so besotted with th' little creatures."

Dianna listened in confused silence. It had been Captain Welles, not Kit, who had brought the food to the passengers, yet Hester would know the two men far better than she. Loud voices outside interrupted her thoughts, and both she and Hester hurried to the window.

"I'll see t'my own granddaughter, Sparhawk!" Asa was shouting angrily. He had jerked off his hat and was shaking it for emphasis. "She don't belong to ye, mind? Ye can't make Mercy take th' place o' the one that be lost!"

On his way from the stables when he'd met Asa, Kit held his long-barreled rifle in one hand and the string of bloody partridges in the other, and even from the window Dianna could see the anger in his green eyes. "You're a trapper and a trader, Wing. You've no place in your life for a child. You can't go off with Jeremiah and leave Mercy behind in that house alone!"

"But I'm telling ye, she won't be alone!" insisted Asa. "That's why I brought Annie back from Saybrook!"

"Worse than alone, then! Did Welles tell you why she's here? What kind of woman she is?" Dianna felt her face grow warm. Better he should have left her to die in the smoke than to have to suffer through this!

"I'll not hear you speakin' ill of Annie! She seems a good lass t'me, an' if she's made mistakes, she's a right t'leave them behind."

Kit slammed the stock of his rifle down on the ground. "But to leave a sweet child like Mercy in the care of an ignorant hussy like Dianna Grey—"

It was too much for Dianna. She charged past Hester and out the door, and with both hands shoved into Kit's chest as hard as she could. "I am neither ignorant nor a hussy, you great mindless bully, and—"

But before she could finish, Asa's open palm caught her square on the jaw. Off balance, she tumbled backward onto the ground. She rolled over quickly, ready to fly at Asa now, but the shocked look on his face stopped her.

"Don't ever shame me like that again, Annie," he said, his voice shaking, almost pleading. "Master Sparhawk be a selectman an' colonel of the militia an' the magistrate, too, an' yet in your temper, ye struck him. Annie, he could have ye whipped in Wickhamton for less!"

He glanced briefly at Kit, then down at the ground. "The lass meant no harm, Master Sparhawk, an' I'll see she'll not do it again," he said contritely. "Now fetch Mercy, Annie, an' we'd best go home."

It was all Kit could do not to pick Dianna up out of the dirt himself. He had never hit a woman, nor would he ever order one whipped, despite what that old fool Wing had said. She looked so small and pitiful, rubbing the dirt from her hands as she slowly rose to her feet, that he instantly regretted what he'd said about her. No, not what he'd said, for that was the truth. But regretted that she'd overheard him. He wished he could let her leave her mistakes behind and begin all over with her, as he would with any other woman he might meet. But that meant wishing away the past, and not even the Sparhawks had the power to do that.

Drawn by the noise, Mercy came behind him, her small hand clutching the hem of his shirt. For one bittersweet moment, Kit let himself imagine it was his sister Tamsin there instead, giggling, counting on him to rescue her again from whatever mischief she'd started. But he hadn't rescued her when she'd needed him most, and she'd been only seven then, Mercy's age.

With measured carefulness, Dianna smoothed back her hair and brushed the new dirt from the fall off her sooty apron. Only then did she dare to meet Kit's eyes. But instead of the smug satisfaction she'd dreaded to find on his handsome face, there was nothing. His thoughts were clearly a thousand miles away, and she felt his disinterest more sharply than the contempt she'd been prepared for. It hurt her feelings, but more than that, it hurt the one thing she still clung to most: her pride.

She would adapt, and she would learn what they knew. She would survive. She would prove to them all that Lady Dianna Grey could be as clever, as resourceful, as any Yankee woman.

And she would make certain that Kit Sparhawk could never again call her an ignorant hussy.

Chapter Eight

"You will pay for this, little brother," said Kit in exasperation as he climbed down from Thunder's back, "and I'll make certain that you'll pay in blood."

But Jonathan only laughed. "After that debacle with little lost Lady Grey, I thought you'd welcome the chance to restore your confidence with the fair sex. Consider this my last gift to you before I sail. Though you're not being particularly grateful."

"I'm feeling ambushed, that's why," said Kit glumly, wishing he'd told his brother last night that Dianna Grey was now anything but lost. He tied their two horses to one of the rings fastened to the oak tree on the green, then resettled his hat, the dark red plume fluttering in the breeze. "To bring Constance here to Wickhamton, to the meetinghouse on the Sabbath, for God's sake!"

Jonathan shrugged and brushed a nonexistent speck of dust from his coat. "I merely served as the lady's escort from New London so that she might visit her aunt."

"So she might visit herself on me like a plague is more the truth," grumbled Kit. "Well, let's get on with it, or she'll talk the ears off Dr. Manning."

They walked slowly toward the meeting house, Kit measuring his steps to match his brother's limp and in no hurry to reach the young woman waving madly from the porch. She was dressed more for a ball than Sabbath services, her purple, quilted cloak turned back to show a yellow satin gown cut far too low to be appropriate, and the way she was shrieking his name set his teeth on edge. Oh, she was pretty enough with her golden curls and pert little nose, but to have her here, in his own town, where he couldn't avoid her chattering and her husband-hunting tactics, was almost enough to make him join Jonathan on the *Prosperity*.

Inside the meeting house, Dianna sat alone on one of the back benches reserved for servants. Neither she nor her father had been much for church-going, but Asa had been adamant about her bringing Mercy to Sabbath services, though, Dianna noticed, he showed no interest in going himself. Still, the morning had dawned sunny and with the first warm promise of spring, and Dianna was eager to see Wickhamton, at three miles away the nearest town. Even Mercy had seemed less hostile, though she had been quick enough to abandon Dianna to her place with the servants while she joined another family closer to the front.

Dianna watched as the congregation gradually straggled in, hoping Hester would come and join her. Asa had made the service sound like a grim, serious affair, but at least beforehand people were whispering and smiling among themselves, and Dianna wished Hester were here to identify everyone and perhaps introduce her. So far she had received only nods and curious stares in response to her shy smiles, and when, at last, another young woman came to sit beside her, she eagerly made room.

The newcomer introduced herself as Ruth and made a great show of arranging her skirts neatly on the bench on either side of her. "I don't know how my mistress thinks she'd fare in a forsaken place like this," she sniffed. "She'd perish, she would! Our meeting house in New London's ten times finer than this, with silver candlesticks an' carving on th' pulpit!"

True, the Wickhamton meeting house was plain, the walls simply whitewashed and the benches pegged together from pine. There were no statues and no stained glass, none of the rich cushions for kneeling or embroidered hangings that Dianna remembered from the churches in London. But she doubted the New London meeting house was so much grander that Ruth had reason to complain, and, besides, Dianna liked the building's simplicity, much as she liked Plumstead's and much, too, as she already disliked Ruth. "You are visiting?"

"My mistress be here by th' especial invitation of a certain gentleman," said Ruth archly. "Though, of course, as is proper, she stays wit' her aunt, Madame Bass."

Before Dianna could ask the man's name, Ruth leaned forward excitedly. "Oh, there they be now! Did ye ever see a more handsome couple?"

Dianna looked, and her heart sank. Walking proudly to the first bench was Kit, his dark green velvet coat the ideal color for his eyes, the white linen of his shirt in striking contrast to his sun-browned face. No other man there could even come close to him, decided Dianna sadly, except perhaps Jonathan, though Dianna found his darker coloring less appealing than Kit's gold.

But while under one arm Kit carried a wide-brimmed beaver hat with a plume, tucked beneath the other was the hand of a young woman every bit as fair as himself. She was elegantly tall, her movements fashionably languid. Her blond hair was artfully dressed in a tumble of curls, crowned by a tiny lace cap, and her skin was pale and perfect. As Kit stepped to one side to let her pass, she smiled brilliantly at him and boldly brushed her skirts across his legs as she moved by him.

"That be my mistress, Constance Lindsey," whispered Ruth importantly. "Don't that gown become her? It's in the latest fashion at court."

"Nay, it's not," Dianna whispered back. It was small of her, she knew, but she couldn't help herself. "No one's worn turned-back petticoats for at least three seasons. I'm new arrived from London myself," she added hastily as Ruth eyed her with suspicion.

"Well, no matter, it does become her," said Ruth firmly. "And when she marries Master Sparhawk, then he can take her to London an' she can see for herself. Master Sparhawk be rich enough t'give her whatever she fancies."

Dianna tried to keep her whispered voice level. "They are betrothed?"

Ruth tossed her head. "Well, nay, not yet, but they will be before she goes back to New London." Behind them an older woman shushed Ruth loudly, and Dianna realized that, while they'd been whispering, the service had begun. She bowed her head with the others, glad no one could see the unhappiness she knew clouded her face.

Miserably she pictured herself as she must look in Lucy Wing's worn grey linsey-woolsey, her hair braided beneath a plain white cap. Her hands were red and rough from the cold, and when she'd caught sight of her reflection this morning in a polished pewter bowl, she had been shocked by how pale and thin her face had become. She had never been a beauty like Constance Lindsey, but, oh, how she wished Kit had seen her, just once, before her father's death, when she had been plump and merry and beautifully dressed!

Trapped. That was how Kit felt. Trapped, with Constance pressing into him as she pretended to study her prayer book. At least she held it right side up; he doubted she was smart enough to know the difference. He glanced down at her half-naked breasts, and she simpered slyly back at him. He liked female flesh as much as any man—more, perhaps—but so much of Constance on display on a Sunday morning was vulgar, not seductive, and again, he doubted she knew the difference. If he had anything to say about it, she would be on her way back to New London in the morning.

"Of course, my mistress will send th' little chit packing," Ruth was whispering crossly. "Look at her, sitting plain as day between Master Christopher an' Cap'n Jonathan!"

Dianna saw Mercy's small head barely showing above the bench, her little white cap flanked by the two broad-shouldered Sparhawk men. As she watched, Mercy tugged on Kit's sleeve, and he bent down to listen. Dianna smiled. She didn't know how Mercy had managed it, but Dianna was delighted for once to see her claiming her share of Kit's attention.

"My poor mistress!" sputtered Ruth indignantly. "To be forced t'bear such shame! That he would bring his little bastard wit' him into meeting! He might not care about th' gossip, but, oh, poor Mistress Constance!"

Her thoughts spinning, Dianna once again bowed her head. There was nothing beyond this woman's gossip that said Mercy was Kit's daughter, no resemblance between them. Yet it could explain so much. What had Asa said—that Mercy could not replace the other Kit had lost. Was the other Lucy Wing, the wife of a man he called his friend? First the woman in Saybrook, and now this. Troubled and confused, Dianna found herself praying for the strength to keep away from Kit Sparhawk.

Kit knew Dianna was there. He had found her the moment he'd entered the door, and her presence only made Constance all the more unbearable. He felt badly about what had happened yesterday. Servant or no, Asa should not have struck her, and he should not have let it happen. That Hester had railed at him about the girl while she slammed pots and kettles about in the kitchen hadn't helped, either. He was surprised that Dianna wanted to learn from Hester. He hadn't expected that from her, any more than he'd expected her to fly at him for merely calling her a hussy. He still thought her a strumpet, though Jonathan had scoffed and called him a righteous prig and said the girl could not be blamed for the gossip of others.

Almost unconsciously Kit's eyes strayed back to the servant's bench, where the morning light streamed over Dianna's small figure. He liked her in the pale, simple clothing, a foil to her aristocratic features and dramatic coloring. The sunlight caught her in profile, outlining her nose with the little bump on the bridge, her full lower lip, her dimpled chin. Kit could not believe that Jonathan had dismissed her as a little wren: there was more grace in the line of Dianna Grey's throat than in Constance's entire body. If she were a little wren, then Constance was an over-bright, squawking parrot and Jonathan was welcome to her.

Somehow Dianna sensed he was studying her and she turned her face toward him, her lips slightly parted with surprise. For a moment, across the rows of bowed heads, their eyes met. A soft flush colored her cheeks and she quickly looked down.

Reluctantly Kit tried to return his attention to Dr. Manning's sermon. This was his first Sunday home after a long and difficult journey and he had much to be thankful for: Jonathan's recovery, a profitable voyage with the loss of only one man, a good harvest at Plumstead while he'd been away. And yet all his best intentions toward prayer were pushed aside by the thought of Dianna behind him.

When the break in the services came in early afternoon, Kit was the first to his feet, impatiently searching for Dianna. He wanted to find her, talk to her, not to apologize exactly, but to say he understood how difficult Asa could be. But with Constance hanging on his arm and a crowd of neighbors welcoming him home, he was one of the last to leave the meetinghouse. Outside, the congregation dawdled in the churchyard in the warm spring sunshine, chatting among themselves as the baskets with cold suppers were unpacked from wagons and horses. Kit spotted Dianna at once. She was hard to miss, with Jonathan in his scarlet coat dawdling beside her, giving her the full benefit of his considerable charm. Kit almost swore, remembering in time that it was the Sabbath. But it was so like Jonathan to saddle him with Constance and then go after Dianna himself.

"I swear you've not heard a word I've told you, Christopher," Constance was saying petulantly. "You'd sooner see me starve than fetch me my supper!"

But before Kit answered, a man on horseback cantered up to the meetinghouse, sending children and a neighbor's chickens scurrying for safety. The rider laughed and cruelly jerked the horse's head around, scattering flecks of spittle and blood from its mouth. He was a heavy-set man and strong, easily controlling the horse with one gloved hand. His round, florid face was framed by a black, curling beard streaked with white, and his hair was carelessly tied back with a limp riband. A single pearl on a gold loop dangled from one ear. His clothes were expensive, velvet and broadcloth, though stained with neglect, and his tall boots, too, were scuffed and mud-stained, the silver spurs glinting in the sun.

"Sparhawk!" the man called to Kit, challenging. "*Sacré sang,* the savages for once did not lie, and your filthy English soul is back among us!"

"Haul your black carcass out of the sight of decent folk, Robillard," answered Kit evenly, but the threat in his voice was clear. The crowd around him had melted away, leaving an open path between him and the rider, and even Constance had vanished.

Defiantly, the man dismounted and sauntered toward Kit. "You have no power over me, Sparhawk. Your *Anglais* laws mean nothing, just as your *Anglais* borders and your *Anglais* treaties mean nothing, either. You are the interlopers, the intruders, here merely by the whim of *Nouveau France,* and when she wishes to be rid of you, she will."

Every muscle in Kit's body tensed. He hated Robillard, hated him with a passion that had been handed down from his father. "This land belongs to us, and to England, Robillard, and there's an end to it."

Robillard laughed, his velvet-covered belly shaking. "You talk bold, but you know the truth. Someday I will own your land, Sparhawk. I have offered you a fair price for it, and like your father, you were too *stupide* to agree. So I will try other ways, eh? I will take it for *la belle France,* and see you mewling *Anglais* at last gone from my woods."

The Frenchman was close enough that Kit could smell the burgundy on his breath, but he was not so foolish as to judge the man drunk. "I don't discuss business on the Sabbath, Robillard, with you or any man. If you have anything to say to me other than your customary empty threats, you may call on me tomorrow at Plumstead. But now, you will leave Wickhamton." Kit's eyes narrowed. "Now, Robillard. I want you gone *now.*"

As he spoke, Jonathan had come to stand beside Kit, and Dianna wondered how the Frenchman could dare to face both Sparhawk brothers. The tension in the air was palpable; the rest of the congregation stood frozen, watching. She knew that neither Kit nor Jonathan was armed; she had seen the long rifles they always carried left in the back of the church. Robillard, too, had left his gun on his saddle. But she still had a sick feeling that something very bad was about to happen.

She wasn't wrong.

"Fah, Sparhawk, you insult me!" Robillard spat in the dirt before Kit. "Which should frighten me more, eh? Your *imbécile* warnings or your crippled brother?" With both hands he began to scratch his belly, or so it seemed to Dianna. But in that instant Kit was on him, knocking the Frenchman onto his back and pinning him with the length of his own body. The blade of Robillard's knife glittered as it slid harmlessly from his open hand across the packed dirt. A murmur of exclamations swept around the others as Jonathan bent to collect it.

It was the other knife that held Dianna's attention, the one Kit held poised across the Frenchman's throat. The blade was long, the hilt carved from horn, and the ease and swiftness with which Kit handled it shocked her. His eyes were hard, his mouth a grim slash, and Dianna realized how ruthless a man had to be to survive in this land. If he'd had to, Kit would have slit Robillard's throat. And what was worse was knowing that the Frenchman would have done the same.

Slowly Dianna let her fingers uncurl and release the apron she'd clutched into a knot, and she followed the others back into the church as Jonathan and Kit shoved Robillard toward his horse. In England, gentlemen did not scuffle in the dirt. Disputes were not settled with knives. But everything was different here. Civility was a luxury, hesitation a weakness that invited death.

Oh, Lord, how was she going to survive in such a place?

"I would've gone if I'd known there was going t'be a fight," said Asa sadly as Dianna cleaned the plates from their supper. Mercy was already in bed in the loft, asleep, worn out after the day's excitement. "Kit's a rare man with a knife, an' Robillard's cunning enough t'make it a good match. I'm sorry t'miss it."

"Even if you'd been there, you might have missed it all if you'd blinked an eye. It was over that fast. I don't understand why they had to fight at all."

Asa snorted. "Ye don't waste words with a scoundrel like Robillard. Frenchies like him, don't understand'em, Annie. He's been a thorn in th' side of th' Sparhawks for twenty years, always a-yammerin' about English land belongin' to th' priests an' the King o' France instead. Kit treated him no worse'n he deserved.''

''Perhaps. But he might have picked a better place and time to do it.'' Dianna was still unsettled by the fight and didn't wish to discuss it again. She gave the table one last pass with the towel, and then sat across from Asa, her hands clasped before her.

''Asa, I don't know what Captain Welles told you about me,'' she began. ''You needed someone to watch over Mercy and chose me, and I'm grateful. But I'm not exactly what you wanted. For one, I can't cook.''

Sucking on his pipe with his head angled back, Asa studied her through half-closed eyes. ''Supper tonight was fine. More'n fine.''

''I didn't make it. Hester Holcomb did.'' Dianna smiled ruefully. ''Hester has offered to teach me cooking and such, things I need to know to be useful to you and Mercy. But I'll have to go to Plumstead, and I'll have to take Mercy with me.''

Asa merely listened, watching her through the tobacco haze.

''I know you don't like Kit Sparhawk, but I'll be there to watch Mercy,'' Dianna plunged onward, from his silence expecting him to say no. ''And it will only be until I can make do on my own.''

Still considering, Asa nodded slowly before answering. ''Hester be a good woman. She'll learn ye well. The pair o' ye will keep th' lass safe enough.'' He pushed back the chair, stretching his arms over his head with a cracking in his joints. "An' truth be, Jeremiah an' I be headin' upriver for a fortnight in th' morning. Knowin' Mercy an' ye be wit' Hester will keep me from worryin'. But ye bring her back here at night, mind? This be her home, an' I don't want Kit puttin' other ideas in her head."

Dianna nodded. "Asa, there is one other thing."

"I'm not a-worryin' you'll burn down th' house, if that be it," he said mildly.

"Nay, not that." Dianna blushed, and looked down at her hands. "I want to know about Kit and Mercy. I heard what you told him about replacing the one that was lost. Mercy is wary of me and she doesn't believe that I want to be her friend. If you know something about her that might help me—"

Asa rose abruptly. "There's nothin' ye need to know, girl," he said sharply. "Don't ask questions about th' dead that can only hurt them that still live, mind. There's things that happened long past that be better forgotten."

A little gust of cold night air blew down the chimney, and for a moment the fire flared more brightly. Slowly Dianna lowered her head to her hands and stared into the flames. Like it or not, she had her answer.

During her first week working beside Hester at Plumstead, Dianna found it easy enough to keep Mercy away from Kit, for not once did they see him. He was always gone before they arrived: meeting with the grist miller about the grind for the winter wheat or

with the saw miller about the pine planking he was
shipping to Barbados; overseeing the plowing of the
outer fields or the grafting in the orchards; or confer-
ring with the other officers of the Wickhamton trainband about defenses for the outermost farms. After
seven months away from home, explained Hester,
there was much that demanded Kit's attention. And,
she added with a wink, much to keep him out of the
path of Constance Lindsey.

But on Friday, Constance intercepted him at last by
the river warehouse, and reluctantly he had given over
the day to riding with her. It was late afternoon before the pair returned to Plumstead. Constance's tril-
ling laughter caught Dianna's ear as she peeled turnips
in the kitchen, and she paused to watch them walking
through the yard, Constance's arm looped familiarly
through Kit's as they led their horses to the trough.

Hester followed Dianna's glance and harrumphed.
"She may think she's caught him, but there's nary a
chance Kit will be pulled along like th' horse."

"She's very beautiful," said Dianna wistfully.
Constance wore a lavender riding habit closely tai-
lored to display her figure, and a matching tricorn hat
tipped artfully over one eye.

"An' very stupid, t'come chasing after Kit this
way." For emphasis Hester gave an extra whack with
her cleaver. "Don't know why Kit didn't send her back
downriver with Jonathan on Tuesday."

"Jonathan's gone?" Dianna asked with surprise.
She had assumed he was still at Plumstead, merely
making himself as scarce as his brother.

"Only th' chance t'bedevil poor Kit with that woman brought him back. He's been landlocked too long with that bad leg to stay away from the *Prosperity* more'n he must. So he's the brother you fancy, eh? Nay, don't be shy about it. Every lass in the valley takes to one or t'other of 'em. Though I'd warrant that jade out there cares more for the fortune than the man, more fool she!"

"Are the Sparhawks wealthy?" asked Dianna, glad to divert Hester's attention from her own feelings and the fact that she'd guessed quite wrongly about the brothers.

"Aye, they own enough of th' land in these parts t'start their own country, if they'd a mind. An' with Jonathan's trading an' th' mills an' shops that Kit's begun, along with th' tenants, why, they'd make their grandfather, th' one that come over with Gov'ner Winthrop, prouder'n daylight if he'd lived t'see it."

It was hard for Dianna to comprehend that the Sparhawks could be so prosperous and yet still wish to work so hard. In England no gentlemen ever worked if he could help it. Even her uncle, with his shipping firm, spent more time at the gaming table than in his counting house. And there was her own poor, dear father, for whom making money was as much a mystery as alchemy. But then she looked down to the turnip in her hands and smiled wryly to herself. In England no lady would do such scullery work herself, either.

"But if one o'them don't take a wife soon," continued Hester, shaking her head, "an' get a son or two, then th'whole thing will get carved among th'sisters.

Oh, not that they aren't good girls, Bess an' Grace an'
Amy, but th'land would pass to their husbands an'
away from th' Sparhawks. I don't want t'see that day,
nay, I don't.''

Dianna thought of Mercy, and wondered if Kit
would acknowledge her openly if she'd been a boy.
Surely Hester, who treated the Sparhawks like the
family she didn't have, must know the truth. Yet it
seemed odd to Dianna that she could speak so freely
of Kit and children if she did.

Hester poured water over the vegetables already in
the kettle, then handed the empty bucket to Dianna.
"Here, lass, be a lamb, an' fetch this full for me."

Even empty, the oak bucket was heavy and Dianna
carried it, swinging before her, with both hands. The
well was around the front of the house, but as she
came 'round the corner, she stopped at the sound of
Constance's voice. She and Kit were sitting on the
benches before the front door, and Dianna was reluctant to interrupt. She was trying to think of an excuse
that Hester would accept if she retreated without the
water when Constance began to sing.

Or at least Dianna guessed that was what the other
woman's yowling was intended to be. She barely recognized the song, an old ballad with a new setting that
had been quite popular at court two years ago. As
Constance's off-key rendition wandered farther and
farther away from the melody, Dianna's smile grew
wider. She didn't have blue eyes like Constance or a
lavender riding habit, but her singing voice was pure
gold. She waited until Constance had come to the
sorry end of the song, and then began it herself as she

nonchalantly rounded the corner of the house and walked toward the well, ignoring the two on the bench.

Lowering the well's bucket on the sweep, she let her voice expand with the bittersweet minor notes, the tale of a shepherdess's lost love. As the notes floated into the warm spring air, she forgot her task and her intended audience, too, and lost herself in the pleasure of the music. When the song was done she smiled contentedly to herself until Kit's applause startled her back to the present. With a little gasp of surprise she spun around and immediately locked eyes with the furious Constance.

"Where might a wench like you have learned that song?" she demanded angrily. "Indeed, the music was just brought to me personally on the *Prosperity.*"

From the corner of her eye Dianna saw that Kit was trying not to laugh, one hand over his mouth, and she did not dare look directly at him for fear of giggling herself.

"Aye, madam, the music might have been brought on the *Prosperity* by Master Sparhawk," Dianna said, her silvery eyes glinting mischievously, "but then, I was, too."

"But that air is in the very latest fashion at court!" Constance sputtered.

Dianna shrugged. "Two seasons ago, at the very least. I was in attendance when it was introduced at Lord Rathburn's Twelfth Night masque."

Constance looked down her nose scornfully. "Of all the impudence! Truly, Kit, you must have the baggage whipped for such lies! However could a com-

mon Wickhamton serving girl like you be at Lord
Rathburn's entertainments?"

"The twists of fortune," explained Kit, "fortune
both good and bad, and nothing more. Would you say
otherwise, Dianna?"

At last, over Constance's shoulder, he caught
Dianna's eye and winked wickedly. His grin was wide
and easy, warm with the pleasure of a shared moment. His smile reached his eyes, too, which crinkled
in the corners, and for the first time Dianna felt the
full force of his masculine charm. But there was more.
For the first time, too, she saw admiration in his eyes
and respect for her. Could one song have done so
much, she wondered breathlessly?

"So it's *Dianna,* is it?" Constance demanded suspiciously, narrowing her eyes at Kit. "I won't linger
here any longer, Christopher, now that I see how
things truly are, nor will I remain to be treated so in-
solently by this—this *creature* whom you refuse to
discipline." She gathered her skirts with both hands to
leave, though hesitating as if she expected him to beg
her to stay.

But Kit only smiled past her to Dianna. "You can't
deny she sings a great deal better than you do, Constance." There was an unspoken invitation in his grin,
something that made Dianna's heart race and her
blood turn sweet and slow as honey. Foolishly she
smiled back, oblivious to everything but the pull of
those green cat's eyes.

He had rescued her from rape and from fire, yet she
had kept her heart safe from him. He had called her
names, assumed the worst about her past, while she

had learned things about his that had shocked her and she had tried not to care. He had kissed her and caressed her, and she had held her emotions at bay. But now, with only a shared smile over a silly, showy prank, he could claim her heart, and she knew she had lost it forever.

Chapter Nine

"How did ye know that ye could rid us o'that old Constance Lindsey so easy?" asked Mercy the next morning as she and Dianna walked to Plumstead. "I tried an' tried t'make her leave Kit be, an' she only called me names an' wouldn't go."

Dianna tried to hide her surprise. This was the most the girl had ever said to her, and she was almost afraid to reply for fear that Mercy would withdraw again. "I didn't think she would be so angry as that, but I couldn't bear to hear what she did to that lovely song."

Mercy laughed gleefully. "Ye shamed her right, ye did, an' before Kit, too, with him sayin' how beautiful ye sing an' how ugly she did it!"

"I don't remember him saying it quite like that," Dianna replied, but she was laughing, too.

"He be right, though, ye do sing beautiful." The girl looked shyly up at Dianna. "I've never heard anything like it. Like angels, it was."

"Thank you," said Dianna softly, moved, and when this time she reached to take Mercy's hand, the little girl did not pull it away. "My father loved music, and he saw to it that I had the best teachers. We sang often together."

Mercy's wooden clogs kicked along through the dead leaves. "He be dead, your father. Kit told me I should be kind to ye, on account o' ye bein' an orphan, too, like me."

That surprised Dianna, too. "Sometimes I still cannot believe my father is dead. You must miss your parents very much, too."

"Aye, I do." Mercy sighed. "But having Kit helps. He an' Father were closer'n brothers. He'd keep me at Plumstead if it weren't for Grandfer." She lowered her voice confidentially. "Kit wept at Father's funeral sermon. He didn't think I saw him, but he did."

"Kit is very fond of you, Mercy," said Dianna carefully, wishing the girl's new confidences involved something other than her father, whoever he was. "But your grandfather loves you, too, even—"

She stopped suddenly, and listened. They were on the low side of a small hill crowned by a rocky outcropping, and though the new leaves of the trees and scrub brush around them hid little, Dianna was certain she'd heard something from beyond the hill. She stood perfectly still, straining to hear the noise again.

Mercy continued shuffling through the leaves. "Oh, Dianna, 'tis only a rabbit or squirrel—"

But Dianna caught her and pulled her back, her hand across her lips as she shook her head fiercely. There was the sound again: footsteps, a pair of footsteps, just beyond their sight. She had no idea whether the stranger was friendly or not, and her imagination pictured a man like Robillard or one of the rough traders she'd seen with Asa and Jeremiah. All she knew for sure was that she was a small, vulnerable woman, alone and unarmed, with a child. Quickly she led Mercy to the rocky hilltop, cursing the noise that her own feet made. She pressed close to the flat, grey stones and, her heart pounding, inched up until she could just peek over the top. She gasped and froze, unable to move from fear.

The man below was watching her calmly. He was tall and lean, his prominent cheekbones peppered with smallpox scars, and his skin was a rich coppery brown. He wore a blanket wrapped over his shoulders like a cloak, a breech cloth, patched elkskin leggings and little else beyond a collection of beaded necklaces. More beads were woven into his blue-black hair, and tied around his shoulders and waist were several lumpy packages and bundles. In his raised hand, ready to throw, was a tomahawk.

Dianna's nails dug into the rock. *Oh, dear God, it's an Indian, a red savage....*

Mercy crawled up the rock beside her and looked over the edge. Too late Dianna grabbed for her as the girl bounded over the rocks, slipping and hopping down the hill toward the Indian. Horrified, Dianna stumbled after her, dreading the awful moment when the tomahawk would strike the child.

But instead, a wide grin split the Indian's face, and, lowering his tomahawk, he tucked it back into the sash at his waist. "Tom Wing's daughter, yes?" he said amiably in English. "You've grown, little one."

Mercy was nearly dancing with excitement. "Kit's back, Attawan!"

"Mercy!" Dianna caught the child by her shoulders and pulled her protectively close. Although the man had put away his weapon, she was still frightened by his wild, half-naked appearance, and she remembered every story she'd ever heard about what Indians did to hapless settlers.

"This is Attawan, Dianna," explained Mercy. "He's a Pocumtuck, and he's a friend of Kit's."

"It seems the whole colony is a friend of Kit's." Dianna ducked her head quickly, unsure how one responded to an Indian. She began backing away, pulling Mercy with her, and rattled on nervously. "In truth, he's likely waiting for us now, Mercy, wondering where we are, mayhap even coming to look for us. Farewell, umm, Master Attawan."

But Attawan only nodded solemnly as he tugged his blanket into place. "He is a good friend to have, mistress," he called after them. "A very good friend."

As the miller droned on with his list of grievances, Kit hoped his own expression showed the proper mixture of sternness and concern. He only heard every tenth word of the man's endless litany, and even that took more concentration than he wanted to spare. It seemed that every moment since he'd returned, he'd been listening to some complaint or another, and he'd often wondered how Plumstead and his other concerns had managed to run at all in the months he'd been away. That things might have slipped while Jonathan had been in charge was understandable; he had, after all, been recuperating, and he didn't share Kit's interests under the best of circumstances. But what stunned Kit was that, since he'd returned, he himself rankled under the responsibilities. He had no patience with his tenants or their problems, little interest in the profits of his mills and less in Wickhamton affairs.

It had taken him less than a week to discover why: Dianna Grey. Somehow he'd become bewitched by the woman, and in a way that was beyond his experience. He wished he could take Jonathan's advice to just bed her and be done with it. But he couldn't. She was the servant of one of his tenants, and by extension, one of his own, as well, until her indenture ran out. She wasn't some tavern wench he could leave behind with a handful of coins. And, of course, there still remained all the reasons he hadn't taken her during their voyage.

But even those objections seemed to fade each time he saw her. She never played the coquette with him, and unlike every other woman he knew, she seemed little enough impressed by his position. He could have bought and sold her blasted blue-blood father ten times over, and she herself now belonged to a rootless old trapper, yet she still found him beneath her notice. And the worst part of it was that he *wanted* her to notice him. He liked to be around her because she always surprised him. He smiled when he thought of how effortlessly she had been able to send Constance scurrying back to New London. Lord, and her voice— he'd never heard a voice that breathtakingly beautiful before, and he wondered what it would take to make her sing again, and for him alone this time.

"Nay, Master Sparhawk, I don't see th' mirth in millstones worn almost flat," said the miller, sounding a bit wounded. "If ye can't bring the stone dresser up from Saybrook, well then, I can't answer for th' spring wheat."

"You'll have your stone dresser, Morgan, and within the fortnight," said Kit quickly. If he wasn't careful, he'd have the gossips whispering how he'd lost his wits in London. "You were right to bring it to my attention, and I know you'll be ready when that spring wheat comes in."

Kit left the man preening happily, and soon was on Thunder's back and heading toward Plumstead. It was still early afternoon. Today he would be sure to reach home before Dianna and Mercy left.

"I'm not certain we should be here, Mercy," said Dianna uneasily as the girl led her into Plumstead's parlor chamber. The room was seldom used, the door kept shut, and like most of the house, Dianna had never seen it. The lavishness of the furnishings surprised her: although the furniture was in the old style of King Charles, dark walnut and oak with heavy turnings and carving and cane seats on the chairs, it had all obviously come from first-rate cabinetmakers in London. The window hangings were dark green velvet, as were the chair cushions, and a bright-patterned Turkey carpet lay across the polished pine floorboards. A tall chest, lacquered in red and black chinoiserie, dominated one wall, and along the man-

telpiece sat a row of polished silver chargers. But it was
to a small table near one of the diamond-paned windows that Mercy drew Dianna to as she pointed to a
long, flat box elaborately inlaid with wood and pearl
veneers.

"Jonathan said this be for music-making," she told
Dianna, resting one hand reverently on the top.
"Mayhap ye know how t'make it sing."

Dianna pulled the tasseled stool from beneath the
table, sat and carefully opened the hinged top of the
box. "It's a virginal, Mercy," she explained as the girl
crowded over her arm to peer at the black and white
keys. Carefully Dianna fingered a chord, and Mercy
gasped at the ringing sounds of the plucked strings.
The instrument was sadly out of tune, but after
months of no music at all, the little instrument
brought an unexpected joy to Dianna. With growing
confidence, her fingers danced lightly over the key-
board, and she began to sing softly as she accompa-
nied herself. This time she sang not to outdo another
but to please only herself, and the song she chose was
"Greensleeves," the old ballad somehow suiting the
melancholy sound of the virginal. Spellbound, Mercy
settled on the floor beside her, her knees tucked up and
her mouth open with rapt admiration. Both were so
lost in the music's magic that neither heard Kit's boots
in the hall, nor did they notice him standing in the
doorway to listen, too.

The music brought back a hundred images fresh to
Kit, memories of his childhood, of his brother and
sisters tumbled around on the floor before the fire
while their mother played and the winter wind howled

outside. He saw again the look on his father's face as he turned the pages of his mother's music and the way he would kiss her on the forehead when she was done.

"No one has touched that since my lady mother's death," he said when Dianna was finished. Still half-lost in his own memories, his voice was oddly uneven with emotion.

Startled, Dianna hurriedly shut the instrument and shoved back the stool to rise. "Forgive me, I did not know."

"Nay, do not stop, I pray! It's not for sentiment that the thing's been stilled, but for the lack of a player." He smiled, a sad smile that struck deep into Dianna's grief for her own lost parents. "My sisters had neither the gift nor the patience, and so it has sat idle. Waiting, I dare to say, for you."

Dianna's cheeks brightened at the unexpected compliment. She was a servant, he was a wealthy man, and it was not right for him to say pretty nonsense to her. But to see him there, smiling like that, she could forgive him anything, and once again she felt the power of his undeniable attraction to her. He was dressed simply, a coarse worsted vest unbuttoned over a linen shirt, open at the throat and the sleeves rolled up, and she caught herself staring, fascinated, at the curling dark hairs on his bare forearms and chest. He came closer, mindless of the dust his boots left on the carpet, and Dianna sank back onto the stool, not to play again, but from fear her legs would not hold her.

"You won't play more?" he asked with a surprising wistfulness, and Dianna shook her head, doubt-

ing now that she could fumble through the simplest
piece.

"Then you force me to talk, Lady Dianna, to fill the
space between us." He leaned against one of the arm
chairs, his long legs crossed before him, and wondered why, for the first time, he had called her by her
title without sarcasm. "At least Constance would wish
me to speak to you."

Guilt made Dianna's words rush over one another.
"Oh, Kit, I don't know what the devil made me act so!
She meant to please you, that was all, and I had no
right to shame her for that, especially if she is your
betrothed."

Kit snorted, and Dianna then noticed the teasing
spark in his green eyes, the same one that had been
there when she'd bettered Constance. "She has no
more claim to that title than the spotted sow in the sty,
and, now that I consider it, her singing belongs in the
barnyard, as well."

"Aye, Dianna made th' ninny turn tail an' run,
didn't she, Kit?" piped up Mercy, and the way that Kit
cocked one eyebrow told Dianna that he, like she herself, had entirely forgotten the little girl's presence. She
waited, expecting him to decide whether Mercy would
remain as an unwitting chaperone or be sent from the
room. But that eyebrow cocked a fraction higher, and
she realized he was leaving the decision to her instead.
That eyebrow, and all it implied, irritated Dianna. A
man's comely face was no reason for letting herself be
intimidated. She could quite easily stay in the room
alone with him, and, her composure returning, she
would prove it to him, too.

"Mercy, please go to Hester. Kit and I must talk alone for a few moments, and then you and I shall go home for dinner." The girl began to protest, but one stern look from Kit was enough to send her reluctantly away.

With a swiftness that startled Dianna, Kit shifted from the armchair to her own bench. Self-consciously she tugged her skirts away from him and he chuckled. The bench was small enough that she could not escape his thigh pressing against hers, but she refused to amuse him more by moving again. "I would speak to you, too, Kit," she began, planning to tell him of meeting Attawan, "and it's better said without Mercy."

"Stay, it cannot be more important than what I must say to you." His voice dropped lower, his green eyes watched her closely beneath half-closed lids. "Why do you plague me so, Dianna? In North Boston, they'd try you for witchcraft for what you've done to me."

Her back very straight, Dianna stared down at her hands clasped in her lap. "I don't know what you mean."

"Aye, sweeting, I think you do." Gently he took her hand in his, her slender fingers swallowed in his broad, rough palm. He meant merely to talk, not seduce her. There would be no harm in that. "Would your hand be shaking like this, your palm damp, if you did not know?"

But already her nearness was testing his intentions. In the heat of the kitchen, she had loosened the neckerchief she wore modestly tucked around her throat, leaving the soft curves of her breasts exposed. As she self-consciously pulled the neckerchief back in place, the simple gesture of her graceful fingers twisting in the linen was more seductive than Kit could have dreamed possible. What was it about this woman that had that effect on him? He turned her hand over in his own, coaxing the clasped fingers open by tracing along the pale veins in her wrist, and he felt a shiver run the length of her arm. Slowly he lifted her hand to his lips, and let them retrace the same path.

Dianna could have held firm if he had been demanding with her again, as he had on the *Prosperity*. She was prepared for that. But this gentleness caught her unawares. One by one she felt her defenses flutter and fall before these feather-light, teasing caresses. Through her clothes, she could feel the heat from his body where their legs touched on the bench, and his own special masculine scent almost overwhelmed her senses. Too vividly she recalled how he had kissed her before, and while her conscience weakly tried to rebel, she felt her heart beating faster in anticipation, her lips parting expectantly.

He raised his hand to touch her jaw, turning her face toward his. His eyes held hers fascinated, and for the first time Dianna noticed how their green depths were flecked with tiny sparks of gold.

Lightly he touched a forefinger to the cleft in her chin. "I like this," he said simply.

She closed her eyes to try to break the spell, but his voice, his touch remained. With one final effort her conscience struggled for something, anything, to save herself.

"Today an Indian tried to kill Mercy and me," she blurted out, her eyes still tightly shut. "Down beyond the west field, not two miles from here."

Kit froze, all desire instantly gone. "What the devil are you saying?"

"There was an Indian in the woods, and he drew his tomahawk and threatened us and was most fierce."

"Dianna, by all that's holy, if you seek to mock me..."

Again he saw the place where the path curved to follow the bend in the river, the terrible, unexpected stillness of the late afternoon, the twisted body of his father's yellow dog lying half in the water, her long tail floating gently with the current....

"There are no hostile Indians near Wickhamton," he said hoarsely. "No Englishman has died here by a savage's hand for ten years. The militia, the train-band patrols, have made certain. There are no more hostile Indians."

"But he said he knew you," said Dianna defensively. Why didn't he believe her? "He said his name was Attawan, and he called you friend."

"Attawan. Aye, he has a right to call me that." Kit knew he should be relieved, but the tight coil of pain within his chest refused to unwind. It was more than just hearing his mother's virginal again, though God knows that would be enough. No, it was Dianna herself and the old danger of caring too much.

He let her fingers slip from his own, and Dianna's heart sank when she saw how cold and withdrawn his expression had become. Did she really mean so little to him that her fear was only a disagreeable interruption?

"It matters not if he knew you, Kit. He didn't know *me,*" she persisted. She must have imagined the sympathy between them, for there was none of it now in those cold green eyes. "If I'm to live in this wilderness, I don't ever want to feel that helpless again."

He rose and turned away so she could not see the anguish he was certain was on his face. How could he tell her that the helplessness never ended, that he faced it every day? "You are a woman, Dianna," he finally said, "and gently bred at that."

"And that should be my excuse?" she asked incredulously. "Nay, Kit, I can't accept that. I want you to teach me to shoot a gun like yours."

"You don't know what you ask, sweeting." His laugh was harsh, and the endearment this time was so tinged with bitter mockery that Dianna winced. "A musket is nigh as long as you're tall. If by some rare bit of luck you could hoist the butt to your shoulder, I doubt you've the strength to hold it steady enough to aim and fire. And if the recoil doesn't knock you flat, then what? It's half a minute for a grown man to reload. For you, twice that. In that time your enemy would have his leisure to dispose of you, and I'd be left with the blame. Nay, Dianna, I won't do it."

"You'd rather I stand meekly and meet my fate, and Mercy hers with me, than teach me to defend myself?" She was standing now, too, her hands defiantly on her hips. She hated his contempt, and in that moment she hated him, as well. "Then forgive me for

insulting your curious sense of honor. I'll ask Hester
instead.''

"An' I'll be happy t'teach ye, too," answered the
older woman tartly from the doorway, "if th' grand
fine Colonel Sparhawk can't bring himself t'do it."
Dianna saw Kit's shoulders tense, and knew Hester's
barb had struck home, just before the woman turned
on her next.

"Mercy's eager for home," Hester said bluntly, the
dismissal clear. "Ye be done here this day. Best
t'leave.''

Dianna paused uncertainly, hoping Kit would turn
and look at her one more time. So they had come back
to this once again, back to the distrust and the sharp
words, and all the wishing in the world wasn't going
to change it. Angry tears stung her eyes, and with her
head down, she hurried from the room.

Kit heard her leave. "Mind your tongue, Hester,"
he said sharply. "You forget yourself, and your
place.''

"Devil take your place, Kit Sparhawk," snapped
Hester. "I thrashed your hindquarters when you were
a lad, and I'll do it again if I must. I'll warrant ye been
using that self-same tender part o' your person for
thinkin' rather than sittin' anyways, least where that
girl's concerned. I heard your ravin' clear in th'
kitchen. Dianna Grey's no part o' your demons, Kit.
Unless ye let her be told or tell her yourself—"

"*Nay.*" Through the diamond-paned window, Kit
saw Dianna and Mercy walking hand in hand across
the west field.

"Nay," he said wearily. "It's past. I would not have her know."

That night Asa returned home with Jeremiah, and after Mercy had gone to sleep, Dianna told him about meeting Attawan in the woods. Unlike Kit, Asa did not scoff at her story.

"It's not the Indians that a-worry me," he said, frowning. "But with that rogue Robillard kickin' up dust again, it don't be safe for th' pair o' ye walkin' clear t'Plumstead alone. I'll send Jeremiah t'tell them that ye won't be comin' back t'morrow."

Dismayed, Dianna realized that that was not at all what she wanted. "You have two muskets, Asa. If you left one here for me—"

"Nay, it be my place to keep ye safe," said Asa firmly. "Ye best stay here wit' me, and we'll see what Hester's learned ye since I left."

For the next weeks, until early June, Dianna and Mercy stayed within sight of the Wing house and yard, but with Hester's advice still fresh, Dianna found there was plenty to do. Cooking took more time than she'd ever dreamed, though thanks to Hester, she had become an adept, if simple, cook, and she was pleased when even Jeremiah began appearing at the house at mealtimes. Tom Wing had been a miller by trade, not a farmer, and he had bought or bartered for most of his family's food. But his wife had kept a kitchen garden, now run to seed and overgrown, and it was this that Dianna sought first to reclaim. Next came the house itself, and after scouring and sweeping and scrubbing nearly a year's dirt away, Dianna could finally see the little saltbox as a decent place to live. But best of all was the change in Mercy. Each day the girl seemed to giggle more, her cheeks growing rosier and her eyes brighter, and her periods of solitary grief became fewer and less severe as she followed Dianna around like a puppy.

In these early days of summer, Dianna worked harder and longer than she ever had before. Yet she would have been happier, too, than she'd been since her father's death, were it not for the emptiness left by Kit Sparhawk.

It had taken nearly a fortnight for her to be able to think of him with anything short of outright hostility, and when her anger had faded, she was left with only a dull sadness that was infinitely harder to bear. Her heart loved him and ached to be loved in return, and her body desired him with an intensity that almost frightened her, while her mind and conscience remained painfully aware of how foolish and futile all her hopes were. She saw him each Sunday, of course, sitting there on the first bench in the meetinghouse with his pride and position for company, but when she noted how careful he was to avoid meeting her eyes, she kept her distance. She, too, had pride to protect.

"I wish Grandfer'd let us go back. I'll wager Kit misses us up t'Plumstead," confided Mercy sadly. "I'll wager he be lonely without us."

Dianna had only shrugged and continued her weeding. She could not answer for Kit, but she herself had learned volumes about loneliness.

It was Hester who finally invited them back. "It's been too long since we've seen ye," she said warmly to

Dianna after services. "There be new kittens in the barn, an' I can use another pair o' hands with th' strawberries."

Recognizing Dianna's hesitation, Hester patted her hand and lowered her voice confidentially. "Kit won't be there, if that's a-worryin' ye. I know how you two be always at odds. He be headin' to the upper river sawmill at daybreak."

With reluctant permission from Asa and a promise to return well before nightfall, Mercy and Dianna headed to Plumstead the next afternoon. The day held the first true summer's heat, and the green canopy of the forest offered a welcoming coolness after the brilliance of the sun. The paths that they had crossed with ease in the early spring were now crowded with ferns and other undergrowth, the buzzing of insects mingling with the birdcalls overhead. Indians and Frenchmen seemed improbably remote on a day like this. Wildflowers nestled among the tree roots, and Dianna wove the blossoms Mercy picked into wreaths for their hair. After twenty-two summers of being encased in sweltering layers of stays and petticoats, Dianna felt gloriously free with her feet bare on the moss and pine needles, her single skirt looped ankle-high over her shift. Impulsively she unbraided her hair, and laughing, shook the dark waves free over her shoulders.

"It be well Dr. Manning don't be here t'see ye," said Hester drily when they appeared in her kitchen. "A proper pair o' heathen strumpets ye look t'be."

"Oh, Hester, 'tis almost midsummer's night," teased Dianna as she plucked one of the deep-red strawberries from the baskets on the table and popped it into her mouth. "Soon the Queen of the Faeries will come to dance from those very forests."

Hester frowned sternly. "I'll hear none o' that nonsense. Faeries! Next you'll be beggin' for Maypoles! Wickhamton may not be so strict as them t'the east, but we still be good Christian folk, with no use for such flummery."

Wide-eyed with her chin in her hand, Mercy stared up at Hester. "Dianna's told me of th' faeries, but what be Maypoles?"

"There now, Dianna, I hope ye be happy!" The glance Hester shot her was sharp as a blade, and with both hands on Mercy's shoulders she steered the girl toward the door. "Maypoles be wickedness from Old England, Mercy, with no place in the New. Now come set your hands t'useful tasks an' help me with th' berryin'."

Contritely Dianna gathered up an empty basket to follow, but Hester waved her back. "I'll thank ye t'take those shirts o' Kit's up t'his chamber for me first. My knees have had enough o' the stairs for this day."

"But which chamber?"

"Faith, lass, where be your wits?" called Hester over her shoulder. "His be th' only one that's open!"

Three newly laundered shirts were draped across the back of a chair. Dianna picked one up gingerly and held it outstretched by the shoulders. Lord, he was a giant of a man, she marveled, with more admiration than she'd intended. Where were her wits, indeed?

Hastily she collected the other shirts and ran up the front stairs.

Kit's bedchamber was square and spacious, filling the house's southwest corner. Unlike the parlor, the furniture here was plain, hewn from local oak and maple: a clothespress, a table and leather-covered armchair, the chest she remembered from the *Prosperity,* a poster bed. Easily Dianna pictured Kit here, his long legs sprawled under the table that served as his desk, pausing at his work to gaze out the windows to the river. The table was strewn with papers, bills and letters mostly, but what caught Dianna's eye was a page of ink sketches of Thunder. In a few bold pen strokes, Kit had captured the horse's spirit, and the confidence of the drawings surprised Dianna. Unexpected, too, was the well-worn copy of Aristotle. How did a man who wrestled with knives in the dust come to sketch and read Greek?

With the shirts folded and placed on the chest, Dianna had no reason to linger, yet hungrily she continued to gaze around the room. The uniform coat hanging from a peg, the engraving of Jamaica pinned to the wall, the boyish collection of pinecones arranged by size along the mantel—all were clues to Kit. Slowly she pushed back the dark green curtains to the bed, the horn rings overhead squeaking as they slid along the rod. The pillows were neatly laid against the bolster, the coverlet smoothed in place, but Dianna could still make out the deep impression his broad frame had left in the feather mattress, and his scent still clung to the linens. Lightly she ran her hand across the coverlet and closed her eyes, imagining him lying there.

"Dianna?"

At first she thought she imagined Kit's voice, too, but when he repeated her name, her eyes flew open with horror. He'd caught her trespassing, pure and simple. But her apology died on her lips as she confronted the vivid reality of the man before her.

Hot and dirty from a day's riding, Kit had stripped off his shirt and boots outside and dumped bucket after bucket of icy well water over his head. His hair was still swept sleekly back from his forehead and his bare torso held the sheen of the water, the sun slanting through the windows highlighting the muscles in his arms and shoulders. Stray droplets glistened in the dark curls of his hair across his chest and down lower, across his abdomen to the top of his breeches. There the water had made the wet fabric cling shamelessly to his all-too-male body. How long she stood there, and how long she stared, Dianna could not begin to guess.

Oh, God in Heaven, what must he think of me!

Chapter Ten

What Kit thought was that Dianna was the most enchanting woman he'd ever seen.

He had met Hester in the yard, grumbling about Dianna and faeries, but he'd had no idea that Dianna herself would be waiting in his chamber like some wild woodland queen. Her hair streamed gloriously around her like a cape with wildflowers strewn through the chestnut waves. Gone was the pallor of the long voyage. Her skin was burnished to a rosy gold, her face and body once again pleasingly rounded. As she bent over his bed, her shift had slipped low off her shoulders above her laced sleeveless bodice, offering him a tantalizing view of her breasts. Her lips were half-open with surprise, her pale eyes wide with—with what? Invitation? He had been mistaken about her before, but to find her here this way, with no one else in the house…no, there could be no other explanation than that she wanted him as much as he did her.

And Kit had never desired a woman more. He had spent these past weeks alternately blessing and damning Asa for keeping her from Plumstead, but most often he had cursed himself for driving her away. He tried to be a good man, a kind master and generous neighbor, and yet with her he always seemed to become an overbearing boor. He couldn't blame her if she loathed him. She was as mercurial as the silver color of her eyes, and each time he had tried to hold her, she had slipped from his grasp. Would this, then, be his last chance with her to prove he was different?

"So you've come back at last," he said softly, unwilling to risk frightening her again.

"For the kittens," answered Dianna hastily, and then winced at how foolish she sounded. How could she think at all with him watching her like a great golden lion? She stepped away from the bed and folded her arms across her chest. Where was the apology that she needed to make before she could escape? "And Mercy wished to see you again."

"Aye, and I've missed her, too." The beginnings of a smile played around the corners of his mouth. "But I've missed you more."

"Missed me!" cried Dianna scornfully, all the frustration of these past weeks rising up. "How can you miss me when you scarcely know me?"

"In some way I feel I've always known you. From that night at Sir Henry's—"

"The night you betrayed me!" said Dianna bitterly.

"Ah, you wrong me now, just as I wronged you then," he said with genuine sadness. With her hair loose, it was too easy to remember how she looked that night and the things that had gone so poorly between them since then. He no longer cared that she had been Sir Henry's mistress, nor did he believe that she had tried to kill the man, but he was at a loss to admit it without angering her, and justly. "I would give much to begin again with you, Dianna."

"Master Christopher Sparhawk would care what became of a convict, a ten-guinea bondswoman?" She had intended to be sarcastic, but instead her words came out as a poignant little plea. She wanted so very much to believe him!

"Master Sparhawk cares very much," he said, his voice deep and seductive. Slowly he circled around the bed to come stand before her. Even barefoot, he towered over her. "And you don't need me to tell you your worth, Dianna."

With a lazy smile, he plucked one of the flowers from her hair and brushed the star-shaped petals along her cheek. "Columbine, isn't it?"

Dianna nodded, her own words scarcely more than a whisper. "The roots when boiled are a good poultice for burns and scalds."

He chuckled. "All from this pretty little flower? Hester has taught you well." He let the flower fall, and his hand alone traced along the curve of her cheek. Gently his callused fingertips cradled her chin, and he marveled at her delicacy as he turned her face upward toward his. "And here I always favored columbine for its beauty alone."

She closed her eyes as his mouth swept down. All her senses were focused on his lips upon hers, coaxing her, wooing her with a tenderness she hadn't expected. Without thinking, she uncrossed her arms and rested her hands on his chest, her fingers uncertainly exploring the damp, curling hair over smooth skin. In response his hands found and spanned her waist and drew her closer. Her breasts crushed against his chest, the water that still clung to him dampening her shift above the bodice. She felt the heat of his body against hers, and the coolness of the water, and an unfamiliar warmth began to build inside her.

Gradually her lips parted, and she welcomed his deepening kiss. He pulled her closer, molding her body against his, and she felt oddly soft and pliant against the hardness of his muscles and sinews. Her hands climbed up the wide expanse of his chest, across his shoulders and twined around his neck. Hungrily she stretched herself along his body as his tongue explored the velvety depths of her mouth.

It was all she remembered from kissing him before, and more, for this time, strangely, she was not frightened. She was a virgin, true, but she was not innocent of what passed between men and women. Four years at court had taken care of that. She realized that she would not flee from Kit this afternoon. Right or wrong, she wanted him, all of him, too much to fight him or herself any longer.

Kit felt the hot pulse of his desire throbbing through his veins, and as she moved her lithe form seductively against him, his low moan of pleasure sounded deep where their mouths were joined. It had been too long since he'd had a woman, but, God's blood, Dianna would be worth the wait. Her mouth was unbelievably sweet, and the fire he remembered was there again, searing him with the heat of her unfulfilled passion. He broke free long enough to bury his face in the silky ripples of her hair, relishing the fragrance of her skin mingled with the wildflowers. His lips brushed down her throat, and she stretched her head back with a little shiver, shaking her hair down over his hands.

With unsteady fingers, he untied the ribbons of her skirt and eased it down over her hips, then unlaced her bodice and pulled it off as well. Only her shift remained to cover her, the thin linen clinging damp and translucent to her body where she had pressed against him. He groaned at the sight, and his kisses now held no gentleness, only the fierce demand of his rising passion. His large hands slid down her body and grasped her hips, kneading the soft flesh as he lifted her up against him.

Dianna let herself be drawn into the irresistible spell of his touch. She was light-headed with desire, her breath shortened to brief gasps, and she scarcely noticed when he tipped her back onto the billowy softness of the mattress. His lips left hers to find first the little hollow at the base of her throat, and then moved lower, to the top curves of her breasts above her shift. With both hands he cupped them, nuzzling the valley between as he tugged her shift's neckline lower over the dark peaks. His callused fingers circled and teased her, his skin rough against hers, until she moaned and arched up against him. Her nipples tightened beneath his touch and then beneath his tongue as his mouth repeated the sweet torture. She tangled her fingers in his hair, pulling him closer. Deep in her belly she felt the tension building, the unbelievable yearning that made her heart pound, and she twisted as he tried to free her breasts from the shift. Frustrated, he grasped

the linen and tore it to the hem, baring her pale body
to his gaze. She was even more beautiful, more perfect, than he had imagined.

Driven by his desire, his caresses grew bolder, more
possessive. He would make her forget every other
lover but him, and he would make her his. Kneeling
between her legs, he traced a teasing trail of kisses
along the insides of her thighs until she quivered beneath him, and he caught her knees over his arms and
lifted her to his mouth.

Stunned, Dianna gasped first with surprise and then
with pleasure. Her whole being seemed concentrated
on coiling tighter and tighter around the secret place
he'd found, and her back arched uncontrollably as she
clutched handfuls of the coverlet. Her knees drew
higher, shaking, her body begging for release.

She cried out his name when he came to her at last,
and her arms clutched convulsively around him to pull
him closer. Instinctively she opened herself to him,
and when his fingers slipped between their bodies to
ease his way, her hips jerked upward to meet him, and
he was deep inside her.

Wild-eyed from the unexpected pain, she stared up
at him in confusion. Kit's expression was rigid with the
effort of control; he wanted to prolong the pleasure as
far as he could, but, sweet Lord, she was so hot and
tight. He began to move as slowly as he could, and
with each stroke, Dianna felt the sting fading and the
pleasure once again building. He filled her so completely, this huge man, and she could not swear to
where he began and she ended, he was so much a part
of her. He pulled back and plunged deeply into her,

and then again, and tentatively she began to follow his rhythm, her own hips rising to meet his thrusts until finally it was too much, and she could only cross her ankles over his flanks and trust him to bring her through with him. And he did, carrying her with him to an exquisite level of rapture that neither had dreamed possible.

Her heart still pounding, Dianna lay exhausted beneath him, her mind and body both dazed by what she'd experienced. Surely he must love her, she reasoned joyfully, else how could his lovemaking have been so passionate and wondrous? She smiled shyly to herself and lightly brushed her lips across his chest above her. He made a low growl of contentment, so deep that she felt the vibrations within her own body where they still lay joined.

Slowly he lifted himself up on his elbows to look down at her. With her flower-strewn hair fanned around her face, her lips still swollen from his kisses and her silver eyes liquid with fulfillment, she was unbelievably beautiful. He had never made love to a woman in this bed before, preferring to keep his involvements safely away from Plumstead, but Dianna seemed somehow to belong in this chamber. Already he was planning, quite pleasantly, how to bring her here again. The gossips in Wickhamton would run riot if they ever learned of it, but Dianna was a worldly woman who could be counted on to be discreet. And he hadn't had a doubt he'd pleased her well in return: he'd never seen a woman look so blissfully sated. Much, he thought wryly, as he probably looked in return.

Tenderly he brushed a dark lock of hair back from her forehead. "Ah, Dianna, sweeting, my goddess of the moon and stars," he said lazily. "Though it will be with the summer sun that I'll always see you in my mind's eyes. You're a lovely woman, my Lady Grey. A lovely, tempting woman."

Dianna heard that "always," and her heart jumped. She'd never dreamed she'd be loved by a man so handsome, so perfect, as Kit Sparhawk. Seductively he moved his hips against hers, and with a little catch in her breath, Dianna immediately echoed his motion and arched into him.

Kit groaned with the pleasure she gave him. God, he wanted her again, right now, with a fierceness he found hard to believe possible. "Little vixen," he growled, kissing her throat. "No woman's ever done this to me."

"I've never known another man, Kit," she whispered breathlessly.

"Another man like me," he finished for her. "Aye, sweeting, I've told you that before, and at last you've come to believe me."

A shadow fell across Dianna's happiness. Didn't he understand? He was the first, the only, man, she'd lain with. How could he not have sensed the prize she'd so willingly surrendered to him? His mouth trailed lower, capturing one rosy nipple in his lips, and her doubts fled, forgotten with the desire he fanned within her again. As in a faraway dream, she heard horses, then men calling Kit's name. She pulled him closer, certain these sounds had nothing to do with them, not now.

But Kit raised his head, listening, his face dark with anger. God in heaven, would he never have a moment to himself? With one final kiss, reluctantly he rolled away from her and crossed the floor to the open window.

Two tenants from an outlying farm were carefully lifting another man, wrapped in a blanket, from the back of a horse. He seemed unconscious, injured somehow, for his arms and legs flopped awkwardly against the horse. The Plumstead workers were clustered around them, and there was Hester, too. If it was her aid with physicking the injured man that brought them here, then why did they need him, too? People were forever falling from lofts or clumsily cutting themselves on scythes. Of course, he cared what happened to them, but why this afternoon, of all days?

Then the others moved apart enough for Kit to clearly see the injured man. He was pale as death, perhaps dead already, and the impromptu bandages that swathed his head were soaked through. Kit gripped the windowsill. He'd seen before what a rough-honed scalping knife could do to a man, swiftly, before he'd realized the Indians were upon him. And what it could do to a woman, a child.

He grabbed for his breeches, hastily jerking them up over his legs, and saw the blood on himself. He frowned, uncomprehending, then his glance flew back to Dianna. She lay curled on her side, propped up on one elbow as she watched him, but there was no mistaking the stains on her pale thighs. His conscience screamed that it was not possible, that he could not have done this to her. Virgins fought and wept; they did not wrap their thighs around a man's waist and writhe with pleasure. And what of her uncle and the other men who'd claimed to have known her?

I've never known another man. She had been willing, but he had led her. She'd been so deliciously tight around him, and now he realized why. Her eyes burned into him, uncertain and vulnerable, waiting for him to explain. Oh, God, what had he done?

He heard the voices in the kitchen below, his name called again. Soon they would come upstairs to find him. Hastily he tied the drawstring of his breeches. He longed to kiss her again, but there was no time. "Dianna, I promise we will talk," he said hurriedly, "I swear to it, sweeting, but now I must go."

Stunned, Dianna watched the door slam shut. She had given him her heart and her innocence, and he had sworn to talk. *To talk!* She pressed her palm across her mouth to hold back the tears. Oh, God, what had she done?

With old memories pressing on him like granite, Kit stared down at the man stretched out on the broad trestle table and wondered if he would live. Scalping didn't automatically mean death; it was usually exposure or the fever that came with the wound that killed. This man had been found soon after the attack, and he was young and strong enough that he might survive. Kit prayed he would, if only for the sake of all the families in Wickhamton and the surrounding farms.

If this was to be the end of the peace the valley had enjoyed for nearly nine years, then Kit, as militia captain, needed to know what tribe had attacked the man, how many braves had been involved. There was always the chance that this had been personal, reparation for some dishonor or crime that the man had committed. Kit sighed, knowing he couldn't risk doing nothing. Already he'd sent riders to the farthest settlers to bring the families to the safety of Plumstead, and he himself would lead the first patrol within the hour.

Kit watched while Hester cleaned and dressed the man's wound. He was a stranger, likely French, and a trapper from his clothes. Odd that the Indians hadn't bothered to strip him. His moccasins were almost new, and the glinting saint's medallion he wore on a thong about his neck should have been a great prize. Perhaps the Davies brothers had inadvertently frightened off the attackers when they found the man near their cornfield.

"There's all I can do for him now, Kit," said Hester grimly as she lifted the pail of dark-stained water from the table. "Put him in th' little chamber off th' kitchen an' I'll watch him best I can."

Kit nodded to John and Samuel Davies, and together they began to gingerly lift the man from the table. But as they did, he groaned and his eyes fluttered open. *"Mon Dieu, qui est vous? Je n'ai pas d'argent!"*

"French," said Samuel with disgust. "Wouldn't ye know we'd save a bloody Papist."

Kit silenced him with a frown. "You're among Englishmen, my friend," he said carefully to the wounded man. "We wish to help you. Can you tell us who hurt you?"

But the man only stared up at him, his expression confused. *"Je ne comprends pas. Anglais? Anglais! Mere de Dieu, preservez moi!"*

"We won't hurt you," began Kit again, but the man's eyes were becoming more and more panicked, and Kit feared he would injure himself further. "Pray, be calm."

"Non, non, vous êtes Anglais—"

"Se taire," said Dianna as she entered the room and gently took the man's hand. She leaned over him so he could see her clearly. *"Vous êtes entre des amis."*

"Oui?" the man whispered desperately. *"Des amis, mademoiselle?"*

Dianna nodded. *"Oui, nous sommes amis. Maintenant, reposez vous."* She was relieved when he closed his eyes again and his breathing became regular with either sleep or unconsciousness. She wondered what had happened to him and why he feared them so. As his face relaxed, she could see how young he was, perhaps only nineteen or twenty. His frame still had the rawboned look of adolescence, and his beard and moustache were pathetically sparse.

"Ask him who he be," demanded Samuel impatiently. "Ask him—"

"Nay, Samuel, ye let him be for now," said Hester sharply. "Best to put him t'bed, else he'll never answer yer questions in this life."

As the unconscious Frenchman was slowly lifted from the table, Kit at last caught Dianna's eye. Her hair was once again neatly braided, the flowers gone, and he winced inwardly when he noticed how she'd folded her shift into the top of her bodice so the torn edges wouldn't show. "Thank you," he said quietly. "I did not know you spoke French."

Her chin shot up bravely, her eyes flashing. "There are many things you don't know about me, Master Sparhawk," she answered. "Now if you're done, I promised Asa that Mercy and I would be home before nightfall."

"You're not going anywhere." Fear for her made his tone sharp. "You will stay here."

"You are not my master!" How dare he treat her so coldly after what had just passed between them?

"You will stay, Dianna," he said curtly as he pulled on the hunting shirt that Hester handed him, and took his rifle from the pegs on the wall. "You're the only one who speaks this man's language, and you must be here when he wakes."

"But I—"

"That's an end to it," he growled. Already men were gathering outside the barn, talking excitedly among themselves as they checked their muskets and rifles, and the first wagon full of frightened women and crying children had drawn into the yard. He slung his powder horn over his shoulder and left to join the others.

His manner cut Dianna to the quick. *You're a silly, trusting fool, Dianna Grey,* she told herself miserably, *to dream of love with a man who never cared!*

"You'd do better to send Kit off with a smile, lass," said Hester so pointedly that Dianna blushed, wondering how much the older woman had guessed. "Else we may all end like that poor lad in there."

Dianna's expression was so confused that Hester rolled her eyes and clucked her tongue. "Where be your wits, girl? D'ye think that Frenchman cut himself shaving? 'Twas Indians, Dianna, Indians that took his scalp, and they'll take yours as well if they catch ye out a-walkin'. A head o'hair like yours would look mighty pleasing danglin' from some brave's waist."

Dianna's gaze flew past Hester to the departing men, and in vain she searched for Kit's gold-streaked hair among them. If what Hester said were true, she might never see him alive again.

"Ah, but I disremember, you're fresh from London," said Hester more sympathetically, misreading Dianna's concern. "We'll be safe enough here at Plumstead. Built stouter than most forts, this house. An' Kit an' the rest o' them will come to no harm, neither. Indians be too clever t'attack a force o' armed men. It be the families livin' all alone that th' sneaking savages prey on. That's why we'll be havin' a houseful until Kit sorts this out."

At that moment a woman Dianna recognized from meeting appeared at the door, one child in her arms and four more following, each with hastily packed bundles of belongings. The youngest girl was weeping, and automatically Dianna went to comfort her. From then until long past nightfall, she was constantly busy, from peeling carrots for Hester to melting lead for musket balls over the fireplace coals to rescuing a kitten from an over-ardent child. There

were thirty-four people at supper, and while the men
took turns standing guard from the upper-floor windows, the women and children had to be settled in the
five chambers upstairs, the lucky ones in the beds, but
most rolled in blankets on the floor. It was a tense,
somber gathering, with no one certain what the darkness would bring.

As Dianna scrubbed out the last kettle with a handful of sand, her whole body felt on edge from listening and waiting and trying to be cheerful. She watched
Hester go for one more bucket of water, a man cov-
ering her with his musket from the doorway as she
walked to the well and back. "We've one more task
this night, lass," said Hester wearily as she leaned
away from the full bucket in her right hand. "Ye must
watch me wit' the Frenchman now an' learn, an' then
th' care of him falls to ye."

The small room where the Frenchman lay was sti-
fling. One wall backed on the kitchen chimney, and
the two narrow windows were shut against the harm
of the night air. As Hester lit the lantern over the bed
and began to unwrap the bandages on the man's head,
Dianna gasped with horror. The top of his head was
completely gone, his bare skull white where his hair
and scalp had been. At the sight, Dianna felt the room
begin to spin around her and the blood pound in her
ears.

"Don't faint on me now, lass," warned Hester as
she quickly reached out to steady Dianna. "I can't
take on two o' ye at once."

At the sound of her voice, the Frenchman stirred.
"Solange, c'est tu?"

Hester nodded at Dianna. "There now, speak to th' lad," she prompted. "He needs t'hear his own tongue."

Dianna hesitated, unsure of how to reply, and the Frenchman struggled weakly to rise from the narrow bed. *"Solange? Ou est tu?"*

"Soyez calme, s'il vous plaît," murmured Dianna, gently pushing him back, and to her surprise he grasped her wrist with unexpected strength. "I am here."

"That's good, lass, hold him steady while I finish." Deftly Hester rinsed the wound and began to tie fresh linen strips around his head. "Mind me, now, for you'll do the same come morning. Call me if the wound turns putrid or a fever takes him." She finished at last and looked at Dianna curiously. "What's he been saying, anyways?"

"He thinks I'm a woman named Solange," said Dianna softly. "I thought it best to agree."

"Aye, let him be at ease. We'll not get much sense out o' him for a day or two at least. Mayhap never, if his wits went with his hair." Hester gathered up the soiled bandages and the bucket. "Ye stay with him tonight in case he wakes. Ye shall find more comfort in that chair than some of them upstairs. I'll be in the kitchen if ye need me."

Dianna nodded and looked down at the slow rise and fall of the man's narrow chest beneath his coarse shirt. He had once again fallen asleep, and gently she eased her hand free from his, wondering if she would ever learn who Solange was.

With a sigh, Dianna tried to make herself comfortable, curling her legs up in the rush-bottom chair and resting her head across her folded arms. From the kitchen, she could hear Hester chatting softly with the men on watch, and beyond that, outdoors, the whirring of cicadas in the trees. She was too exhausted to stay awake long. Although she wished it were otherwise, her last thoughts before sleep claimed her were of Kit and how sweet it had been to lie in his arms on an afternoon in June.

Chapter Eleven

It wanted still two hours until dawn and Kit hated to wake Dianna. The single candle's light from the tin lantern washed her figure in shadowy gold as she slept, her face pillowed in her crossed arms, her lips slightly parted. It seemed the one peaceful moment in Kit's world right now, a world gone horribly awry. He longed to find solace in her arms and in her embrace, forget the memories of old tragedies and the fresh, raw images of what he and the others had found beyond Plumstead. But he had no right to her comfort, not after the way he had treated her this afternoon. No, it had been yesterday, he reminded himself wearily. Only yesterday. It might have been a lifetime, given the way he felt now.

The Davies brothers had been lucky. Their house and barn had been burned to charred, smoking timbers, but their horses and cattle at pasture left unharmed. If the brothers had not brought the Frenchman to Plumstead, they would likely have met the same fate as their neighbors, the Barnards.

John Barnard and his three sons had been shot dead in their cornfield, their attackers boldly using the tall,

new corn for cover. From the moccasin footprints between the rows, Kit doubted the Barnards had seen the
Indians until it was too late. Their house, too, had
been burned, and there was no sign of Dorothy Barnard or the two daughters. Women made useful captives, for ransom or to sell as servants to the French,
and, grimly, Kit knew it unlikely that he'd ever see
them again.

Kit and the others had pushed on to the rest of the
surrounding homesteads, continuing to travel long
after nightfall. They had found no more destruction,
but Kit had warned the other settlers and urged them
to come to Plumstead for safety. That most stubbornly refused did not surprise him. Many years had
passed since the country surrounding Wickhamton
had been attacked, and despite the attack on Deerfield to the north in February, newcomers in particular naively scoffed at the danger. But then few carried
with them the memory that had haunted Kit every
hour, every day, since the year of his twenty-second
birthday.

It had been early autumn, still warm in the after-
noons, though the leaves had begun to change and the
first, weak frosts marked the ground at dawn. Kit's
mother, Amity, had spent the night with a friend in
Wickhamton, easing her through a difficult birth; with
six children of her own surviving infancy, Amity's
comfort was much in demand. It was Kit's task to
bring his mother home, but at the last moment, for a
reason he never could remember, his father had gone
instead and taken his youngest daughter, Tamsin, with
him. When they did not return by supper, Kit had

ridden out to meet them, certain his mother had, as usual, dawdled to gossip with friends and that his father would welcome his elder son's company.

Instead what Kit had found were the slaughtered bodies of his parents and sister scattered across the Wickhamton road like mangled dolls.

If he'd only gone instead of his father...

If he'd left to meet them even a quarter-hour earlier!

No one held him to blame except himself. If Kit had been there, too, his friends had argued, then he would have perished as well. Even the minister had told him he'd been spared by God's infinite mercy. But Kit did not believe them then, and he did not believe them now. Some part of him had died that afternoon along with his parents and sister. Methodically he had tracked the four Mohegans responsible for the killing, and as he watched them hanged, he had realized the empty satisfaction of his revenge. He had thrown himself into running Plumstead and governing the land around it as his father had done, building the mills to lure more settlers, and expanding into trade with Jonathan and other captains. But nothing had helped. Nothing had eased the anguish or given back to him what he'd lost.

How could he ever explain it to Dianna? He let himself watch her sleep a little longer, knowing he was wasting the short time he could spare to be alone with her. Even if he found the words, how could she possibly understand?

Even before she woke, Dianna sensed Kit was there. Her eyes opened and met his warily, uncertain what to expect. He stood on the other side of the injured Frenchman, his unshaven face streaked with dirt and sweat, and bits of leaves and brambles stuck in his hair. His eyes were red-rimmed from lack of sleep, his mouth a hard line that would offer no sweetheart's promises, and she steeled herself to be equally cold and unyielding.

"We need to talk, Dianna."

Dianna shook her head fiercely. "There is nothing to say."

So this was how it would be, thought Kit wearily. A "nothing" like that from her meant he could talk from now until Christmas and she wouldn't hear a word of it. But he had to try. "Dianna, dearling, I regret—"

"I want none of your regrets and none of you!" she answered hotly. "I'm sorrier than you will ever be about—about what passed between us yesterday, and I will thank you never to mention it again."

"Dianna—"

"Nay, I'll not hear more!" She scrambled out of the chair and grabbed a handful of the fresh bandages that she and Hester had torn last night. "This man needs to be tended, Master Sparhawk, and I'll ask you to let me go about my work."

Kit sighed and rubbed his forehead. How could he set things right with a half-dead Frenchman lying between them? If he weren't so tired and discouraged, he might have laughed. "Has the man said anything of use?"

"Nay," Dianna swallowed hard, concentrating on both cleaning the wound as Hester had shown her and not fainting before Kit.

Kit hadn't imagined her as a nurse and was surprised by how gently she tended to the Frenchman. The man stirred and groaned restlessly beneath her touch, and Dianna murmured to him softly in French. The unknown words in her low voice struck Kit's ear as impossibly seductive, and as the man relaxed, Kit felt the first twinge of unexpected jealousy. "What are you saying to him?" he demanded impatiently.

Her eyes narrowed at the unmistakable suspicion. "You don't know how to trust, do you?" she said tersely. "I've said nothing to him that I wouldn't say to Mercy."

"Damn it, Dianna, there are four men dead, a woman and two girls missing, and yet you expect me to—"

"Colonel Sparhawk!" The man pounded unceremoniously on the chamber door. "The messenger's ready t'ride to th' garrison at Northfield."

His expression black with anger, Kit threw open the door and stalked into the kitchen filled with the men from the trainband. They all believed he'd been questioning the Frenchman, and Kit felt like a fool for concocting an excuse merely to talk to a woman who refused to listen. "Where's Eleazer? I'll need another copy of this letter to send to Lord Bellomar, and two more for Albany and New Haven. If it is the Sagomutucks again, then other Englishmen should be warned."

"Eleazer's gone t'warn 'em at Deerfield, Colonel," said John Davies uneasily. "Ye sent him there yerself."

Kit swore and dropped heavily into the chair at the end of the table. "Why the devil did I do that?" he demanded of no one in particular. From the corner of his eye, he caught Dianna's small figure slipping among the men, the bucket held before her. "Eleazer's the only man I trust to write a decent hand. Ah, well, there's no help for it but I must write the letter again myself." He reached for his pen and another sheet of paper.

"I can copy it for you," said Dianna quietly. Every man turned to stare at her, but she stood with her head high and her hands folded before her. "It takes no great manly strength to wield a pen, you know."

Kit looked up at her from under drawn brows, weighing her offer for only a moment before shoving the paper and pen toward her. "I need three copies for my signing by the time I return tonight, one to Lord Bellomar in Boston, and one each to the governors of Connecticut and New York. And mark that they're neat and true, for I want their lordships to read every word."

As all around him the other men rumbled and nodded in agreement, Kit finished the tall flacon of cider Hester had brought him. He should, he knew, eat something as well, for he intended to visit the farthest points of his settled land today, a good day's hard riding at best. But he was still too concerned about what he might find to linger at Plumstead any longer, and restlessly he rose to leave. Only at the doorway did he let himself pause to look back at Dianna, bending over the table to study the letters she was to copy. Let her read them, he decided as he left. Then perhaps she would understand.

Dianna stared down at the letter before her, the words blurring before her eyes. She wanted to take Mercy and go home, never to see Kit Sparhawk again. She needed time alone to think. She felt trapped in his house, trapped as much by his overwhelming presence as by the danger waiting in the forest. He hadn't bothered to thank her for copying his infernal letters, let alone bid her farewell. Because she had rebuffed his attentions, she knew she could expect no better. But, oh, how it hurt!

She forced herself to read the letter before her. Kit's handwriting was irritatingly like him, bold and confident and masculine. But the events his words described made her soon forget her own concerns. In short, blunt sentences, Kit described the massacre of the Barnard men and the kidnapping of the women, the scalping of the Frenchman and the destruction of barns and houses. And this, he concluded, might only be the beginning of a long, bloody conflict in the river valley.

''Is this true, Hester?'' Dianna asked hoarsely, her face drawn with horror.

''If Kit's written it, then true it be,'' replied Hester. ''Poor Dorothy Barnard! She be a timid soul anyways, and then t'lose her men an' her home on th' selfsame day must be too much for her to bear. God preserve her an' restore her an' the lasses back to us!''

"But surely when the governor sends us the soldiers Kit has asked for—surely then they will be rescued!"

Hester shook her head sadly. "There's no certainty in this world, lass. This be a big land, and th' governor has many calls for his troops. One poor Wickhamton family don't account for much wit' those fine folks in New Haven. An' even if the soldiers come, why, th' trail will be so cold by then that Goodwife Barnard's sure to be lost t'English eyes forever."

"Can't Kit and the trainband men go after them?"

"Don't believe he hasn't thought on it!" exclaimed Hester ruefully. "But those roguish savages could lead them clear t'Montreal, an' who'd be left here? Trainband men have farms an' families t'tend, an' Kit— faith, there's hardly a soul 'round here that don't depend on him for something."

"What will the Indians do to the women?" asked Dianna. She thought of the day when she and Mercy had met the Indian in the woods. What if he hadn't been friendly?

"If they didn't kill them outright, they'll likely sell them in Montreal, where th'priests will try t'beguile them into turning Papist," said Hester with true Protestant contempt. "Else they'll keep th' women for themselves an' turn them into heathen squaws. Me, I never could decide which fate'd be th' worst."

Dianna had heard enough. With a sigh, she carefully began to copy Kit's letter as Hester, a broad wooden spoon in her hand, bent over Dianna's shoulder to watch.

"Then it be true? Ye can read an' write like a gentleman? I never learned beyond makin' my mark," she marveled. "With your French an' writin' an' all, ye can do more good for Kit than th' rest o' us womenfolk combined."

But when Dianna remembered the cold expression on Kit's face, she knew he'd only one use for her, a use that would bring no good to any of them.

For the next two weeks, Dianna was never far from Kit's thoughts. Again and again, as he rode across open meadows and through uncleared forests, he could think of little beyond her—her smile, her laugh and, most of all, how she'd looked wearing nothing more than wildflowers—and again and again he cursed himself for being so besotted. It was dangerous, for one thing. He could be mooning away after Dianna and not see the glint of a musket or knife in the tree overhead until it was too late. Too many people were counting on him for him to risk his life and theirs by acting like a lovelorn schoolboy.

It was all Dianna's fault, of course. He'd tried to apologize, and God knows he'd never had to do that to a woman before, but she'd just stuck her haughty little nose in the air and dismissed him, there, in his own house. In front of Hester, she had shrugged off his thanks for copying the letters with a brusqueness that bordered on being rude, and had given him no opening to admit to the misspellings she'd corrected, an admission he'd felt sure would have melted her resistance. With Plumstead full of women, she was the only one who didn't look to him for reassurance, or smile at his jests when he sought to cheer them. She kept her distance, but her small, slender figure was always there, taunting him with her proximity alone until he thought he'd go mad from wanting to touch her. How could she have given herself so freely to him that one perfect afternoon and now not even deign to meet his eye?

Perhaps if he'd had more success in the forest, he could have borne her rejection more gracefully. Each day he and the others rode out on ever-varied patrols, checking on the farms and houses that had been so hastily closed and searching for any signs of the Indians that had killed the Barnards. But at dusk they returned to Plumstead with no news, and it ate at him that he still didn't even know which tribe was responsible. They had struck and then vanished, their identity and motives mysteries, and Kit had little patience with mysteries weighted against the lives of English women and children.

Kit's last hope for a clue lay with the Frenchman, and even that was fading as fast as the trapper's life. He had never regained consciousness to be questioned about his assailants, and when the fever had settled into his weakened body, Hester and Kit each knew without speaking that the man would not survive. Only Dianna tenaciously believed he would recover and spent long hours talking to him in French and bathing his body with cool, damp cloths. Her attentions irritated Kit, not only because they struck him as so misplaced—before the attack, the man had probably been as coarse and wolfish as any other French trapper, certainly company Dianna would have taken pains to avoid—but also because it was at Kit's own order that she had begun tending the injured man in the first place. To be jealous of a dying man was ludicrous, yet Kit was, and knowing it didn't make it any easier to bear. Being jealous meant he cared about her in the way that he'd been doing his damnedest to deny.

Late one evening Kit sat at the kitchen table, moodily swirling the beer in his tankard as he watched Dianna with the trapper through the open door. The candle in the lantern brought out the mahogany streaks in her hair, like a soft red halo around her face. As she changed his bandages she sang, crooning almost, the seductive sound of her voice wrapping around the soft French words.

It was too much for Kit. In three long strides he was in the little room. Dianna's startled face upturned before him as he caught her by the arm.

"What do you want? You've no reason to hold me thus!" Her pale eyes flashed her anger.

"You wanted to learn how to fire a musket," he replied, "and by God, I'm ready to teach you."

"But you refused before—"

"Things are different now." He pulled her along after him, pausing in the kitchen only to grab a musket, bullets and powder, before he led her out the door and away from the house. Dianna struggled to break free, twisting and jerking back, but his grasp was too strong to break, and she followed stumbling after him.

"You said we all had to stay near the house!" she yelled at him. "Your orders, *Colonel* Sparhawk!"

He ignored her, intent on reaching the small copse of beech trees. The moon was just past full, the meadow they crossed almost as brightly lit as by day. He stopped before the trees, releasing her so suddenly that she reeled to one side.

"You're mad, you are," she said as she flung her loosened hair back out of her face. She was breathless from fighting him, and breathless, too, from being alone with him. For a fortnight she had been able to keep her true feelings about him buried behind a careful mask of indifference, but she did not trust herself without the safety of others around her. "To fire guns after dark with all the country fearful, we'll likely be shot ourselves! I'm going back to the house now—"

"You'll stay," he said as he unshouldered the musket, "and you'll learn." Before she could protest, he had caught her again and yanked her back hard against his chest. Holding her within the circle of his arms, he began to load the gun, shaking a little powder into the priming pan and snapping it shut with two fingers.

"This is the firelock. Make certain it's at half-cock before you begin, and only a smidge of the powder here." Deftly he then sloped the musket down, steadying it with one hand while with the other he shook more powder down the barrel. Next went the wadding and the ball. Then, after drawing the ramrod from the barrel's loops, he gave it three quick strokes to shove the ball in place. In spite of herself, Dianna watched him, fascinated by the practiced ease with which he loaded the musket. The confidence with which his long-fingered hands moved was almost graceful, and she remembered too well how those same hands had moved across her body.

Loading a musket was a task Kit could probably do while drunk, asleep or both, and considering the effect Dianna was having on him, it was just as well. Small as she was, she fit so neatly against him, her soft curves especially designed, it seemed, to complement the harder planes and hollows of his own body. Beneath his nose her hair smelled clean, like meadow grass, and he longed to bury his face in it. He handed her the musket, holding it steady while she found her aim, noticing how smooth and silky pale the skin of her shoulder looked beside the darkened maple of the musket's butt.

Dianna tried to concentrate on the tree branch that Kit had chosen as her target. Once her father had let her fire one of his small hunting guns, and, to his great amusement, the recoil had landed her on her backside. This musket was heavier and longer, and she dreaded giving Kit one more reason to scorn her. Feeling his warm breath just below her ear did nothing to help her concentration, nor did the way he guided her aim with one hand gently at her wrist. She took a deep breath, braced her legs apart and fired.

The gunshot exploded in her ear, the impact throwing her back against Kit. He stood firm, unmoving as she quickly scrambled away from him to peer out into the moonlight. The bark on the bottom of the branch had cracked and splintered, the leaves around it bouncing wildly from the impact. Elated, she spun around to grin at him, clutching the musket like a prize with both hands.

"Why did you not tell me you were a maid?" he asked softly, his eyes hidden in shadow.

Dianna stiffened, her excitement gone in an instant. "Would it have made any difference to you?" she demanded, her head high. "Maid or not, what could I ever hope to be to you beyond one more of your harlots? Another pitiful lass fallen under the spell of the irresistible Kit Sparhawk?"

"Merciful God in Heaven," murmured Kit to himself in disbelief. This was not what he'd expected, not at all, but when had Dianna ever been predictable?

"Is it because I'm but a woman, a lowly, base creature, you won't bother to defend yourself?" Her laugh was brittle, the strain of the last weeks catching her at last. "What of Patience Tucker then, and the babe she's likely borne you by now? Would you defend *her?*"

"If you were a man," said Kit quietly, "I'd call you out for speaking such nonsense."

Why doesn't he deny it? thought Dianna wildly. *Please, please, tell me I'm wrong!* She felt the tears welling up behind her eyes and roughly dashed them away. "And what about Mercy? She's your daughter, too, isn't she?"

Dianna was sobbing now, lost in her misery and disillusionment, and blindly she turned toward the house. But Kit caught her by the shoulders first, holding her straight before him. Having grown up with four sisters, he was generally unaffected by weeping

women, but the desolation in Dianna's crying shocked
him. Had he really hurt her that much?

"Listen to me, Dianna," he said urgently. "Listen
to me!"

She shook her head and looked down at the grass,
letting her tears fall unchecked, as the musket dropped
to the ground. His hands slid along her shoulders and
up her neck to turn her face up toward his. "Patience
Tucker's husband was second mate on the *Prosperity*.
When he was lost in the last gale, it fell to me as owner
to tell her. I've never laid eyes, let alone anything else,
on the lass before or since. As for Lucy Wing—sweet
Jesus, Dianna, her husband was one of my closest
friends! I know you're from a different world where
such things may not matter, but I would never have
done that to Tom if Lucy had tossed herself before me
naked as Eve!"

"But Asa says—"

"Then Asa lies," said Kit firmly. "He never took to
Lucy, or to me, either, for the time his son spent with
us instead of him, and now he feels the same with
Mercy. I love the little minx, aye, but where's the harm
in that?"

Gently he stroked her cheeks with his thumbs,
striving to reassure her with his touch as well as words.
"I've never claimed to be a saint, sweeting, and there
are women enough who can spin pretty tales of Jonathan and me both. But not Lucy, not Patience, and no
bastards. I'm not nearly so free with my seed as you
believe."

She blushed at his frankness, though she knew it
was no less than she deserved. Through the tears she

searched his face, hoping, praying that she could trust him.

He saw the doubt in her eyes and sighed. "Believe what you will, Dianna, but I swear by all that's holy and dear to me that that's the truth." His voice was deep and low. "Now why did you not tell me you were a maid?"

"I did not think I had to," she whispered hoarsely. "I thought you were different. I thought you would believe me instead of my uncle. But I was wrong, wasn't I? I was wrong...."

She spoke without malice, yet her words cut straight to his conscience and to his heart, too. "Nay, dearling, not wrong, but wronged," he said sadly. "I've no right to ever hope for your forgiveness."

She listened, incredulous, and tentatively touched her fingers to his rough cheek. "Ah, Kit," she breathed, her smile fragile and tremulous. "We are neither of us, I think, quite so good nor quite so bad as we each might fear."

He caught her hand in his and brushed his lips across her open palm. "I love you, Dianna Grey," he said simply, and he realized he had never meant anything more in his life than those words. "How much I love you!"

"No more than I love you, Kit Sparhawk, my perfect, precious love!" And now, at last, she believed him, and knew, in her heart, she always had.

This time when their lips met, their kiss was at once heated, urgent and wild. Dianna seized at the passion he offered and arched herself into him, opening her mouth fully to his demands. She forgot everything but

him as she twined her limbs around his, and swiftly Kit
scooped his arms under her knees and carried her into
the purple shadows of the beech trees. Collapsing into
the rustling leaves, she showered him with kisses, wet
and soft, on his face and throat and chest, and tangled her fingers in the lion-like mass of his hair. She
lay atop him, her breasts crushed against his chest, her
legs slipping apart over his hips, and through their
clothes she could feel the heat of him, hard and ready
against her belly.

Kit's hands swept along her length, caressing and
stroking her as he drew her even tighter against him.
He kissed her hard, his tongue filling her mouth as he
longed to fill her body. She tasted so impossibly sweet
that he was sure he could kiss her forever and never
tire of her. Hungrily he reached between their bodies
and tugged her bodice open, the silky fullness of her
breasts spilled over the lacings and into his palms. He
cupped them gently, marveling at the softness of her
skin as his fingers played across the crests, her nipples
swelling and tightening. She moaned into his mouth,
wanting more, needing more, and he jerked the rough
wool skirt over her hips. He reached to stroke the
backs of her thighs, the curves of her hips and buttocks, the little dimples at the base of her spine, and
she arched back, gasping, as he caught one rosy nipple between his lips. Convulsively her fingers worked
in the muscles of his shoulders, her head thrown back
and her hair streaming over her shoulders.

Kit was almost shaking with the force of his desire.
With a groan he separated from her only long enough
to unfasten his breeches. He rose to his knees, and she

threw her arms around his neck, climbing him, her movements frantic with need. His breathing harsh, Kit shoved her skirts up and found her wet and ready. As his fingers touched her, Dianna gasped raggedly, and then his hands were grasping her thighs and lifting her, her legs wrapping tight around his waist as he slid deep into her. With his hands spread to cradle her, he moved her powerfully against him, and she cried out in wonder. He was a part of her and she a part of him, joined in heart and spirit as surely as they now were joined in flesh, and as together they soared higher and higher, it seemed that their love, like their passion, would be ever boundless.

Afterward they lay together, coupled still, listening to the whirring of the cicadas and the muted calls of night birds as the pounding of their own hearts grew gradually quieter. Dianna wondered if she'd ever move again, so contented was she, and mindless of the wanton way she lay sprawled across Kit with her skirts rucked up and her bodice unlaced. His shirt beneath her cheek was damp with sweat, and she snuggled closer as his fingers twined randomly in her hair.

"I love you, sweeting," he murmured into the top of her hair. He could not remember feeling so contented, so at peace, as he did now with Dianna. "I would keep you here with me all night and let the white-faced cows find us come dawn."

Dianna giggled at the image and propped herself up on her elbows to study him. His face looked so relaxed, the dark lashes sooty shadows on his cheeks, that she wondered if he were asleep, and she spoke softly in case he was so he would not wake. "I love you too, Kit, and not even white-faced cattle can change that."

With his eyes still closed, Kit snorted. "At least my cows would keep their own counsel, which is a sight more than our good neighbors will be able to manage. I'll talk to Asa on the morrow and buy you out of that ridiculous indenture, and then—"

But Dianna silenced him with her fingers across his lips. "Hush, love. I want no promises, no plans from you tonight." No plans, no promises that could be broken along with her heart. "Knowing you love me is enough."

His arms tightened around her, praying she was right. How could love survive when life itself seemed so fragile? One by one, he kissed her fingertips and she shivered with delight.

"But cows or no, we cannot truly stay all night, can we?" she asked wistfully, though she knew the answer.

"Nay, there's no help for it, my love." He opened his eyes and smiled, his teeth blue-white in the moonlight, and Dianna thought she'd never seen such a beautiful man. Carefully he plucked a leaf from her hair. "Come, I'll play your lady's maid and help set you to rights."

They dressed slowly, pausing often to kiss and caress each other, and by the time they headed toward Plumstead, the only light left in the house came from the little lantern in the sickroom. As they walked through the tall meadow grass, already heavy with dew, Kit laughed ruefully and stopped to pick up the musket they'd left behind.

"Here's proof enough how I can think of nothing beyond you," he said, shaking his head. "The whole country in alarm, and here I leave musket, powder and balls for any savage to find."

Although he tried to make light of it, the gun was a sharp reminder of all they'd been able to forget in each other's arms. Irretrievably, the mood was gone, and each felt the loss sorely. Mindful of the two men on watch at the house, they walked self-consciously, as close as they could without actually touching. As they drew closer, one of the guards ran toward them, waving.

Kit frowned, fearing the worst. "What in blazes—"

"Colonel Sparhawk, sir," the man said quickly, tugging on his hatbrim before he impatiently turned to Dianna. "Where ye been hiding yerself, lass? Mistress Holcomb's been raisin' the devil tryin' to find ye! That ruddy Frenchman o'yours is dyin'!"

Chapter Twelve

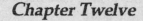

Kneeling at the Frenchman's cot, Dianna noticed the change at once. She had never seen anyone die before, but there was no mistaking the man's condition now. He'd seemed to shrink into himself somehow, his breathing slow and labored, and beneath the white bandage his skin was waxy and oddly translucent. Already he looked more like a corpse than a man.

"He'll not see another dawn, lass," said Hester as she rested her hand on Dianna's shoulder. "Ye've done all ye can for him, but it be th'Lord decides these things, not us."

"How can he die?" said Dianna unevenly. "I never even learned his name."

From the doorway, Kit heard the catch in her voice, and he yearned to comfort her. He felt no jealousy for the Frenchman now, only a terrible sense of waste. He'd seen it so often, too often, Kit thought wearily, one more man's life cut short before its time.

But at the sound of her voice, the Frenchman moaned and strained upward toward her, and with obvious effort his eyes half opened. "Ah, Solange, you are here."

"Dormez, mon ami," said Dianna as she touched her hand to the dying man's cheek, his skin hot and brittle.

"Tell François I saw him, Solange," he rasped in French. "He tried to hide, the swine, but I marked his face, and I tell you now!"

Dianna drew closer, aware of the significance of the man's words, and aware, too, that his time was short. *"Ou est François, mon ami?"* Where was he?

"He waited in the trees...but I saw him. I saw Robillard, damn him, the coward!"

At Robillard's name, Kit leaped forward. "What did he say, Dianna?" he demanded urgently. "God in Heaven, if Robillard's filthy hand is in this—"

Dianna's eyes never left the Frenchman's wasted face. "He said he saw Robillard hiding in the trees when the others attacked him."

Kit leaned over her shoulder. "Ask him who the others were!"

But as Kit spoke the Frenchman slipped back, and Dianna watched the last bit of life drain from his face. *"Au revoir, mon ami pauvre,"* she said as Hester closed the man's eyes for the final time. *"Au revoir!"*

They buried the Frenchman the next morning; with the summer's heat, there was no reason to delay. Dianna and Kit were his only mourners. Some, like Hester, stayed away because the man had been French and a Papist, but most were simply too busy leaving Plumstead to bother with a stranger's burial. At dawn Kit had told the families in his keeping that they could return to their homes, that as much as he could guess, the danger was past for now. Still, he sent soldiers from the Northfield garrison along with each wagon and warned the men to keep watch for trouble. Now that Kit knew the attacks had come from Robillard, not Indians alone, he knew it was up to him to make some sort of move.

And Kit still wasn't certain what that move should be. To call in more soldiers to lead an attack in retaliation on French settlements to the north seemed pointless to Kit, though the governor's men, safe in Boston, would probably counsel it. All that would bring would be more French soldiers or French-sponsored Indians and more suffering to the English families in his protection. And yet to ignore Robillard's attack was cowardly and just as likely to bring more slayings and more kidnappings.

It was Sparhawk land that Robillard wanted, plain and simple. Kit believed that the man had only intended to cause enough damage to frighten away the English settlers on Kit's holdings and weaken his claim, although, thought Kit grimly, Robillard had shown typical French disregard for English tenacity where good, rich land was concerned. The poor French trapper must have had the misfortune to wander through the Davies' fields at the wrong time. Likely he'd been one of Robillard's own trappers to know him by name. Kit wondered if the other men had been French, as well, or Indians, Mohegans or Abenakis, in Robillard's hire. Not that it really mattered. Murder was the same in any tongue, and Kit wanted no more of it in his valley.

The two gravediggers tossed the last loose soil onto the new grave, hoisted their shovels over their shoulders and began the long walk back to Wickhamton. Dianna bent to lay a circle of wildflowers on the new grave, murmuring softly in French that, this time, Kit did not ask her to translate. Her eyes were dry, but her face was pale and solemn. The Frenchman's death had shaken her more than she wanted to admit, and Kit longed to be able to spare her from such sorrow. He'd grant that her spirit was as strong as any woman's, and her temper, too, but he could not forget that she'd been gently bred, and today her eyes were shadowed and her shoulders bent from sleeplessness and fatigue.

As they walked home in silence, Kit let his hand rest comfortably about her waist. Beside him she seemed so small, almost fragile. Yet there was no denying the strength of the passion that burned in that delicate frame, and at the memory of last night, his fingers slid down from her waist, fanning to caress the soft curve of her hip and buttocks. He heard her breath catch as she glanced up at him through her lashes, her eyebrows arched expectantly as her cheeks flushed.

"You tempt me sorely, lass," he growled as he bent to kiss her neck behind her ear. "I should toss you here, in plain sight of the house, to show you how dangerous your game can be."

Dianna smiled shyly. Why was it with one touch he could make her forget everything else except him? "Tonight, then, by the beeches," she whispered, feeling daringly bold. "I swear I won't keep your cattle waiting."

It was all Kit could do to steady himself. With all her chattering about illegitimate children, she'd never mentioned herself. Even now his child could be growing in her belly, and for the first time the idea of fatherhood warmed him with pleasure. Pleasure, but responsibility, too, and he knew then what he would do about Robillard.

"Nay, lass, not tonight. I'll say farewell to you now," he said, too abruptly even to his own ears. "There won't be time alone when we're back among the others before I leave."

She stared up at him, uncomprehending.

"I'm going to find Robillard myself," he explained hurriedly. Merciful heaven, why did those beautiful eyes have to be so full of questions? "It's me he wants, and it's me he'll have, and perhaps then he'll listen to reason. My land's English, not French, and there's no law or treaty that says otherwise. I'll haul him clear to Quebec to prove it, if I must."

"You'll take soldiers with you?"

"Nay, I don't want to give him any reason to send his men out to greet me with less than kind hospitality." The miserable jest fell flat, and he plunged on. "I'll go with Attawan, if I can find him on my way, but that's all."

Dianna stopped and yanked her arm away from his. "Of all the braggartly, half-witted schemes—"

"Dianna, I've lived all my life on this land and know it as well as my own parlor."

"That's not the point, is it?" she asked incredulously. "You're going to dance right into the arms of a man who'd like nothing more than to see you dead, a man who's killed your own tenants to get at you. And just so you can have the honor of playing hero!''

She waved wildly at the fresh grave behind them. ''Look what he did to one of his own countrymen! Why do you think he'll be willing to change just because you asked him genteelly?''

''Is that really what you believe? That it's only selfishness that makes me want to save the lives of my people? Aye, and your life, too, for I'm doing this as much for you as for anyone.'' The depth of his feelings for her was still so new that he felt clumsy trying to put it into words. ''I do care what happens to you, Dianna.''

''Precious odd way you have of showing it, Master Sparhawk!''

''Dianna, listen to me—''

''Nay, you listen to me! It's your ludicrous man's pride that makes you want to toss away your own life. Empty, vain, puffed-up pride that's not worth a tinker's dam!'' Kit tried to take her hand, but she shoved him away so hard, she herself stumbled backward. ''Don't you understand that every moment I spent with that poor man, I thought of how I'd feel if it were you lying there instead, with your life's blood slipping away?''

Her voice caught on a sob, her words rising in an anguished wail. ''I hate this country! I hate how it turns every man into a murdering savage, and I hate the blood-letting and the revénge, and I hate—oh, damn it, I hate how I'm crying, too, as if I truly cared what happened to your prideful, selfish hide!''

Once again Kit reached for her, and this time caught her wrist, but again she jerked away, her eyes bright with tears. "That's how you are with everything, Kit. Take it and force it to bend to your will, just because your name's Sparhawk. But it won't work with François Robillard. And it won't work with me."

Dianna turned and fled, her bare feet flying beneath her skirts as she left Kit standing alone on the rutted dirt road. Her heart felt near to bursting, not from running, but from all that she'd heard and said. She needed desperately to be alone, and she headed for the barn, hoping that at midday, all the workers and animals would be in the fields. The wide doors were thrown open to catch any breeze, and she paused in the doorway, her breath coming in great shuddering sobs, while her eyes grew accustomed to the shadowy barn.

"Dianna!" Mercy stepped from one of the empty stalls and grinned. Cradled in her arms was a white kitten patched with black, sleeping blissfully against the girl's chest. Automatically Dianna reached out to straighten Mercy's linen cap and pluck bits of straw from her apron.

"I'm glad you've come at last t'meet my Lily," said the girl proudly. "Lily, this be Dianna. She'll be nice to ye, Lily, an' she won't shoo ye away like Hester."

The girl held the little cat's paw out to Dianna to shake. "She be a fine catkin, my Lily," Mercy said fondly, stroking the sleeping kitten. Suddenly she noticed Dianna's tear-streaked face.

"Ye be mournin' that Frenchman, don't ye, Dianna?" she said with surprising empathy. "Well, ye grieve howsomuch ye want out here, an' I'll not tell Hester.''

Not trusting her voice, Dianna knelt down and took Mercy in her arms, holding her tight until the kitten between them yowled in protest. With a shaky smile, Dianna sat back on her heels. She'd had little time to spend with Mercy these past weeks, and she'd missed the girl's company. ''We'll make a special bed for Lily when we go home tonight, up in the loft with us. That way you can talk to her if she gets frightened in the night.''

Mercy's grin widened, and with a pang Dianna noticed she'd lost another baby tooth. ''I want you and Lily to say goodbye to Kit and thank him for having us as guests at Plumstead. Hurry now, I think he's likely at the house.''

''Nay, Mercy, he's right here,'' said Kit, and Dianna's head whipped around. He stood with his legs widespread, a dark silhouette in the doorway against the bright afternoon. Though unable to see his face, Dianna could hear the anger barely contained in his voice, and she rose slowly as Mercy ran to meet him, poor Lily jiggling in her embrace.

Kit swept the little girl up into his arms. ''Mind you take good care of Lily,'' he warned. ''I don't give Tiger's kittens to just anyone.''

Mercy giggled happily. ''Nay, 'cause ye keep them all t'yerself! Hester says th'barn be so overrun with cats Jonathan'll have t'bring in rats from th' shipyards t'keep 'em busy.''

''Aye, and right she may be. It's well you're taking Mistress Lily with you.'' He kissed the top of her head before setting her back on her feet. "Now off with you, poppet. I've things to say to our friend here."

There was an ominous sound to that which Dianna did not like, and she squared her hands on her hips, ready for a battle. He loomed before her, the sunlight behind him turning his tousled hair golden like a halo. *Halo, ha! More like the flames of hell, come to claim their own!*

He didn't waste any time. "I may be prideful and selfish, but I don't run away at the first sign of a fight. It makes me madder than a hornet in a bottle the way you keep flying off like that, and I won't have you doing it again!"

Dianna's chin jerked higher. "I believed, sir, our conversation was at an end."

"Not by half, it wasn't. Only a coward would say otherwise. And you, my lady, are no coward."

In an instant his hands were around her waist, drawing her closer. This time her pride kept her from rebuffing him, from confirming the accusation he'd just made. Defiantly she tried to raise her eyes to meet his, but somehow the path was slower than she intended, from the triangle of curling hair at the open throat of his untied shirt, along the stubborn strength of his jaw, already stubbled, to a mouth that, even set with sternness, could make her remember the sensual promise of kisses given and shared. She was certain she'd be betrayed by the pounding of her heart. Whether it raced from anger or desire she curiously couldn't decide, and for the first time she realized how closely twined the two passions could be.

He tried to remember all the things he'd decided as he followed her here, but his mind was empty except for the vibrant reality of her before him, her pulse thrumming there in the softest place on her throat. Swiftly he plucked Dianna up as easily as he had Mercy, and perched her on the edge of a tack-box so that their faces were now level.

"You're no coward, Dianna," he repeated as his thumb found the little cleft in her chin and he tilted her face toward his. "You're brave and beautiful and unlike any other woman in this world, and I'm so in love with you that to leave you today will be the hardest thing I've ever done."

He caught her around the waist and slid her against him as his lips crushed hers. There was no coaxing or beguiling this time, no gentle seductions, only a raw urgency, a primal intensity that left both of them panting as their mouths met and moved hungrily against each other.

Then suddenly he pulled away, his breathing harsh. He closed his eyes and shook his head with the effort of stopping, and let his head tip forward until their foreheads touched. "Dianna, sweetheart, this is how I'll take my leave, with both of us half mad from wanting," he said. "Now you'll believe me when I tell you nothing will keep me from coming back. Nothing could keep me from loving you, and I swear to you on my heart and honor that nothing will!"

And believe him she did.

Kit set off soon afterward. He decided to travel by canoe instead of horseback, knowing that in high summer the rivers would be both easier and swifter than making his way through the heavy brush. With his provisions and gunpowder bundled in a moose-hide to keep dry, he followed the Wickham River southwest, to where it joined the far larger Connecticut, and then headed north, toward Springfield and Deerfield, and Canada beyond. Even by water he guessed the journey would take him ten days, perhaps a week if the fair weather held, and then he planned to make certain all was well with his upriver sawmills. Only once before had he travelled to Robillard's holdings, and that was long ago, with his father. But though Kit's recollection of the route was hazy, he trusted his pathfinding instincts enough to be sure he'd find it again.

The sun was hot on his shoulders, and he welcomed the physical exertion of paddling against the current and the solitude and the beauty of the land and river around him. Overhead wild ducks flew against the brilliant blue of the summer sky, and through the trees he caught glimpses of curious deer and moose watching him. This was what he'd missed most when he had gone to England for Jonathan, this sense of boundless freedom. He began humming to the rhythm of his strokes, a tune he later realized to his amusement was the one Dianna had sung so much better than Constance.

At twilight he paused only long enough to stretch his legs and eat the cold ham and cornbread that Hester had packed, and then he was off again. He was too restless to need sleep, too unsettled. He continued through the night by the same full moon's light that had washed over him and Dianna the night before, and he marveled at how long ago that already seemed.

On the second night, he stopped at a small island, pulling the canoe well up beyond the sharp rocks of the riverbed and hiding it in the scrub pines. As boys, he and Jonathan had often come here, pretending the island was some Caribbean pirate stronghold. Strange to think that they could come all this way and still be on Sparhawk land, or so at least the parchment from his grandfather's time called it. Kit remembered his grandfather well, a fierce old Puritan with cropped white hair. He had been a soldier with Cromwell at Marston Moor, rewarded with a grant in land too wild for lesser men to tame. His grandfather had taught Kit much about combat and swordplay and leading other men to fight, lessons that had saved his life more times than he cared to count.

Foregoing the small luxury of a fire, Kit contented himself again with cold food and water, and rolled his tired body in a blanket to sleep, his rifle and knife beside him. Then, with the sound of the river running soft in his ears, he let his thoughts turn to Dianna: the way she smiled, the husky way she called him her love, the way her lips parted so eagerly to welcome his.

She might not wish to think of the future, but he couldn't help it. When he returned home, he meant to marry her. He frowned and quickly amended his thoughts. He would *ask* her to marry him and pray she agreed. For all his land and position in the colonies and for all she swore she loved him, he still remembered her grand family and how his in England had been minor west-county gentry at best. People like the

Greys didn't wed for love, and he could only hope she was different. She had to be.

By the time Kit saw the other man's arm, bright in the moonlight over him, it was almost too late. He threw himself sideways, the knife already in his hand as he tossed off the blanket and clambered to his feet.

Attawan rested the butt of his musket on the ground and leaned nonchalantly on the barrel, his face all angles and planes in the moonlight. "You grow careless, Sparhawk," he said, shaking his head. "I could have killed you ten times in your sleep."

"And I might have slit you in two before I opened my eyes, Attawan," Kit replied with a grin. He and Attawan had been friends since boyhood, when Kit's parents had taken Attawan's mother in after she had been wounded by an English scouting party. "You've been a stranger to my home since I've returned, my friend."

Attawan shrugged. "This spring your English have been too quick with their muskets, Sparhawk." As always he ignored the clipped Yankee pronunciation of Kit's name, emphasizing the "hawk" instead.

Kit's smile vanished as he dropped down onto the ground with a sigh. "I can't fault them, not after Deerfield, and now Wickhamton, as well."

"Abenakis and Mohegans," sniffed Attawan scornfully. "Not Pocumtucks."

"A woman and two girls are gone, four men dead, and on my land," said Kit with sharp impatience. "I can't fault quick fingers after that."

Attawan squatted down beside Kit, spreading his blanket out to dry after wading to the island. "So you go by yourself to avenge this?'' he asked. ''One man against ten times ten in Quebec?''

''I don't think the men who attacked my people are the same ones who sacked Deerfield,'' said Kit slowly. ''I think it was someone who'd like me to believe that. I think it was Robillard.''

Skeptically Attawan raised his eyebrows, waiting for Kit to explain.

''The trapper they scalped lived long enough to tell me Robillard was with the party. I'm guessing he hopes we'll all flee, like they did at Deerfield, and leave everything to him. I plan to tell him how very wrong he is.''

Attawan stroked the barbs of the turkey feather in his hair, considering Kit's words. ''You're a man with more courage than wisdom to go alone,'' he said at last.

Kit's smile was tight-lipped. ''You're not the first to tell me that,'' he said softly, remembering the tears in Dianna's eyes. ''But Robillard is a coward. He only fights when he's sure others will stop him. He'll bluff and bluster, but he won't risk doing me any real harm. He's made his feelings about me too well known, and he'll have all New England on his tail if I don't return. Same way I don't want all of New France on mine.''

''This man Robillard keeps many worthless Abenakis in brandy,'' said Attawan. ''You've grown so soft, you'll need someone to make sure the thieving curs don't find your back.''

Kit reached out to grasp the Indian's shoulder. ''I was hoping, my friend, that you would feel that way.''

* * *

For a man who fancied himself a gentleman, François Robillard's home was an unkempt shambles. Wary as Kit was as he and Attawan paddled up beside the makeshift dock, he couldn't overlook the meanness of the place. The gossip said Robillard was French born, a wily veteran of the Turkish wars. But one glance at his house confirmed what Kit had always suspected, that Robillard was no more than a back-country trapper, a coureur de bois who'd made enough money from lucky trading to become a first-rate bully.

Sitting at the crest of a rocky hill overlooking the river, the large house was more of a stockade built of rough-hewn logs and chinked with dingy lime plaster. Oiled skins filled the narrow windows instead of glass, and the yard was bare, dry dirt. To the back was a lean-to used for storage, and a small stable. Two mongrel dogs wrangled over a goose carcass before the house's open doorway, while three Abenakis and a French soldier in haphazard uniform wagered on the outcome. When Kit and Attawan pulled their canoe onto the bank, the four men at once forgot the dogs, and their expressions turned hostile as they reached for their muskets. The French soldier barked an order to one of the Indians, who scurried into the house as the others trained their guns on the newcomers.

But Kit ignored them, nonchalantly taking his time as he took his own rifle from the canoe and swung it casually across his shoulders. Beside him Attawan had not taken his eyes from the men at the house. Kit could sense his friend's tension and disapproval. When Kit began to whistle the little tune of Dianna's, Attawan spoke so sharply in his own tongue that Kit smiled to himself, certain he was being soundly cursed. So far, everything was just as he had hoped.

Kit loped up the hillside, his boots crunching on the shale. He didn't like those muskets aimed at him any more than Attawan did, but he'd be damned if he'd let Robillard know it. He was within twenty paces of the house before the soldier called to him.

"Faire halte!" he demanded. When Kit shrugged his incomprehension, the man switched to garbled English. "What go there?"

"Christopher Sparhawk. Your master will know the name." The soldier scowled and did not move, and Kit sighed impatiently. "I'd be obliged if you'd tell him I'm here."

From the corner of his eye Kit caught the movement in the doorway, the sun glinting off the pistol's long barrel. *"Bonjour, Sparhawk,"* said Robillard. He laughed, but the gun in his hand remained steady. With a muted click he drew back the hammer. "Or is it *au revoir,* eh?"

Chapter Thirteen

For one sickening moment, Kit wondered if he'd miscalculated. There were five of them, five guns, odds a coward like Robillard would favor. At point blank like this, he and Attawan wouldn't have a breath of a chance.

But even as Kit was considering this, Robillard laughed again, his big belly shaking. He uncocked the pistol and tipped it back against his shoulder. "Even I would not kill you like this, Sparhawk," he said scornfully. "You are a *fou gros* to come here, eh? Did not your other *Anglais* tell you I would shoot you, bang, bang?"

He waved the pistol at Kit, laughing again at his own wit. Kit wanted nothing more than to knock the foolish wind out of the man, but he knew how precarious his position remained; the others still had not lowered their guns. "Aye, they warned me," he said, swallowing his temper, "but I believed you would wish to talk first."

Intrigued, Robillard scratched his jaw with the pistol's barrel. "Come, then, I would hear you talk."

"Nay, Robillard, not here. Inside. And alone. What I have to say needs reach no other ears than your own." Confident that the Frenchman would agree, Kit began walking toward him. "I'll leave my own man here, as well."

Robillard shrugged. "Eh, if you wish it. Your life is in my fist anyway."

Kit waited until the Abenakis and the soldier laid down their guns and reluctantly slumped back down beside the wall. He ignored Attawan's scowl of disapproval as his friend chose to sit far from the others, his musket still cradled in his arms. Only then did Kit follow Robillard into his house, ducking his head beneath the low doorway.

The front room was probably the finest in the house. The tall-backed chairs had cushions of padded leather, and a bright Turkey carpet was draped over the massive walnut table. A costly crucifix, carved and painted, hung between the windows. But the pewter candlesticks were dull with dirt, and the prints of saints' martyrdoms that were tacked to the log walls were fly-specked and yellowed.

Imperiously Robillard waved Kit toward a chair and dropped into an armchair that groaned beneath his weight. Kit ignored the seat the Frenchman had offered, choosing instead one that put his back to the wall and gave him a clear view of both the door and windows. Much like Attawan, he kept his rifle in his arms, although, he decided idly, indoors he'd likely do better with the knife.

"So you come to visit me in my home like a *gentil-homme,* Sparhawk?" asked Robillard jovially. "It's a fine holding, *oui?*"

Glad his visit had fed the man's pride, Kit was nonetheless thankful Robillard had never visited Plumstead. "Aye, a fine holding," he agreed. "A gentleman's house. But the deeds I've come to discuss are not gentleman's deeds, nor—"

He broke off as a young Abenaki woman entered the room with two leather tankards of brandy. As she set them on the table, Robillard reached out to caress her bottom, and the woman smiled and moved wantonly against his hand. He pulled her, giggling, back into his lap, her legs splayed over his knees and her deerskin dress riding high over her thighs.

"You do not like squaws, do you, *Anglais?*" asked Robillard as he freely fondled the woman. Kit shook his head, disgusted. Reluctantly Robillard pushed the girl to her feet, smacking her hip as she scurried away. "It is a pity you do not. She has a sister, that one, another plump beauty."

A sudden grin split the Frenchman's face. "But then I forget you will soon take a wife! *Félicitations!*"

Kit frowned. Surely he could not mean Dianna. No one knew that, not even her. "You must be mistaken, Robillard."

"Ah, but I have heard of this Lindsey girl, your *fiancée, non?*"

"Nay, she is not." God's blood, had Constance's aspirations really spread this far? "There is no betrothal between Mistress Lindsey and myself."

"Then you shall have my chit's sister. I swear it, she will do anything you wish with her mouth—"

"Enough!" said Kit abruptly, striking the table with his fist hard enough to bounce the tankards. "You've killed four of my men and carried off three of my women. I want the women back, unharmed. I'll even pay their ransom, if I'm certain the gold goes to the Indians and not you. And I want you to swear you'll never venture anywhere near my land again."

Robillard's face grew shuttered, and he tucked his jaw low against his chest. "I know nothing of this. What you say is the work of Indians. We all have such troubles with *sauvages*."

"Nay, you forget, Robillard," said Kit, his voice rumbling with quiet menace. "Your men struck one of your own, as well, lifted his scalp and left him to die. But he did not die at once, not before he told me you were there, too."

"Do you not believe that Indians kill *Français,* as well?" Robillard blustered, but from the furtive panic in his eyes, Kit knew for certain he was bluffing, lying again. "Like all men, I have my enemies. This dead man must be one. Why would I have gone along to that *Anglais* farmer's house, to his corn field, eh?"

"Why you went matters not. But that you did, I don't doubt for a moment." Kit's eyes narrowed. "I didn't tell you the man was a farmer or that he was murdered in a corn field. It seems, Robillard, that your memory is improving."

Kit rose to his feet, towering over the other man. "I don't want war, Robillard, any more than you do. At present this is between us alone. Do as I say, and I'll leave you in peace. But cross me again, and so help me, I'll be back with an army to burn your precious gentleman's house and see you hang for murder.''

Kit's voice had dropped to scarcely more than a whisper. ''Mark well what I say, Robillard. The three English women back and you off my land.''

He turned on his heel without waiting for the Frenchman to reply, and walked out the door and down the hill to the canoe. He heard Attawan hurry to join him, but he didn't turn, unwilling to give Robillard anything more satisfying then the sight of his back. While a small part of him wondered how many French bullets might find their way into that same back, the larger part was confident not one would dare.

Finally Robillard roused himself, stalking to the doorway as Kit and Attawan pushed off into the current. Swearing under his breath, he watched them go, all too conscious of the man who had come to stand behind him in the doorway. ''I told you Sparhawk was a *fou,* a *très gros fou,*'' he blustered. ''I should have shot his head from his shoulders when I had the chance!''

''You are the only fool here, Robillard,'' snapped Lieutenant Hertel de Rouville. Irritably he rapped his knuckles on the doorframe, his sword in its scabbard swinging back and forth from his hip. That he, the man who had destroyed that pitiful English village of Deerfield; he, Jean-Baptiste Hertel de Rouville, the special agent and friend of the Marquis de Vaudreuil, the governor of all Canada—that he should be reduced to dealing with a fat peasant like this Robillard, was almost beyond bearing. "You couldn't have shot that man had he held the pistol for you."

His pride wounded, Robillard's head jerked up and he sniffed loudly. "Sparhawk is not worthy of my scorn, not him, nor his father, nor his father before him."

"He is worth ten of you," said Hertel de Rouville with disgust. "If you'd harmed him today, the forests would have been alive with English soldiers in a fortnight. He wouldn't have come here unless his governors knew of it. You cannot kill men like Sparhawk without consequences."

"But you promised me his holdings if I helped you," said Robillard peevishly.

"My mission is to drive these English from French land, not to make you rich," declared Hertel de Rouville impatiently as he flipped back the lace-trimmed cuff on his shirt to scratch his wrist. There had been fleas in his bed last night, and God only knew what kind of vermin on the Indian woman who'd been waiting naked beneath the coverlet for him. The sooner he could return to the civilities of Quebec, the better. "Sparhawk must die, that is so. But it must be arranged so that no blame can fall to us. We must draw him to us of his own will, away from the others."

"If only he had a wife we could take as bait, eh? He is a *galant,* that one. He would follow."

"No wife, perhaps, but there is some lady he holds dear. Didn't you mark how he started when you asked of the Lindsey woman?" Hertel de Rouville chuckled, quite pleased with himself. "You will go to his home, Robillard, and you will learn the name of his *amourette.*"

Robillard shook his head. "I do not think that a good plan, *mon ami,*" he said doubtfully. He was reluctant to question a fine gentleman like Hertel de Rouville, but his own neck was the one at stake. "You heard Sparhawk. He'll kill me if I go to Plumstead."

"Not if you come with news of, say, those three English women. You may even claim the ransom for aught I care."

"You will give them to me to take back?" asked Robillard incredulously.

The lieutenant shrugged carelessly. "Not possible, I fear. The oldest one could not keep pace and perished. The two girls will find a new life of grace with the good sisters in Quebec."

De Rouville laughed to himself as he gripped Robillard's shoulder, his fingers tightening into the older man's flesh. "You tell Sparhawk whatever he wishes to hear, *oui?* And you do not return here until you know the woman's name and where she dwells. Then, *mon ami,* it will be high time for our Abenaki *compatriotes* to pay her our compliments."

"If we return tonight," suggested Attawan hopefully, "we could kill him while he sleeps."

"And be killed ourselves in the bargain," said Kit matter-of-factly as he tossed a stone into the water. They sat on a rocky outcropping high above the river, Kit watching the sun dip behind the Green Mountains to the west while Attawan cleaned the two bullheads he'd caught for their dinner. Earlier, in the afternoon's heat, Kit had stripped off his shirt, and now, while the stone beneath him still held the warmth, the evening breeze felt pleasantly cool on his bare back.

"There were four men that we saw," Kit continued, "and doubtless others who chose not to show themselves. Besides, I'd warrant Robillard expects us to be the same sort of skulking cowards he himself is and will double his watch tonight just in case."

Attawan struck his thigh with his fist. "I am not afraid, Sparhawk."

"So who is more brave than wise now?" asked Kit, grinning. He leaned back on his elbows, his legs outstretched comfortably before him. "Nay, much as I'd like to throttle that man's fat neck, 'tis better this way. Once Robillard returns the Barnard women, I'll be free to hunt down the Abenakis responsible and bring them to Wickhamton for trial."

Attawan snorted, shaking silvery fish scales from his fingers. "*If* he returns your captives. I don't believe he has the power to find them."

"If he can, he will. He no more wants English soldiers in his fields than I want French ones in mine."

"Even if they're already there?"

Kit frowned, sitting upright, waiting for Attawan to continue.

"The Abenakis and Mohawks who destroyed your Deerfield were led by French soldiers. Two hundred soldiers on snowshoes, it is said."

Kit stared at him, stunned. "Would you swear to this?"

Attawan didn't answer, wounded to have his word questioned, but Kit was too disturbed to soothe his friend's feelings. "Why didn't you tell me of this earlier?" he demanded. "One hundred and forty-two English were lost that day, and all has been blamed on the Indians alone!"

"These French are not foolish," said Attawan reasonably. Having misdeeds blamed on Indians was nothing new to him, and though he called Kit friend, he didn't share his horror for the killed or kidnapped English and judged the fighting between French and English no different than the skirmishes among the Seven Nations. "They let the Abenakis attack first, and when the killing is done, they followed. It was the same at your English village of Pascommuck, too, though not so many of your people were taken."

"Nearly two score," said Kit grimly, tugging on his boots. "We're heading for Deerfield this night and talk to Captain Ferris. They must be warned. I knew the French had leagued with the Indians to the east, but I didn't think they dared to come here. I've been away too long, Attawan. I should have known this was happening. If I hadn't gone to England in my brother's stead—"

The second boot caught on his foot, and in his frustration Kit yanked it off and sent it sailing into the brush. Calmly Attawan went to retrieve it.

"Your scars run deep, my friend," he said gently as he dropped the boot into Kit's lap. "These are your people, aye, but they're not your family again. You cannot change the past, and you must not let it blind you to the future."

Kit wished he could. He wanted no more killing, no more families torn apart, no more nightmares of

Tamsin's screams. All he longed for was peace and a life with Dianna at Plumstead. God in Heaven, was that so very much to ask?

The musket fired, and as the gunsmoke drifted clear, Dianna could see the rock she'd set on the fence post as a target was gone, shot clean away without touching the wooden post.

"Aye, ye be a finer shot than most o' th' men now," said Hester with considerable satisfaction. "I don't care what that old fool Asa says. It be a good thing ye know how t'handle a gun, with ye an' Mercy all by yerselves in that house."

Carefully Dianna cleaned out the gun's barrel, remembering all that Hester had warned her about fouled firearms. "We'll be safe enough, Hester. We're too close to Wickhamton and Plumstead to be attacked. Besides, Asa and Jeremiah are never gone for more than three nights running now. Asa promised."

"Well, ye keep that musket o'yours primed an' ready like I told ye. Just because we haven't been plagued by any more o' the savages don't mean they're not waitin' and plannin' t'strike again. Mind, 'twas four months 'twixt Deerfield an' the Barnards," warned Hester. She shaded her eyes with her hand, gauging the time by the sun's height in the sky. "Come, 'tis time I turned th' joint, an' time, too, ye an' Mercy headed back. Kit would have my head if I let ye tarry after dusk."

Dianna busied herself with collecting her powder horn and bullets, her face lowered so Hester wouldn't notice how she blushed at the mention of Kit's name.

She always did. Having him gone more than four weeks hadn't changed that, nor had she stopped missing him every hour, every minute of each of those thirty-one days. It was a part of being in love that she hadn't expected, this constant caring laced with fear. She was certain he'd be back, but she worried about all the dangers that might threaten him. What were his assurances against arrows and hatchets?

For distraction she threw herself into a hundred tasks, from gathering herbs to dry for physicking, to learning how to shoot a musket, to teaching Mercy how to read from the one book that Asa owned, an Old Testament. But no matter how busy she kept her hands, Kit remained to haunt her thoughts by day and her dreams by night.

Yet it was Hester now who spoke, seemingly reading Dianna's thoughts. "I wish th'lad would get himself back here soon," she said uneasily. "He's been gone too long t'suit me."

Swiftly Dianna stood upright. It was bad enough to worry alone, but infinitely worse if Hester, who had lived here nearly all her life, was concerned as well. "You don't believe some ill has befallen him, do you?"

Hester sighed deeply, shaking her head. "Nay, I've no real reason. He's young an' strong an' a good man in a fight, an' he knows th' woods better'n any other Englishman. An' he be clever, too. If he reckons talkin' with that lout Robillard's going t'set things to rights, then we must trust him t'do what be best. But I don't have to like it." Her voice rose indignantly.

"Nay, not a bit o'it! The Sparhawks be too unlucky with th'Indians for Kit t'be off testing fate like this."

"Unlucky?" echoed Dianna faintly. "How so?"

At once Hester realized her indiscretion. "So he hasn't told ye?" she said uncomfortably, looking past Dianna to avoid her eyes. "Well, it don't be my tale to tell."

"I know his father led the militia before him," Dianna persisted, determined not to be put off. "Was he killed by the Indians? Was that it?"

"Aye, lass, poor Master Samuel was, indeed," Hester agreed eagerly, seizing on that much of the truth. "Shot an' scalped wit' nary a chance t'defend himself. 'Twas Kit who found him."

"Oh, poor Kit!" breathed Dianna. She knew the pain of losing a father suddenly, but she could not imagine the shock of finding his mutilated body as well. Now she understood why Kit had reacted so violently when the wounded French trapper had been brought to Plumstead. She'd been so swept up in her own concerns that she hadn't realized Kit's anguish or been able to recognize it for what it was. Oh, how she wished he'd told her himself!

"Aye, ye can see why I worry over him," said Hester vehemently, her eyes snapping. "An' him off with one of th' blood-thirsty savages, too! Oh, I know Kit says that Attawan be different, that red men must be judged a-piece, same as Englishmen, but I ask ye, was it Englishmen that burned Deerfield? Master Samuel and Mistress Amity an' all their children were both thick as family wit' Indians, an' no good ever come of it, t'my mind. Th' sooner they all be driven away or killed for good, the better for us Christian folk!"

Then, to Dianna's surprise, the righteous anger vanished from Hester's face and her mouth seemed to crumple as her eyes grew shiny with tears. "I've no kin o'my own, you see," she explained hoarsely. "No younglings t'worry over. But those two Sparhawk lads, aye, an' their sisters, too, they've been more'n enough t'love. An' if any harm comes to Kit, why I'd feel it as if he were my own flesh."

Near to tears herself, Dianna threw her arms around Hester and hugged her tightly. "He'll come back, I know it," she said fiercely, as much to convince herself as to reassure Hester. "He swore he would, and you know Kit Sparhawk would never break his word!"

"That be true enough, lass." Embarrassed by her emotions, Hester stepped back and wiped her eyes with the corner of her apron, sniffing loudly. "An' enough of this foolish old woman's fancies, too, ye be thinkin'. There'll be naught worth eating tonight if we don't go back."

They hurried back to the house and self-consciously, neither of them mentioned Kit again. "Now ye take that cheese wit' ye, like ye promised," said Hester as they entered the kitchen. "There be a nice piece for yer supper that surely will go wantin' here otherwise."

Leaving Hester to poke at the roast on the spit, Dianna stepped into the cool shadows of the little buttery off the kitchen to search for the cheese. She paused, listening, when she heard the heavy footsteps in the kitchen, and a man's voice she didn't recognize. None of the field workers should be back at the house this early anyway, she thought, frowning. Then came the sound of shattering crockery, and Hester's voice raised in angry protest. Dianna peeked through the half-opened door just as the heavy-set man pinned Hester's arms behind her back.

Dianna pulled back quickly into the shadows, praying the man hadn't seen her. She recognized him as the one who'd challenged Kit outside the meeting-house, Robillard himself, and she remembered, too, how quick he'd been with a knife. Now she would have to be even faster if she wanted to help Hester. *Why was he here? Where was Kit?* She shoved the doubts away. She could see her musket where she'd left it, leaning against a chair. Three steps and she would reach it. She took a deep breath to steady her nerves and lunged for the gun.

Before Robillard even noticed her, she had grabbed the musket and trained it on his startled face. "You let Mistress Holcomb go free," she ordered, her heart pounding with adrenaline, but her voice surprisingly calm. "Then off with you! You've no business in this house."

Dianna watched the man's expression change, the surprise changing to disbelief and then to bemused contempt. "Eh, I should be frightened by a *petite fille* like you?"

That contempt angered Dianna and steadied her, as well. "Better a little girl than a *cochon énorme!*" she answered tartly, squinting down the barrel as she cocked the trigger. At this range she'd no doubt she'd hit the Frenchman. The challenge would be missing Hester.

Robillard frowned, the older woman he held forgotten. This wild girl with the pale eyes puzzled him. She was dressed as commonly as any English settler's wife, but she held herself proud like the grand ladies he'd seen in Quebec, and she was good at orders, too. Such a girl should not be trusted with a musket, and he swore in French.

"Don't sully my ears with your filth!" replied Dianna in French. "Now let Mistress Holcomb go free, and pack yourself off before I help you on your way."

Sacré bleu, could the chit be French? Robillard stared at her, his confusion growing. "What are you doing here, eh, *ma petite?*" he demanded, wondering if this could possibly be the woman he sought. He'd always thought Sparhawk a pious, self-righteous prig, like all Englishmen, and never dreamed he'd keep a mistress right here in his blessed Plumstead.

"Don't go a-tryin' her patience, Robillard," warned Hester. "Her temper's short as th' rest o'her."

"Fah, and what of my patience, eh?" With a flourish Robillard released Hester and shoved her away. Rubbing her wrists, Hester quickly ran to safety behind Dianna, and Robillard snorted with disgust. "You do not care that I bring to you a message for your master?"

"Master Sparhawk's not here," said Dianna sharply.

"And did I not know that already, *ma petite?*" he said, sneering. "My message is both for him and from him."

Hastily Dianna lowered the gun. "A message from him?" she asked eagerly. "You have seen him then, and he is well?"

Slowly Robillard smiled. So she *was* the woman, after all. She was not as beautiful as he'd expected, but beneath the coarse clothing, she was pleasingly rounded, and her lips were full enough to welcome a man's kisses. And she was at least part French: that alone would make her more desirable than the other English spinsters he'd seen. In fact, the more he studied her, the more he understood why Sparhawk had refused the squaw. *Mon Dieu,* why shouldn't he, with such a little delight waiting at home?

His smile widened to a leer, and he ran his tongue along his lower lip. "When Sparhawk was at my house, he was well enough. But that was long ago, maybe a fortnight. I thought he would be home by now, eh?"

He watched the fear flutter across Dianna's face and his last doubt about her disappeared. How he wished he could see Sparhawk's face when he learned the Indians had taken his mistress! "When he comes, tell him I have found the warriors who hold the English women, and they will be returned as soon as he pays the ransom."

He stepped forward, meaning to take the gun from her, but Dianna snapped it back to her shoulder, flushing at her own carelessness. Where were her wits to let this man toy with her? Likely everything he said was lies anyway. "Why should he pay any ransom to you?"

Robillard's smile twisted to a sneer. "You give him my message, *ma chère,* and that will be enough. He doesn't need a woman to make his decisions for him, eh?"

"If you've nothing more to say, then get out now," said Dianna irritably. "Though I've almost *decided* to shoot you now and save Kit the trouble."

"I'm going, *mademoiselle,* I'm going." Slowly Robillard retrieved his hat from the floor where it had fallen and inched his way toward the door. "You be a good girl and give my message to Sparhawk. If he wishes to see the women alive, he pays me the ransom."

Dianna followed his movements with the gun as he left the house and climbed onto the horse he'd tied near the well out front, not lowering the weapon until he had ridden from sight. Only then did she realize how tense she'd been and how her arms ached from holding the heavy musket. Sighing, she let her shoulders sag and rubbed her wrists.

"I don't believe he knows anything at all about the Barnards, do you, Hester?" she asked wearily. For a long moment Hester didn't answer, standing in thoughtful silence beside Dianna with her arms crossed over her chest as she stared after Robillard.

"You an' Kit," she said at last, and clicked her tongue. "Why didn't I see it coming?"

Chapter Fourteen

"An' where d'ye be headin' this day, eh, Annie?" Asa asked Dianna as she and Mercy swept out two large baskets they'd found in the barn. "Ye know I don't want ye two rangin' far."

"No farther than the apple orchard at Plumstead," said Dianna, frowning at Mercy behind Asa's back. If the girl didn't stop her nervous giggling, Asa was sure to suspect something unusual was planned, and harmless as Dianna judged a picnic to be, she wasn't sure Asa wouldn't forbid them to go. "We're going to gather the early windfalls so I can make my pies for tomorrow."

"Pies for tomorrow? What pies be those?"

"For the supper after training day," explained Dianna for what seemed like the hundredth time. "You promised you'd take us."

Asa sighed. "Aye, I warrant I did. Though training day's likely far more serious this year than you might be expectin'. If th' lads have any conscience, they'll spend more time learnin' their drills an' less chasin' maids. I warrant that Captain Tyler will see they're worked proper, better'n when Colonel Sparhawk be here. He be too gentle by half wit' th' men, that one. Too eager t'get to th' women an' spirits hisself.''

Asa lit his pipe, puffing as the spark took, and looked closely at Dianna. ''There not be some lad ye favor in the village, eh? Mind ye be bound t'me for seven years, an' I'll not have ye spoken for 'til your time be done. Ten guineas be too dear a sum t'toss away for naught.''

''Nay, there's no one in Wickhamton,'' said Dianna with carefully chosen words. How could any other man compete with Kit? ''I wish to go for Mercy's sake. She sees too little of children her own age.''

''Aye, there be no harm t'that,'' Asa agreed, reaching for his hat. ''I've business o'my own in Wickhamton this day, but I'll take ye back on the morn, as ye asked. Are ye certain ye will be safe enough without me here today?''

''Oh, Grandfer, you go on your business, an' Dianna an' I will go on ours,'' said Mercy airily. Asa harrumphed, but kissed the girl indulgently before leaving.

Dianna finished packing a third basket with food and cider for their supper. She liked planning little surprises and outings like this one for Mercy, just as her own father had done for her long ago. Lord knows it seemed to Dianna that Mercy had done precious few things for the pleasure of them alone. Even now the girl was dancing with excitement by the door, the little cat, Lily, jostling in her arms.

Dianna slung the basket with the food over one arm, handed the empty ones to Mercy and then pulled her musket out from its hiding place behind the cupboard. She often wondered which would upset Asa more: that she had the gun at all, or that it had come from the Sparhawks' collection. But after this summer, nothing Asa could say would dissuade her from keeping it now, and she never left the house without it.

There was a crispness to the day that hinted at autumn, and already the topmost leaves of the maples and oaks were beginning to change color. The apple trees were heavy with fruit, the branches bowed beneath the weight, and the fragrance of apples was sweet in the air. While Lily chased and pounced on every whirling leaf and imaginary mouse, Dianna and Mercy soon filled their baskets. They would come back again next week to help the field men and women harvest the bulk of the crop, and in return, Dianna would receive a share of the apples to press for cider or dry for winter cooking.

"May we eat now, Dianna?" begged Mercy. "I think this be the perfect spot, and Lily is near to starving."

Dianna glanced down doubtfully at the little cat, already grown plump from all the milk and scraps Mercy managed to send her pet's way. "'Tis early, but if Lily deems it time to dine, then I shall not be the one to deny her."

"So this be truly what lords an' ladies do in London?" asked Mercy excitedly as Dianna spread a homespun cloth on the grass and began to unpack the food. "They'd rather take their meals under a tree than in a fine dining hall?"

"Even the finest dining hall can grow tiresome," replied Dianna with mock seriousness. "Of course, we should have let the footmen bring the hampers, and have the dishes arranged before we arrived. The musicians would be waiting, too, to play for us while we ate, and then, after perhaps only a half-dozen dishes—for we are being quite informal—we might sing ourselves and dance on the grass with our beaux."

The more she had told Mercy about her past, the less real it had become, the people and places she'd grown up knowing reduced to a kind of fairy tale. And what was most curious, when she thought about it, was that she was far more content in her tiny shingled house, making do for herself, than she ever would have been in a grand home in London with a score of servants. If only Kit would come back, she thought longingly, then quickly amended her thoughts. *When* Kit comes back . . .

"What kind o' shoes do ladies wear for dancing?" prompted Mercy eagerly.

"Slippers made of calf-skin so fine that one night of dancing will wear them to pieces," said Dianna grandly. "All over embroidered with silk-thread flowers and tiny silver stars, and perhaps they'll fasten with buckles set with paste brilliants that sparkle like diamonds when you kick your feet high in the air!"

As she listened, Mercy's eyes sparkled like the paste brilliants, and Dianna thought with pleasure of how much the girl had changed these past months. Then suddenly Mercy's face twisted into a stern grimace.

"Grandfer says dancing's wicked," she said, sounding uncannily like Asa. "He says it be wicked sport, born o' idleness."

Dianna hesitated. She did not like to scoff at what Mercy had been taught by Asa, but faith, what harm could possibly come of music and dancing? "When the day's tasks are done," she said cautiously, "then I don't see the wickedness in dancing."

Mercy pressed her cheek against Lily's fur and glanced impishly up at Dianna. "Then if you teach me how, 'twill just be another secret best kept from Grandfer."

Dianna gasped, then laughed. With both hands she caught the girl by the waist and twirled her around and around, their skirts and aprons flying in a giddy circle around their bare legs. "Oh, Mercy, you shouldn't say such things! 'Tis disrespectful and—"

It was the flicker of movement that caught Dianna's eye, the tall figure easing among the shadows in the trees. Swiftly she shoved Mercy behind her and grabbed for the musket beside the basket. She shook her head to clear it as she raised the gun, cursing the silly spinning game that had left her dizzy, the trees before her eyes still careening wildly. Blast, she knew the man had to be there somewhere!

"I'm not afraid of you!" she called out defiantly, her heart pounding.

Dianna felt Mercy's fingers tightening in her skirts behind her, and she hoped the girl could not sense her own very real fear. The musket held but a single bullet. She had only seen the one man and prayed he was alone. She would have just one shot to kill him if she had to.

"Come out and show yourself or I'll shoot, see if I don't!" she called again, and this time she heard the desperation in her voice.

At last the trees had stopped spinning. She could make out a fringed hunting shirt, the glint of a rifle barrel as the man moved. He was very tall, broad-shouldered, and he was walking toward them, daring her, it seemed, to shoot. She swallowed hard and cocked the dog-latch.

"Isn't this a fine welcome home!" exclaimed Kit as he stepped into the sunlight. "I didn't dream I'd find the women-folk here as mad with blood-lust as any Abenaki brave!"

Simultaneously Dianna and Mercy cried his name, but it was Dianna who reached him first, flinging her arms around him as if she'd never let go. "Oh, Kit, praise God you're back! I feared so that you were gone, lost—"

"And so you hoped to finish the task when I returned?" he teased. So many elegant speeches he'd rehearsed for this moment, and here he was, instead, taunting her as though she were one of his sisters. But it still seemed impossibly right to have her in his arms again. At once he forgot how tired he was, forgot the desolation he'd seen and the sorrow he'd heard and how many miles he'd travelled to be here with her again.

Dianna drew back indignantly. "I might have killed you!"

"Not the way you were weaving, likely to trip over your own feet. I'd swear you'd brought hard cider in that jug, my lady, and had your share of it, too."

"Nay, Kit, it's not like that," said Mercy seriously. Self-consciously Dianna and Kit separated, though Kit kept hold of her hand. He had to reassure himself that this was real and not another dream. "Dianna and I are having a—" She stumbled over the foreign words "—having a 'fate sham-pader.'"

"A *what?*" asked Kit.

"A *fête champêtre,*" answered Dianna, delighting in the incredulous look on Kit's face. Despite the dark beard that hid half his face, she thought he had grown even more handsome, his hair streaked with pale gold and his skin tanned as dark as Attawan's. She guessed that, wherever he had gone, he must have met with success to be looking so happy. "A country feast, a picnic. Not everything French is evil, you know."

"Aye, Kit, it be something that all the lords and ladies do in *Paris,*" explained Mercy, pleased to prove her new knowledge to Kit. "They eat outside instead o' in."

"Then you mean to say Attawan and I have spent the last six weeks having these *fêtes,* and we didn't even know it?" He twined his fingers around Dianna's marveling both at the delicacy of her hand and at the new calluses that marked her palm.

Mercy frowned and folded her arms across her narrow chest. "Nay, Kit, you're jesting now. A *fête* needs dancing an' music an' gentlemen t'be our beaux." She sighed dramatically. "But since you're here now, I warrant you must be our beau, else you'll have naught of our food."

"I warrant I must, since it's your food I'm after." Kit's eyes met Dianna's over the girl's head. He grinned, and Dianna felt herself melt. "Among other things. And besides," he said to Dianna, "by my reckoning, you owe me for a certain stewed chicken. Most savory it was, as I recall, before you seized it from my own table and carried it off."

"'Twas not for myself, as well you know," she answered staunchly, but unable to keep the smile from her lips. "I took it for others who were a great deal more hungry than you were."

"A claim you'd be hard pressed to make this day." He sat cross-legged on the grass and began exploring the contents of the supper basket. Gingerly he lifted out the meat pie, sniffing the fluted crust with such a look of intense expectation that Dianna laughed out loud. In the short time since she'd known Kit, there had been precious little time for laughter, and it was good to feel the tension and worry slip away.

"The pie's squirrel," she explained, her voice still merry, "and there are pickled onions in the little jug, and a carrot sallet and cornbread wrapped in the cloth, and the little bundle, there, has a slip of honeycomb."

"You are a marvel, Dianna, an angel to a starving man," proclaimed Kit as he stuck his knife deep into the pie. "I did not tarry at the house when Hester said I might find you here, but she should have told me, too, that she'd provisioned you, as well."

"She didn't, Kit," said Dianna proudly, sitting back on her heels with her hands at her waist. "Like it or not, 'tis all of my own making."

He cocked one eyebrow doubtfully, balancing a slice of the pie on the blade of his knife as the sauce dripped and the pastry began to flake before he slid the entire piece into his mouth at once. He groaned with contentment that was not entirely due to the pie. Not a quarter of an hour had he been with her, and already he felt happier than the entire time he'd been away.

"I'll take that as well meant," Dianna said as he cut himself another piece. That there would be little, if any, left for her or Mercy mattered not. She would have given him anything he desired, anything at all.

"*I* made the cornbread!" declared Mercy jealously. She pushed herself closer to Kit, practically sitting in his lap to get the attention she felt she was missing.

"Then I must try that next," said Kit with his mouth full. With a great flourish, he cut into the yellow cake while Mercy waited expectantly, her hands clasped, for his verdict.

"Wait, you'll want honey." Carefully Dianna unwrapped the comb and trickled the honey onto the cornbread he held before him. Some trickled onto her fingers, and before she could wipe them in the cloth, Kit lifted her hand to his lips and licked them clean himself, sensuously tracing the length of each of her fingers. The touch of his tongue, soft and wet, on her fingers made Dianna shiver, and her thoughts flew back to how she and Kit had parted in the barn, each breathless with unfulfilled longing. She felt herself being drawn back to that moment, her gaze locked by the power of Kit's eyes and her own desire, and she leaned closer toward him, her lips parted.

"Oh, fah, Kit, how can you do *that?*" exclaimed Mercy, her turned-up nose wrinkled with disgust. "To lick another's fingers!"

Embarrassed that she'd so forgotten Mercy, Dianna tried to pull her hand away, but Kit held it fast. "Mercy, sweeting," he said, his eyes not straying from Dianna's. "Where's Mistress Lily? I can't believe you'd let that fine little catkin stray."

With a stricken look, Mercy's head whipped around, searching for the cat. She bounded to her feet, calling the cat's name, and scurried off to search for her pet.

Kit's smile was slow and lazy as he lifted Dianna's hand to kiss the pulse of her wrist. "I missed you."

"And I you," said Dianna softly, reaching forward to stroke his cheek. "To have you back is like the spring after winter's cold."

"You would turn poetess on me?"

"Poetess or fool, more like." Dianna's cheeks pinked. "Mayhap I am too much alone, with only Mercy and the beauty of the land for my companions."

"Nay, my love, never a fool," he said, chuckling, as his hands slid down around her waist to pull her closer. "But last you swore you hated this land, and all of us in it."

Dianna winced, hoping this was only more of his teasing. "Words I did not mean," she said quickly, "spoken in passion."

Their faces were nearly touching now, his voice so low that only she could hear. His easy, jesting manner had vanished, and to her surprise, she saw his eyes grow guarded.

Kit tried to swallow his rising doubt. Was she perhaps speaking in riddles to save his feelings? He knew well that often women, and men, too, mistook passion for love and used the words interchangeably. Could it be that the first time he truly cared about a woman, she did not care about him in return?

"Tell me true, Dianna," he asked quietly. "Were there other words you did not mean, too, words spoken in passion?"

"Other words?" she repeated slowly, searching his face for some clue as to what he asked.

"Damn it, Dianna, do you love me?" he demanded. "Because I love you, and if you don't love me back—" He broke off abruptly and looked away, unwilling to let her see the raw emotion her hesitancy raised.

"Oh, Kit," she murmured, her smile tremulous. She took his jaw in both her hands, cradling his face as her fingers sank into the rough bristles of his new beard. "I loved you before and I love you now, and I believe in my heart that I always will."

She kissed him lightly at first, her lips barely brushing their sweetness across his until, with a possessive growl, his mouth came down hard on hers, wild and rough with passion. Fearlessly she surrendered to him and the rising desires within herself as her fingers tightened on the hard muscles of his shoulders.

"Dianna, love, how you tempt me," he said roughly, his breathing harsh. "But not here, not now." Yet even as he protested, he was pushing her back against the grass, tugging the linen cap from her hair to tangle his fingers in the rich, dark strands. "Mercy will be back—"

"Mercy!" Awkwardly Dianna pushed Kit back and struggled to sit upright. She had once again, to her chagrin, completely forgotten the little girl. With fingers clumsy from interrupted desire, she tried to comb her hair back to neatness beneath her cap. "To find us thus would hurt the child to no end, and I'll not have her lose her trust in me because of you!"

Sprawled on his back, Kit watched and listened before the laughter erupted from deep inside him. Dianna had switched so completely from a woman abandoning herself to lovemaking to a prim, concerned goodwife that he couldn't help it. Yet he loved her all the more for putting the little girl's feelings first. Perhaps now, if he were wed to Dianna, Asa would at last let him adopt Mercy. Happily he realized he might have both a wife and daughter with him at Plumstead before the first snowfall.

"Dianna," he said softly, reaching out to rest his hand on her thigh. "I have so many things I wish to say to you. Tomorrow is training day in Wickhamton—"

"I know, and Asa is taking Mercy and me to the supper afterward."

"Then meet me at dusk on the rise behind the burying ground. I would have you alone, with no others to spy or listen."

Behind him Dianna saw Mercy skipping toward them, the cat swinging from her arms. Quickly Dianna touched her fingers to Kit's lips.

"Tomorrow, then," she whispered. "And I swear I'll listen to every pretty word you wish to tell me."

"You're sure she is Sparhawk's woman?" demanded Hertel de Rouville skeptically. "A serving wench?"

"Je le tiens pour certain," replied Robillard confidently. "Though it is strange. In the village, they say he brought her with him from London, and yet she lives in a wretched house with an old man and a child."

Hertel de Rouville shrugged. "It sounds to me that this woman is merely a convenience for Sparhawk. Otherwise why would he bother with a creature so low-bred?"

"Ah, but Lieutenant, one look at her and you would see that she is not common." Eagerly Robillard leaned across the table. "She is a little goddess, *mon ami,* a beauty with the manner and the temper of a noble lady."

"So you would have her for yourself, is that it?" Hertel de Rouville asked with a weary sigh.

Robillard's dark eyes glittered in the candlelight. It had been long since he'd had a white woman, even longer for one so young who spoke his language. And how he would doubly enjoy her knowing he had robbed the Englishman! "She would be a small prize to share if you capture Sparhawk."

The lieutenant downed the last of his brandy and tapped his fingers on the empty glass. "If, as you promise, she is the right bait to draw Sparhawk to us and if we succeed in capturing him, *and* if the woman herself survives, then, Robillard, then you may consider her a gift." His smile was cold as a frozen river. "But if you have promised wrong and she is of no more use to us than any other *Anglaise* drab, then you shall watch the Abenakis kill her. Slowly, painfully, however they choose to amuse themselves. And you, *mon ami,* will be next."

Chapter Fifteen

"Five, six, seven, eight—*ouch!*" Dianna jerked her hand out of the brick-lined oven, shaking her fingers to cool them. At last she judged the oven hot enough to bake the six pies waiting on the table. She'd begun the fire before dawn, raking out the coals twice until she was satisfied that the heat was right to crisp and brown the pastry. The other women in Wickhamton would be harsh critics, and Dianna's pride wouldn't permit her first offerings to them to have soggy crusts or underbaked apples. And then there was the special pie they'd never see, the one fancifully trimmed with pastry hearts, that was reserved for Kit alone.

She smiled happily to herself. He was home and he was safe, and he loved her. *He loved her!* He might tell her times beyond counting and still she'd never tire of hearing it. All night she'd stayed awake, anticipating today. As leader of the militia, he would be much in demand on training day, and for him to arrange to see her alone showed how much he, too, longed to be alone. She chuckled, remembering how he'd sent Mercy scurrying away yesterday in the orchard. Perhaps he'd be as eager to kiss sweet apple from her lips as honey from her fingertips.

Quickly she shook off her daydreaming and with care, slid the first two pies off the long wooden peel and into the oven. Her pies would be done, but unless she wanted to greet Kit with a face shiny from the kitchen's heat and clothes blotched with flour, she'd have to hurry to be ready when Asa came to take them to the village.

Together she and Mercy bathed in the stream down the hill from their house, shrieking as the icy, spring-fed water puckered their bare skin with goose bumps. Dianna rinsed her hair first with vinegar for shine, then crushed lavender for fragrance, and sat in the sun before the house to comb it dry.

At Mercy's request, Dianna braided the girl's hair in sevens and bound the thick tail with red yarn. Her own hair Dianna left unplaited and drawn back loosely from her face so the dark chestnut waves tumbled freely down her back. Today, too, she refused to hide it beneath a cap or kerchief. Oh, there'd be talk enough among the older people about her immodesty, but she remembered how Kit liked to tangle his fingers in her hair when it was loose, the way it had been the first time they'd made love, and she was determined to wear it like that again today, for him.

Likely, too, there'd be gossip about how she was dressed. What Dianna lacked in skill as a seamstress she had more than made up for with ingenuity. She'd stood through enough fittings for gowns to absorb the tricks even quality dressmakers used by turning a facing here, adding a cuff there. Beginning with a plain grey bodice of Lucy's, Dianna had lowered the neckline and narrowed the waist to flatter her own smaller figure. The tattered remains of her black silk gown had been ruthlessly torn into narrow strips that Dianna had braided and appliqued along the seams and neckline. Finally, she'd found an old pair of Tom Wing's breeches, faded from maroon to pink, and from these she had fashioned the rosettes that crowned her shoulders and were scattered across her skirt. The final effect was not half as stylish as what she'd worn in London, but still considerably more frivolous than any other woman in Wickhamton would choose, certainly any other servant. But as she dressed, Dianna worried that perhaps she'd gone too far. Nervously she tugged at her neckline, wishing she had a mirror to see just how much of her breasts showed. She'd sewn every stitch with Kit in mind, and if he hadn't returned in time, she would have worn something else. But what if Asa found her dress too worldly and made her change before Kit had had the chance to see her?

"Oh, Dianna, but ye do look grand!" said Mercy proudly, hugging her knees as she sat on the bed. "Like the Queen o' Faeries again."

Dianna plucked at one of the rosettes on her skirt. "You don't think your grandfather will judge me too bold?"

"Aye, he will," agreed Mercy amiably. "But he'll be too 'shamed t'tell ye so."

Dianna chewed on her lower lip, considering. "Perhaps I should tuck a kerchief in the front."

"Nay, don't change it!" declared Mercy. "This way you'll make Kit blind t'all th'other lasses, see if ye don't!"

Dianna looked quickly at the girl, wondering how much she'd guessed about her relationship with Kit. She considered telling her the truth, at least as much of it as she herself knew, but Mercy's face was full of admiration and nothing else, and Dianna relaxed. "He'll be so busy with training and telling everyone about his journey that he'll have little time to spare for any of us lasses."

Unconvinced, Mercy reached across the coverlet to pull Lily into her lap. "Kit always has time for his friends. Ye know that. Else he wouldn't have come t'see us yesterday."

Friends or not, Dianna decided it was time to change the subject. "I'm afraid you'll have to leave Lily here. She'd be lost among all the people, and the guns might frighten her."

Mercy sighed heavily and let the cat climb from her lap back up the bed to the pillow. The front of the girl's dark blue skirt was covered with white cat fur, but Dianna kept her reproof to herself. "Say farewell to her now, Mercy, and then join me below," she said instead as she climbed down the ladder. "Your grandfather should be back soon, and we don't want to keep him waiting."

Taking care to keep her clothes clean, Dianna slid the last pie from the oven and balanced it on the open windowsill to cool. The long-handled peel was still in her hand when she heard the door swing open behind her.

"We're ready to leave whenever you wish, Asa," she called gaily. "I'd like to see the shooting if we—"

But as she turned, the words dissolved into a stunned gasp. In the doorway stood two Indians armed with muskets and tomahawks, their bare chests painted red and their faces striped fiercely with black and white.

There was no time for Dianna to think or plan, only react, as the first Indian came toward her. As the man reached for her, she swung the peel as hard as she could. The wide paddle caught him flat across the face with a smack, and though he stumbled backward from the impact, he was still able to yank the peel from her hands. Desperately Dianna longed for her rifle, tucked beyond reach behind the cupboard across the room. But the paring knife still lay on the table, and she lunged for it just as the Indian grabbed her around the waist.

As he shoved her back across the table, she turned and twisted in his grasp to face him. His long black hair flicked across her cheek, and she could smell the bear grease that glistened on his skin. She raised her feet and kicked him hard in the stomach, glad today that she wore shoes. But though she felt her hard leather heels strike against his muscled flesh, the Indian only grunted and tightened his fingers on her waist as he arched her back against the table. She clutched the little knife convulsively at her side, breathing a prayer of thanks that he hadn't noticed it in her hand. She must kill this man if she could. She had to. She jerked the knife upward, aiming for his chest.

But the Indian sensed her movement before he saw it and deftly rolled away from her. The knife slashed instead across his upper arm as he caught Dianna's wrist and squeezed it until she cried out from the pain. Her fingers sprung open and the knife dropped harmlessly to the floor.

For an endless moment he held her hand forced overhead, her body pinned beneath his as the warm blood dripped from the cut in his arm onto her bare shoulder. Panting, Dianna struggled to control her fear and panic. Desperately she reminded herself that she was still Lady Dianna Grey, and Greys were never cowards. She swallowed hard, and forced herself to meet his gaze. The Indian's eyes were dark, almost black, and so bright with undisguised hatred that Dianna shuddered.

Roughly he pulled her to her feet. She winced as he twisted her arms behind her back and held her wrists together with one hand, his fingers as tight as an iron band.

"Dianna!" shrieked Mercy pitifully, her face white with terror as she clung to the ladder, Lily struggling in her arms. The cat broke free and scrambled back up to the loft just as the second Indian reached up and plucked the girl from the ladder. Mercy wailed with anguish, tears streaming down her cheeks as she stretched out her arms toward the lost pet.

"Lily will be fine, sweetheart," said Dianna unsteadily, trying to keep the tremor from her voice. "God gave cats nine lives, and Lily hasn't squandered one of them yet. She'll be fine."

Far better than we will, thought Dianna miserably. Through the open door she saw they'd set fire to the barn, the flames ate greedily at the dry thatched roof, while squawking chickens ran foolishly back and forth across the yard. The second Indian shoved Mercy at Dianna, and as the girl buried her sobs in Dianna's skirts, he retrieved the peel from the floor. He tore the linen curtain from the window, wrapped it around the peel's blade, and thrust it into the hearth fire. Immediately the gauzy linen ignited. Holding the improvised torch before him, the Indian methodically set fire to the remaining curtains, baskets and the rush-filled mattress of Asa's bed.

"Nay, stop!" cried Dianna, her voice wild with emotion as she watched the flames begin to curl and lick at the house's wooden beams. "You heartless rogues! You have *us!* Why must you destroy our home as well?"

For answer they shoved her and Mercy through the door and away from the burning house. They paused by the fence while the Indian with the brand returned to light the roof shingles, dry from the summer's heat and quick to burn. The other man contemptuously let go of Dianna's hands, confident now that she would not flee. She sank to her knees and wrapped her arms protectively around Mercy. The Indian took the tomahawk from his waist, pantomimed striking with it and nodded meaningfully as he slipped it back into his belt. The simple gesture chilled Dianna's blood more than any words of warning. God in heaven, what had they done to deserve this?

Dianna held Mercy more tightly as she watched the orange flames twist through the door of the house. *Her* house. In these past months, in a thousand little ways, she had made it her own. She thought of the herbs she'd hung to dry from the rafters, the musket Hester had given her, the pumpkins and Indian corn and turnips she'd grown herself for the coming winter, all lost forever by the hand of one vengeful savage.

She fought back the tears that stung her eyes, blaming them on the grey, acrid smoke. If only Asa had returned an hour before, she thought bitterly, then they would have been safe with the others in Wickhamton. How long would it be now before Asa came to find them gone, and how long before he could gather men to follow after them? By then she and Mercy would be on their way to Quebec and irretrievably lost from the English world. She pictured Kit waiting for her at dusk by the burying ground, wondering impatiently why she didn't appear.

Oh, Kit, my dearest, I may never see you, kiss you, love you again!

The second Indian rejoined them, and together the two men motioned for them to leave. Dianna kissed Mercy on the forehead, and with the girl's fingers clutched tightly in her own, she followed their captors. Her last glimpse of her happily ordered life was distorted by the waves of heat from the fire: an apple pie on a windowsill silhouetted against orange flames.

For Kit, the best part of the training day came last with the shooting competition. Even though as colonel he'd long ago had to disqualify himself, he enjoyed watching the other men vie for the ten-pound prize and the praise of the young women so willing to be impressed. Greybeards from the east grumbled to Kit that more time should be given to proper exercise with pikes and musket volleys, but Kit disagreed. Against an enemy that could vanish at will among the trees, battles would be won by a single man's marksmanship, not a synchronized volley by a line of musketeers.

Kit grimaced as one over-eager apprentice's shot went wildly awry to the jeers and whoops of his friends, and he wondered if the hard cider, ale and rum that traditionally ended militia day had already begun to appear. He wished the men would take the practice more seriously. Most were too young or too new from England to have seen action in King Philip's War, and in the absence of obvious danger, crops and harvests still claimed their first attention. Perhaps what he'd told them today about the raw desolation he'd seen at Deerfield and the dozens of missing women and children would make them practice a bit harder.

Kit shook his head as another woeful shot missed the target. From what Hester had told him, Dianna could outshoot them all. It surprised him how much he liked the idea of her small, straight figure there at the line, aiming and firing better than the men. Once again he impatiently scanned the crowd of spectators, searching for her familiar face.

Damnation, she and Mercy should be here by now! He should have insisted on bringing them himself instead of relying on Asa. For all Asa's pious cant about family duties, the old fool had no sense of time or responsibility, and an unseasonable fondness for the bad French brandy he got from trading. Likely that was where he was now, sleeping it off somewhere, Kit fumed, but his irritation at Asa was only a part of the growing uneasiness he couldn't shake off.

He left the competition and went striding off to where the older women were preparing the evening meal. He recalled Dianna was baking pies. Perhaps she'd come here first. Again his gaze swept over the women, seeking the one that wasn't there. That morning, for Dianna, he'd taken special care with his red uniform coat, polishing the gold buttons and retying the silk sash across his chest a dozen times before he'd been satisfied, yet now he was oblivious to how even grandmothers turned to gawk with open admiration at him in his sword and plumed hat.

"She don't be here, lad," said Hester before he could ask, "and it don't be like Dianna t'be late. Ye didn't have words yesterday, did ye?"

The way Kit's face changed at once into a blank, emotionless mask was answer enough for Hester. "Then like as not, it be Asa that's kept her," she said hurriedly, "an' they'll be here directly."

"I'm going back for them."

Hester's forehead furrowed with concern. "Take some o' the others with ye, then. It's likely nothing, but then ye can't be sure...." Her voice trailed off, with what was left unspoken still painfully clear between them.

"It will be quicker if I go alone." He knew she was afraid of what he would find and what it would do to him, and he hated her concern, for it mirrored his own.

"Kit, ye can't go alone, not again," pleaded Hester anxiously. "Ye leave now, an' the whole town'll be talking, they will!"

"Let them," he called back as he headed for the horses. "I'll be back with Dianna and Mercy, and God help Asa Wing when I find his shiftless old hide!"

Kit let Thunder have his head on the Wickhamton road, and they soon were near to the Wing house. Kit drew the horse in as they cut through the woods, but even though the last light of day filtered through the trees, the stallion was unusually skittish, his pointed ears swivelling to hear Kit's reassurances. But at the clearing near the stream, Thunder suddenly snorted and balked, then reared back as a score of crows rose like a noisy black curtain from the tall rushes before him. While the crows danced and chattered in the branches overhead, Kit fought to calm the horse, and then, reluctantly, dismounted to investigate.

A dead deer, he told himself automatically as he stepped through the swaying rushes. Animals often came to die at the same places they drank, but the carcass should be moved before it fouled the water. With the long barrel of his gun, he parted the rushes and found Asa's body.

The dead man lay face down in the marsh, felled by the bullet wound in his upper back, and though his wispy grey hair still fluttered in the breeze untouched, his murderer had looted and stripped his body before abandoning it to the crows.

Kit reeled back, his knees suddenly weak. He had seen worse things, far worse, and yet now when his eyes squeezed shut, it was not poor Asa that he saw in his mind's eye but his parents and his sister, and Dianna and Mercy.

"Nay, not Dianna!" he rasped out loud. He steadied himself against a tree, the blood still pounding in his ears, and cursed his own weakness. Not Dianna, not Mercy. He had no proof they weren't still waiting on the other side of the hill. Quickly he swung himself up onto Thunder and urged the horse across the stream. But as soon as they crested the hill, Kit smelled the smoke and his last fragile hope shattered.

The Barnard farm had looked much the same as the scene now spread before him. The fire had burned itself out, leaving the charred outline of the house, the thick, blackened beams still upright around the chimney. Of the less substantial barn, nothing remained but smoking rubble.

Kit drew closer and called Mercy's and Dianna's names on the slim chance that they might have escaped and be hiding nearby. He tied Thunder to the fence and forced himself to search the ruins for bodies. To his grim satisfaction, he found none, but near the doorway he did find footprints, two sets of moccasins and two smaller, heeled shoes. His spirits rose to know that they had been taken from here alive. In their arrogance, the Indians hadn't bothered to sweep away the tracks, and the footsteps across the dusty yard were a trail a blind man could follow. Until, of course, they had reached the forest. Then Kit knew it would take every bit of tracking skill he possessed to follow them.

And he *would* follow them. There was no question of staying back this time. From the warmth of the timbers, he guessed they had at most six hours lead on him. He'd lose another hour returning to Plumstead to change his clothes and gather provisions and leave word where he'd gone. Two Indians were manageable odds, odds he could accept. A dozen militiamen might panic the Indians, and Dianna and Mercy would be the ones to suffer. Besides, by now there wouldn't be a single man in Wickhamton sober enough to be worth the delay. No, Kit would go alone. He owed it to Dianna, and he owed it to the two men who dared take her from him.

As he turned to go, something round and half-blackened caught his eye in the rubble, and he knelt to look closer. The pie had cracked when it had slid to the ground, but the two pastry hearts were still intact. Lightly he traced their outline and crossed the filling that trickled from the crack. On his fingertips the cooked apples were sweet and spicy to taste, and still warm, and the sense of loss and desolation that swept over him was almost unbearable.

Something brushed against his leg, and he started and jerked his rifle to his shoulder. Lily mewed forlornly, her white fur singed and marked with soot she hadn't been able to lick away. With one hand Kit scooped her up against his chest.

"We've lost them, haven't we, catkin," he whispered hoarsely into Lily's fur as the cat rubbed her head against his thumb. "But I'll bring them back safe, I swear it. This time will be different. I swear to God, this time I won't fail them."

Chapter Sixteen

For ten days Dianna and Mercy travelled with the Indians. The men were careful to avoid other houses and farms, keeping to hidden trails through the forest. With the afternoon sun always over her left shoulder, all Dianna knew for sure was that they were heading north. She could not tell how many miles they had already walked or how many more lay ahead. She was thankful that both she and Mercy were accustomed to walking, for the pace the Indians set was rapid and their breaks for sleep only a few hours long each night. Dianna often remembered the evening she'd first arrived with Asa and how after months of inactivity on the *Prosperity,* even that short journey from the river to the house had left her aching and breathless. Her captors now did not have Asa's patience.

Each long day she stared at the back of the man ahead, the one who always walked first. It had not taken long for Dianna to see the differences between the two Indians. The one she had wounded was clearly the leader, both in his imperious posture and in the way the other deferred to him. His name was Mattasoit—though Dianna did not understand their language, she had figured out that much from the context of their conversations—and he was tall and lean and strong, his movements as spare and lithe as a panther's. Like Kit, she'd caught herself thinking more than once; before this she hadn't realized how unlike most Englishmen Kit was or rather, how much more like an Indian. She found the idea unsettling and concentrated, instead, on noting the differences.

For one, there was Mattasoit's hair, shaved clean on either side of his head, with the top crest left long and flowing. Two turkey feathers were tied into his hair, along with several strands of beads made from purple shells. Beneath his paint he was tattooed, dark dots across his cheekbones and the mark of a deer on one arm. On his other arm was the cut Dianna had given him. From the way he ignored the wound, purposefully leaving it uncovered, Dianna sensed her action had caused far greater injury to his pride, and secretly she rejoiced. There on his arm was the proof that she had not always been so helpless!

Though in appearance the second man looked much the same, there seemed to be a hesitancy about him that lessened the fierceness of his painted face. While he was quick enough to prod Dianna with his musket if she slowed, he was more patient with Mercy, helping the girl if she stumbled and offering her berries and parched corn from his pack. But Dianna remained wary of his kindnesses, remembering that this man had torched their house. Mattasoit called him Quabaug.

Both men were bare-chested, with trading blankets looped over their shoulders in place of shirts or jackets. Dianna envied them their leather leggings and the ease with which they glided through the brush as again and again her own skirts caught on branches and twigs. The invisible paths they followed were not meant for English petticoats. Impatiently Quabaug would yank the fabric off, tearing it rather than working it free. At first Dianna thought with dismay of all her careful handiwork shredded so ignominiously, but then she noticed how the scraps of torn fabric were left behind. They would, she realized, be an easy trail to follow. As often as she dared, she began to catch her skirts on purpose, and prayed that their rescuers would spot the scraps.

If, that is, there were any rescuers. Desperately Dianna wanted to believe that she and Mercy would be saved, but too well she recalled all the reasons why the militia hadn't gone after Goodwife Barnard, and she knew this was no different. How could she reasonably expect them to come after a servant and a child?

Because Kit loves you, her heart answered fiercely. What had he thought when she hadn't joined him on training day? Had he been angry when she didn't come, or worse yet, had he despaired, believing she had changed her mind? She remembered how surprisingly insecure he had been about her loving him, betraying a desperation that she didn't understand. It was strange to think of a man like Kit so vulnerable, and she never wanted to hurt him, not even this way, when she couldn't help it. But surely Asa would have explained, once he'd seen the burning house and gone to Wickhamton for help. Asa was unpredictable, but he did love Mercy.

And Kit—Kit loved *her*. Even before he'd known her name he had rescued her from the nightmare in her uncle's house, and so much had changed between them since then. He would come for her and for Mercy. He would. Over and over Dianna repeated the words to herself as they went deeper into the wilderness.

She was worried most about Mercy. Once they had left sight of their home, the girl had stopped her weeping and instead had seemed to draw into herself, her face empty as she let Dianna draw her along by the hand. She did not seem to hear Dianna, nor did she speak in return, and when they stopped to rest, she would curl herself into a tight little ball with her eyes squeezed shut. To lose her parents, her home and her pet, too, was more than any child should have to bear, and the unfairness of their capture tore at Dianna. Nor could she tell how much longer Mercy could bear the strain. Each dawn she was harder to rouse, and her slender body was growing visibly weaker from the hardships.

The night they crossed the river brought reality to Dianna's fears. The Indians had not stopped at dusk as usual, but continued on, and in the darkness unseen branches lashed at Dianna's arms and face and roots and rocks seemed to rise from nowhere to trip her feet. The night was cold, too, with the chill of winter in the autumn air, and Dianna shivered in her tattered dress without a shawl or cape. Mercy's little hand was icy, and the child was almost weaving from exhaustion.

"We must keep up, Mercy," Dianna urged, as much to encourage herself as the child. "We're warmer walking than if we stop."

Dianna heard the rushing water ahead as they came through the trees. The river was narrow here, scarcely more than a wide stream as it raced over and around a cluster of large rocks. Mattasoit easily stepped from the bank to the first rock and then jumped across to the next in line. When he was half way across, he turned and beckoned sharply for Dianna and Mercy to follow.

"Nay, Dianna, I can't!" wailed Mercy, shaking her head as she backed away from the water. "I'll fall an' drown, an' they—they won't care!"

"*I* care, lamb, and I have no intention of letting you drown. See, the water's scarce a foot deep here, just like the stream at home." Gently Dianna tried to draw Mercy toward the water. She could feel the impatience radiating from Mattasoit. She didn't want to frighten Mercy, but this was definitely not the time to dawdle. Kit said that the trail between Deerfield and Quebec had been littered with the corpses of English women who had faltered. "At home you'd be hopping over these stones like a leap-frog. I'll hold your hand, I swear, and I won't let go. But we must go now, Mercy. Now!"

Whimpering, Mercy let Dianna pull her to the water's edge. "I'll count, Mercy, and we'll go together. One, two, three, jump!"

The rock was wet and more slippery than Dianna had expected, and their shoes skidded across the surface before Dianna could steady herself enough to stop. She took a deep breath as she looked at the next rock, the black water foaming and churning around her feet. She didn't like this any more than Mercy did, but there stood Mattasoit ahead of them, one hand on the tomahawk at his belt. Lord, how she hated the threat the gesture implied, and how much she hated the man who made it!

"Again, Mercy." They had come this far, and she wouldn't falter now. "One, two, three, *jump!*"

Fourteen rocks they crossed until only the last step remained to the bank. "Almost there, Mercy," coaxed Dianna, "and you've done it, just like I knew you could."

Mercy smiled tremulously up at Dianna, and for the first time dared to let go of her hand. "'Twas not so very hard," she said and took the last hop on her own. But she hadn't counted on the marsh grass that lined the bank, and though she scrambled frantically for a foothold, she tumbled back into the water with a shriek. The water here was not deep, and Dianna at once dragged her, weeping, to the river bank.

"Hush, Mercy, you're safe enough," murmured Dianna as the little girl clung to her neck. The water coursed from Mercy's skirts and petticoats into puddles around her sodden shoes and stockings, and the cold, wet wool clung to her legs. Already Dianna could feel her shivering.

Yet Dianna felt Mattasoit's hand on her shoulder as well. She did not need to understand his words to know that he was angry with the delay and demanding that they continue. Slowly she disengaged herself from Mercy's embrace and rose to face the Indian.

"We cannot go on, not tonight," she told him firmly, forgetting that the man knew no English. "The child needs to dry her clothes and to lose the chill with the warmth of a fire."

Mattasoit's eyes narrowed, and he pointed once again to the trail into the woods.

"Nay, I will not go," said Dianna angrily, her silver eyes flashing. "I refuse to risk the child's health so that you might continue to drive us like animals!"

Furiously the Indian raised his hand and struck Dianna across her jaw. She stumbled back from him, but kept her footing. Instead of subduing her, his blow only fanned her temper more, and all the indignities and fears she'd borne in the past few days came rising up.

"You have no right to treat me thus!" she said defiantly. "I'm not one of your heathen squaws, but an English gentlewoman, a lady, and nothing you can do or say to me can change that! You think you are such a brave warrior to bully and torment a woman and child! Mercy and I are ten times braver than you. Nay, a hundred times! You are a coward, and so I'll tell everyone in Quebec! *Vous êtes un très gros poltron!*"

Mattasoit's whole body tensed with fury as he answered her in flawless, unaccented French. "If you were not worth so much to me unharmed, I would cut your tongue from your mouth so I would hear no more of your lies. You will call me master and you will obey me."

Stunned, much of Dianna's anger evaporated with the knowledge that they could now communicate. "Then you must understand—"

Swiftly his hand sliced the air before her face. "I must do nothing you ask!" he said sharply. "Through your English cunning you have concealed from me that you speak the Frenchman's tongue, and as your master, I am displeased. I have sworn to deliver you unharmed, but not so your child. Perhaps she shall suffer in your stead."

"Nay, you can't!" protested Dianna wildly. Her gaze flew back to Mercy, huddled miserably on the river bank with Quabaug crouched beside her. "Do whatever you wish to me, but leave her alone! She is innocent, she has done nothing!"

Mattasoit smiled triumphantly, his lips curling back over even white teeth. "So, you give me the secret to your obedience."

Another master, another man who demanded she obey. But for Mercy's sake, Dianna abandoned her pride and softened her voice with supplication. His belief that she was Mercy's mother could only add weight to her requests. "My child is weary, and she will sicken if you refuse her the comfort of a fire's warmth. If she becomes ill, she'll only delay you longer."

Mattasoit shook his head, the beads in his long hair clicking softly against one another. "It matters not. If she cannot keep up, she will die." His smile widened. "Monsieur le Lieutenant Hertel de Rouville will give me four gold pieces for an English child's scalp."

"Nay, you could not!" gasped Dianna, horrified.

"Your words continue to be harsh to my ears, *Anglaise,* and unfit for your master. I care nothing for your child. It is Quabaug who wanted her, not I." He waved dismissively toward the other Indian. "He wishes to make a gift of her to his sister, to replace another claimed by death. I believe yours is likewise sullen and sickly, an unworthy gift, and I have told him so. But he will not listen and fancies her all the more."

While Mercy had been frozen by fear and cold, Quabaug had gently pulled off her wet socks and chafed her icy feet until the blood had returned. Modestly she had quickly tugged her skirts back down over her toes as soon as he was done, but she had not run away to Dianna's side, watching instead as he emptied his leather pack. At last he drew out a pair of child's moccasins, embroidered across the toes with porcupine quills. He held them up to Mercy's feet and frowned. He stuffed the toes of the moccasins with dry leaves until, satisfied that now they would fit, he held them shyly out to Mercy. The girl hesitated only a moment before accepting his gift. While Quabaug beamed and nodded, she slipped them on with a tentative smile and pointed her feet toward Dianna for approval.

But Dianna's eyes were on the contents of Quabaug's pack, piled neatly on the grass beside him. On the top was a white linen shirt, an Englishman's shirt, worn and crisscrossed with mending and covered with the stiff, dark blotches of dried blood. Dianna noted how the old shirt's collar had been turned and resewn to lengthen its wear; she had done the work herself not a fortnight before. Slowly, as if in a dream, she forced herself to see Quabaug's musket, still cradled protectively in his lap. Why hadn't she noticed before the two wedge-shaped notches in the stock, the notches that were Asa's special mark?

She wrapped her arms tightly around herself and dug her nails into her own skin, fighting back the impossible urge to laugh. No one was coming for them because no one knew they were gone. In her elegant courtier's French, she was left to barter for her life with a half-naked savage who painted his face like a skunk's back.

By the time they finally halted for the night, several hours before daybreak, Mercy's eyes were unnaturally bright and her cheeks were flushed with fever.

"I'm so c-cold, Dianna," she said, stammering with the chills that shook her weakened body as she sank to the ground.

One hand across the child's forehead told Dianna all she needed to know, and quickly she turned to Mattasoit. "Please, I beg you, my daughter needs hot food to eat. If you or Quabaug can bring me anything, a squirrel or a rabbit, I can make us all a stew."

"You would have us fire muskets, would you?" Mattasoit snorted with scorn. "So that every Englishmen will know we are here? I am no fool, *Anglaise.*"

"A fire, then, just a small one," pleaded Dianna, "so that she might warm herself and her clothes."

"A fire and musket-shots? Why don't I let you go to the highest hill, and shout so that all might hear you?"

"But there is no one!" Dianna's voice cracked with the admission. "Please—"

"Do not test me, *Anglaise,* for you know my answer," he snapped. "We leave at sunrise."

Numbly Dianna watched as the two Indians rolled themselves in their blankets and were, it seemed, instantly asleep. Curled on the ground, Mercy, too, slept, but restlessly, her arms and legs thrashing as she muttered in her dreams. Taking care not to wake the girl, Dianna lay beside her and wrapped her own body around the sick child's to share what warmth she could. Mercy's breathing was harsh in her chest, a wheezing rasp that meant the chill had settled in her lungs. Dianna hugged her closer, trying not to think of tomorrow. She had truly come to love Mercy as her own, yet there was nothing she could do to save her or even give her comfort. Hot tears of fear and frustration slid down her cheek and angrily she wiped them away with her fingers. Weeping would serve no purpose to either of them.

Gradually the first light of the false dawn began to filter through the yellow leaves of the tall oaks overhead. A low mist drifted over the ground, enveloping the dark tree roots like an eerie shroud, and muffling all sound, for the woods were strangely silent in these last moments before the true dawn. Dianna remembered the elves and faeries and other woodland creatures that her father had used to amuse her as a child, but here their world seemed strangely real, and Dianna's heartbeat began to quicken at what she felt but could not see.

Mercy shifted uneasily in her arms, her eyelids fluttering open. "Dianna?" she asked hoarsely, each breath an effort.

"Hush, lamb, 'tis not time to rise yet." Dianna stroked the child's hair. Oh, Lord, she was so very hot to touch.

"But it hurts t'breathe!"

"Then here, sit upright in my lap, and perhaps that shall be better." Mercy climbed across Dianna's legs and rested her head against Dianna's chest. With each breath came the wheezing that meant congestion in her lungs, and Dianna's heart sank when she remembered the long day before them. She could not let them leave the child behind. Better to let them kill her, too, than abandon Mercy, and she curled her arms protectively around the girl's limp body.

"Would ye sing t'me, Dianna?" rasped Mercy. "The pretty song wit' th'queen's lament?"

Dianna hesitated, unwilling to disturb the sleeping Indians, but Mercy persisted. "Please, Dianna, th' queen's song be my favorite."

How could she refuse what might be the last favor the girl asked of her? "Oh, aye, if that's your favorite," she said, trying unsuccessfully to tease the way they always had before. Mercy's favorite was from an old-fashioned opera by Lully, and though Dianna was hazy as to which queen was doing the lamenting, the aria had always been one of her best pieces. She began softly, her own voice rough-edged from the chill, but soon the old beauty of the music filled her throat, and, closing her eyes, she let the notes rise and soar into the early morning mists.

When she was done, she kept her eyes closed just a moment longer to savor the vanishing pleasure of the music. When she opened them, Mattasoit loomed before them, and instinctively Dianna clutched at Mercy.

"You are *Me'toulin, Anglaise?*" he asked with a tentativeness that surprised Dianna. "They did not tell me that when I said I'd take you."

"*Me'toulin?*" repeated Dianna uncertainly. He was hanging back from her, unwilling to come too close, and Quabaug remained farther still, his dark eyes round with fear in the half-light.

"*Me'toulin, me'toulin.*" Mattasoit fanned his fingers, searching for the comparable word in French. "You have the gift to speak to the spirits, yes? You can make magic for them?"

Slowly his meaning dawned on Dianna. Her singing, that was it. Perhaps the Sun King's opera would sound like magic to ears that had never heard it. "Aye, I speak to them," she answered boldly, her chin high, "and they listen to me, too."

Mattasoit drew himself up confidently, but Dianna saw the fear come into his eyes now, too. "What did you tell them, your spirits, your gods?"

"I told them about you." Dianna paused for emphasis. "And I told them the truth."

Mattasoit flicked his hand, and Quabaug scurried forward. "We are within two days' journey of a village, *Anglaise,*" he said with an unwarrior-like nervousness. "There your daughter will be well tended. And she shall not walk further. Quabaug will carry her, and she shall have his blanket to warm herself. You will tell all this to the gods, *Anglaise?* You tell them so they will listen of Mattasoit and Quabaug?"

Dianna nodded. "They will listen," she said softly, and somehow, she thought they already had.

Chapter Seventeen

"You are right, Sparhawk," said Attawan as he rejoined Kit. "The woman and the child are within the village."

Kit swore and slammed his hand down hard on the ground in frustration. They had been so close, not more than half a day behind. "Did you see them? Are they well, unhurt?"

Attawan dropped the bag of cornmeal he'd traded for a Dutch knife, his excuse for visiting the village, and sat on the log beside Kit. "The woman is well, but the girl has been ill with lung fever. They carried her here."

Kit shook his head, remembered the time they'd wasted. When Mercy's footprints had changed first to moccasins and then disappeared completely, he had insisted they search the surrounding woods in case she had been abandoned. He owed that much and more to Tom Wing and to Asa, too. *And to Tamsin . . .*

And instead the Indians had carried Mercy. A simple explanation, really, for only one of a hundred small missteps. The fleeing Indians had not gone north toward Quebec as Kit had expected, but northwest, farther into the wilderness claimed by the French than he'd ever ventured before. The falling leaves had obscured the trail more effectively than snow, leaving only a bent branch here, an overturned stone there, to mark that any had passed before them. The first little flag of Dianna's torn skirt had seemed like a miracle, and when Kit had found enough to realize she'd done it intentionally, his admiration for her rose even higher. He'd saved each scrap like a talisman, a tattered reassurance that she still lived. And now she was just ahead, beyond one more hill and one more stream.

"How many guards are there?" he demanded impatiently. "Are they kept in a house or out of doors? Is there—"

"I didn't judge it wise to be too inquisitive, Sparhawk."

"Damn it, Attawan, I didn't let you come along so you could pass judgment!"

"You did not 'let' me. I chose to come. If I weren't here, you would now be bound and waiting for the village women to torture you." Attawan slipped a finger inside his moccasin and scratched his heel, considering whether to take offense or not, and decided once again to let Kit's outburst pass. It was the ghosts that spoke, not his friend, and it was a good thing that he, Attawan, was here to protect Sparhawk from letting those ghosts steal the Englishman's wits completely. "You forget the Pennacooks have no love for things English, and that includes big bull-heads like you."

Kit sighed heavily and rested his hand on the Indian's shoulder. "Aye, bull-headed I am," he admitted, "and I couldn't have come this far without you. But I want them back, Attawan. Tonight I will come with you, and together we'll find them."

Attawan nodded, satisfied by the words. He reached into his bag for his pipe and a flint, for despite Kit's impatience, they would not be going anywhere until nightfall at the earliest. "They are prisoners of a brave named Mattasoit, an Abenaki, not of this tribe. They don't like having him here, but they fear him and let him stay. What is strange, Sparhawk, is how he treats this woman as a great prize, yet in your English village, she is only a slave."

"A servant, Attawan, not a slave," said Kit automatically. "But you're right, it makes no sense."

Attawan shrugged. "I heard Mattasoit believes her to be a *me'toulin,* that she can speak with the gods."

Kit stared in disbelief. "What about Dianna Grey would make him think that? She is a Christian lady, not some kind of Abenaki witch!"

Attawan's expression grew serious. "Then hope Mattasoit doesn't learn this Christian lady has lied to him. He would be dishonored, and he would beat her, maybe kill her, if others laugh at him. She would not be much good as a servant after that, Sparhawk."

The smoke from Attawan's pipe filled Kit's nose, the tobacco's familiar scent pungent and oddly comforting. It was time Attawan knew the truth. "She won't be a servant when she returns to Plumstead," he said softly, trying to blot out the image of Dianna's being tortured by Mattasoit, and remember instead the way she laughed, her little cleft chin tipped back. "If she'll have me, Dianna Grey will be my wife."

Attawan showed no surprise, and only nodded thoughtfully behind the haze of smoke. "Then tonight we shall find your woman."

Dianna and Mercy were given a small wigwam to themselves near the center of the village. Although Dianna realized that they had displaced the wigwam's regular occupants only that they might be more carefully guarded, she still welcomed the privacy of the little house's windowless walls of woven mats. Their only visitor was a stout, wary woman who never raised her eyes from the water and food she left on the floor before retreating backward out the deerskin flap that served as a door. And, of course, Mattasoit and Quabaug, who did not leave their post outside the doorway.

With a small fire in the center of the packed dirt floor, the house was pleasingly warm, and Dianna was relieved that Mercy's breathing had eased and her sleep had grown more peaceful. Gently Dianna stroked the child's hair if she stirred, and settled the blanket higher over her shoulders. Whenever Mercy woke, Dianna urged her to eat—fried cornmeal cakes, baked beans and small strips of roast moose. The villagers had obviously offered them their best, but even their hospitality made Dianna uneasy. At Plumstead she'd heard many stories of Indian captivity, and not one of them had included Englishwomen as pampered guests in a village. But then none of the other captive women had been called a *me'toulin,* either.

In the afternoon of the second day, she waited until Mercy had fallen asleep again, and then drew back the deerskin to speak with Mattasoit. She had not realized how dim the house was until she stepped into the bright autumn sunlight and squinted, shading her eyes with her hand.

"Take yourself back inside, *Anglaise*," ordered Mattasoit with a touch of his old arrogance. He had freshly painted his face, and there were more beads and feathers woven into his hair. "It's not fit that you show yourself."

Dianna raised her chin imperiously, remembering the haughtiest of the dowager duchesses at court as good inspiration for an aspiring *me'toulin*. "Clearly these people are not yours and this is not your village," she said, declaring what was obvious even to her. These villagers bore little resemblance to Mattasoit, and were obviously intimidated by him. "Why do we remain here with them when they are such lesser warriors?"

She could have sworn he preened at the compliment. "We wait here for the men who seek you."

"What men are these?" she asked quickly, unable to keep the excitement from her voice. Maybe he meant the men who made and carried the ransom for captives. This would be as far as she and Mercy would have to travel before they could go home.

"The Frenchmen will come first," he said, and Dianna's hopes plummeted. "Forty gold pieces the fat one offered me to take you. He wants you badly, that one."

"What is the man's name?" Somehow her voice remained calm, almost offhanded. She had been chosen, kidnapped by design. The fat Frenchman must be Robillard; no other knew of her. She remembered the coarse hunger in his face when he'd looked at her at Plumstead, and she knew Mattasoit was right. Robillard did want her, and the certainty sickened her.

Mattasoit looked at her shrewdly. "The spirits haven't told you?"

Dianna returned his gaze levelly. "I can only hear what they tell me, and they don't bother to speak of fat Frenchmen."

Mattasoit shrugged carelessly, and with his thumb wiped a smudge from the barrel of his musket. "A Frenchman. I know not his name, and it matters little to me if he brings his gold pieces. He'll have you, and Quabaug shall have your daughter. Then shall come the Englishman." He smiled, his teeth startling against the black warpaint. "You are like a fawn, set out to tempt the big wolf to come before the hunters."

Suddenly, horribly, she understood. She was the bait to trap Kit. "He's not coming," she said too rapidly, fighting against the tightness in her chest. "If he had followed us, he would have found us already. Don't you hear me? He's not coming!"

"He will come, and he will die. You will go to the Frenchman, and your daughter will go to Quabaug's sister." Mattasoit's smile faded, and he tapped three fingers together lightly on his lower lip. "Listen to your spirits, *me'toulin,* and you will hear that all this is true."

Dianna jerked back the deerskin and stumbled back into the little house, the world swimming before her. Now that she knew Kit must not come for her, she was certain that he had. Somewhere, not far away, he was waiting to try to steal her and Mercy back. He would die trying, and it would be her fault. She needed no spirits to explain it. She balled her fingers into a fist and pressed it silently to her lips as if she could take back all the words she'd spoken to bring her to this place.

"What is it, Dianna?" asked Mercy, her face by the firelight still puffy with sleep. "What has happened?"

Dianna took a deep breath, the effort sharp as a blade in her lungs. "It's nothing, lamb, nothing at all."

But outside they heard the jingle of horses' bridles and more voices in French, angry, agitated voices. Dianna seized Mercy and drew her to her breast.

The man who thrust himself into the house was ruddy-faced above his neatly clipped beard and moustache, his chest as round and solid as a hogshead barrel and his legs bowed as if from the weight of his body. But what Dianna noticed first was the silver cross around his neck and the neat white collar above his dark cloak that marked the man for what he was: a minister, or more likely, since he seemed a Frenchman, a priest. Surely a man of God would help her escape!

"So this is the Englishwoman who claims to have gifts from God," he said coldly. "It is no more than

Protestant trickery. With such blasphemy she dishonors you, Mattasoit, and damns her own soul.''

Behind him stood Mattasoit. ''Beware, *mon père,* she speaks your tongue.''

''Aye, sir, and I'll not be shamed by anything I've done,'' said Dianna vehemently as she rose to her feet, her arms still tight around Mercy's shoulders. ''If I have spoken less than the truth, I've done so to save my child.''

The priest ignored Dianna and glanced instead over his shoulder at Mattasoit. ''You did not tell me there was a child with her. The lieutenant has no use for innocents.''

''The child is my prisoner along with the woman,'' said Mattasoit stubbornly. ''She will have a home among my people.''

''Where she will become another soul lost to the true faith.'' The priest slid the polished cross between his fingers thoughtfully. ''I have decided. Come to me, child. Your mother has chosen the path to damnation, but there is still time for your redemption. The holy sisters will nurture you and teach you the ways of goodness that come from Our Lord's Blessed Mother.''

The French words were meaningless to Mercy, but she understood well enough the beckoning hand of the man in black and clung more tightly to Dianna.

''You can't take her from me!'' cried Dianna. ''Roman or not, you are still a Christian, and no true Christian would separate a child from her mother!''

''If you truly love her, *madame,* you should thank me for saving her immortal soul,'' said the priest coldly. "She will be well cared for, much better than you yourself seem presently capable of."

Angrily Mattasoit gripped the man's arm. "I tell you, they are both mine!"

The priest stared pointedly at Mattasoit's hand, and suddenly on some unseen cue, two French soldiers appeared at the narrow doorway, only their boots and the muzzles of their guns visible, but enough to make Mattasoit release his grip with a furious shove.

"You expect compensation for your efforts," said the priest calmly, and tossed the Indian a handful of coins. Scornfully, Mattasoit did not catch them but let the coins fall to the dirt floor. The priest's lips curled beneath his neat moustache. "As you wish, so shall it be."

With unexpected swiftness, he grabbed Mercy around the waist and jerked her from Dianna's arms. The child screamed as Dianna lunged after her, but as soon as the priest was safely through the door, the soldiers barred Dianna's way with their muskets. Dianna shoved against the cold metal, struggling to reach Mercy as the priest tossed the thrashing child onto his saddle and climbed behind her. One soldier shoved Dianna back into the doorway, and then the soldiers, too, mounted their horses. Dianna's final glimpse of Mercy was her skinny bare legs in the new moccasins, kicking vainly against the horse's side.

Dianna stared after the three horses, not caring that she wept before the silent crowd of curious Penna-cooks. Her father, her name, her home and now Mercy and Kit: there was nothing left for her to lose.

It was Mattasoit who at last grabbed her shoulder and shook her roughly to break the spell of her own misery. "Come, we are leaving."

Uncomprehending, Dianna looked at him through the haze of her tears. "We're going after them?"

"Why? I've told you before that the child means nothing to me." The Indian's face was rigid with fury. "English and French, you have all lied, and betrayed me, and I will suffer it no longer. These white men will come for you, but you will be gone, and I will be the one to laugh at them as fools!"

His fingers tightened on her shoulder, his nails leaving crescent-shaped marks in her skin even through the wool of her bodice. "If you were true *me'toulin,* you wouldn't have shamed me before the priest. But you are false, like all your kind. And by the time we reach my village, you will beg me to have sold you to the French."

Kit and Attawan waited through most of the night, until the last hour before dawn when sleep is deepest, before they crept together into the village. Clouds hid the moon in their favor, but still Kit tied his light-colored hair beneath his hat and shaded his face with soot. Although Attawan had assured Kit that the villagers had no interest in Mercy or Dianna, and would likely not fight to keep them, Kit refused to rely on their goodwill. Instead he planned to kill the two Abenakis, steal their captives and melt back into the night without waking anyone. They'd use knives, not guns. Knives were silent and quick and did not need to be reloaded. He had never come to enjoy killing, hunting other men, white or red, for sport the way some did, but neither did he shy from it. And he wanted this man Mattasoit. God's blood, if he had given even one moment's pain to Dianna or Mercy...

As he and Attawan slipped from the shadow of one house to another, their moccasined footsteps silent in the dust, Kit forced himself to put Dianna from his thoughts and concentrate instead on the long blade of the knife in his hand. But something was wrong. He sensed it with his body before his thoughts agreed, before he saw Attawan stiffen and scowl and gesture toward the rounded wigwam before them.

Neither of the Abenakis were standing guard, as Attawan said they had been earlier. Immediately Kit's gaze swept around the rest of the village, looking to see if they'd moved Mercy and Dianna to another house. But there was no sign of Mattasoit or Quabaug, no movement at all beyond one lame dog drowsily scratching his head. Impatiently Attawan ducked into the house, barking a warning that Kit didn't understand. A woman shrieked and was quickly muffled, and then came a babble of excited voices. Kit followed, his eyes straining to make sense of the mounded figures in the dark house. One, an old woman, waved her arms defiantly in Attawan's face as her shrill words rapidly rose and fell.

"For God's sake, Attawan, what is she saying?" demanded Kit. He could not stand upright against the low, curved ceiling, and bent over he felt awkward and vulnerable. "Where's Dianna?"

Disgusted, Attawan thrust his knife back into the sheath at his waist. "They left before sundown. A

French priest and two soldiers took Tom Wing's daughter, and the Abenakis took your woman."

Kit fought against disappointment so sharp he felt it like a blow. "Strange they would be separated," he heard himself saying as he and Attawan stepped outside. *He had come too late. He'd failed again.* "Any notion of where they've gone?"

Attawan shook his head. "They force us to separate, too. I'll follow the priest." He laid his hand on Kit's arm and looked at him seriously, reading his doubts. "The Abenakis are yours by rights. You will find them, and you will show them that you are worth ten of their worthless braves, that they should not take what is yours. The courage is in your heart, Sparhawk."

He smiled and shoved Kit playfully. "Go now, or you shall feel the sharpness of Dianna Grey's tongue for making her wait."

The basket Mattasoit had tied to Dianna's back was heavy, and the hickory splints dug into her shoulders. She tried not to feel it, tried not to think beyond placing one foot after the other. That was difficult enough, burdened beneath the basket's lopsided weight. But if she stumbled, Mattasoit would hit her and curse her clumsiness. Her lip was swollen from the last time, when she'd tripped across the root, and the coppery taste of her own blood was still in her mouth. He'd been so disgusted that he'd gone on ahead by himself, leaving her with Quabaug's musket—Asa's musket— to prod the backs of her legs. *One step at a time, only one step, then one step more....*

She saw the flash in the fir trees from the corner of her eye, heard first the dry echo of the gunpowder and then the surprised little grunt that Quabaug made as he flopped forward on top of her. Beneath his weight she toppled face first into the dry maple leaves, her breath knocked from her lungs. Gasping, she looked around wildly for the shot's source and tried to pull herself free from beneath Quabaug's sprawling, still body.

Then Kit was there, truly there and not just another dream, the sun bright in his hair and the rifle in his hand as he jumped and ran down the hill through the brambles toward her. And above him, behind the broken oak tree, with one eye squinted as he peered down his musket's barrel, was Mattasoit.

Chapter Eighteen

Until Kit had seen Dianna there with the Indian, he had not realized how part of him already believed she was dead. By surrendering hope, he had tried to defend himself from the pain of losing her yet again. But it hadn't worked: he knew that the moment he saw her again. Without her, his life wasn't worth living, and all the pretending in the world couldn't change that.

From the trees he saw the discolored lump of the bruise on her jaw, the tattered, filthy clothing and the way she bowed beneath the basket she was forced to bear, while that Abenaki bastard ambled behind carrying nothing more than old Asa's musket. Kit's bullet found the Indian's breast in an instant, clean and neat, and too easy a death by half for what he'd done to Dianna. But none of that mattered now, he thought joyfully as he plunged through the underbrush toward her. She was alive, and he meant to take her in his arms and beg her to forgive him and swear to never let her suffer again.

Yet her expression was all wrong. Her mouth was twisted open in terror, her eyes rounded and staring away from him, past him.

Instinct made him dodge and drop to the ground, and the musket bullet rang instead into an alder's trunk, the bark splintering with a crack. Above him he heard Mattasoit's unearthly cry for battle, and Kit had only time to roll to his back as the Indian threw himself down from the hill, tomahawk in hand.

With both hands Kit held his rifle crossways, catching Mattasoit's wrist back against his chest. The Indian's face contorted as he strained to break Kit's hold. He twisted his leg beneath Kit's and threw his weight sideways, rocking Kit over with him. Kit slammed the rifle toward the man's throat and grabbed for his knife. In that half-second the Indian shoved the rifle away and swung the tomahawk upward. Swiftly Kit ducked, but not before a handful of severed gold-streaked curls drifted past his shoulder. He grabbed the Indian's wrist just as Mattasoit's fingers tightened around his own.

Helplessly Dianna watched as the two men tumbled over and over across the ground like wild dogs. They were well-matched in skill and size, each strengthened with blood-lust and anger. It would be a fight that ended only when one man was dead. She hated watching and looked away. There in the grass, not far, lay Asa's musket where Quabaug had dropped it. Her fingers clawed vainly at the loamy ground and leaves as she tried to reach it, her breath coming in short pants of frustration as she stretched toward the gun.

But it was too late. She heard the ragged cry, the last sound of a dying man. Dropping her head onto her arm, she squeezed her eyes shut, afraid to look. *Mer-*

ciful God, she prayed, *let Kit be alive! Let him be alive, and I shall never ask for anything else again!*

And then Kit was pulling her free from Quabaug's body and from the crushed carrying basket. The cry she heard now was her own, and tears of relief tracked down her grimy cheeks as she threw her arms around Kit's neck.

"Oh, Kit, I thought I'd never see you again," Dianna murmured hoarsely against his chest. "My own love, my only love!"

Yet strangely he did not embrace her in return, but held her too lightly with his hands on her shoulders. Puzzled, Dianna drew back, and he seemed to follow, swaying unsteadily, and to her shock she realized he only stood because of her support.

"Behind that hill are—there is a shelter," he said thickly. "You need rest, dearling, you are—"

He did not finish, clutching at her as his legs gave way. He stared blankly at Dianna, his green eyes too wide open and his face oddly pale beneath the tan. Now Dianna saw the dark patches on his hunting shirt were blood, new blood, and not all of it Mattasoit's. The hair over Kit's left ear was wet and red, the curl gone limp.

"Nay, Kit, 'tis you that's wounded," she said as she struggled to keep him upright. Lord, why did she have to be so small a woman in a world of large men? She lifted one of his arms across her shoulder like a yoke and tried to lead him. "Listen to me, love! We must get you to this shelter, but I'll need your help. Nay, don't wobble on me now, Kit!"

Kit heard her voice from far away and smiled, wondering why this pretty little woman beside him should accuse him of wobbling. Wobbling was a damned foolish accusation to make to a man. He was steady enough to dance, if he'd a mind to, and mayhap with this very lass, if only she'd stand still long enough for him to catch her. Her face spun before him, her features crazily unfocussed. Silly baggage, to tease him this way!

Somehow Dianna managed to lead him over the hill, not even sure that the shelter he'd mentioned even existed. But there beside the trickle of a nearly-dry stream were the bent saplings of an abandoned Indian camp. The Indians had taken away most of the woven mats that turned the sapling arches into houses, but one little wigwam remained almost intact, perhaps the last refuge of a villager too old or ill to follow with the rest. It was empty enough now, smelling of musty reeds and squirrels, and there were ragged holes in the walls where the mats had fallen through. Yet the wigwam was better than Dianna had dared to hope, and with one final effort, she half led, half dragged Kit inside. He groaned, muttering something she didn't understand, and at last, his body gave way to unconsciousness.

Dianna pushed her hair back from her face and tried to think what to do next. With a quick glance at Kit, she ran back over the hill to where the two dead Abenakis lay. First she retrieved the basket she had been carrying, loaded with provisions Mattasoit had appropriated from the Pennacooks—two blankets, a brass cooking pot, twice mended, smoked venison, parched corn, walnuts and a bark basket of cranberries that were only slightly crushed. Next she collected Asa's musket and Mattasoit's, too. For a long moment she stared down at Mattasoit's body, flopped on his side with his arms outstretched across the bloodstained leaves. Quickly, before she lost her nerve, she reached down and pried the tomahawk from his stiffening fingers and pulled the powder horn and bag of bullets and patches from around his neck. She did the same to Quabaug, shivering as she tried not to touch him more than she had to, and then, her arms full of all she'd gathered, she ran as fast as she could back to the house where Kit lay.

He had not moved, and Dianna wondered if that meant good or ill. She filled the brass pot with water in the stream and tore the last of her petticoats into strips for bandages. Nothing was as clean as it should have been—what she would have given for a cup of strong soap!—but she made a small fire in the center of the hut beneath the roof hole and balanced the pot of water over it to boil. Finally she knelt beside Kit and as gently as she could, pulled off his blood-soaked shirt.

One cut ran diagonally from his collar-bone, and another crossed his forearm. Neither was serious, and the bleeding had almost stopped. Her hands grazed the dark hair on his chest as she washed the cuts. She'd forgotten how powerfully muscled he was, and how, too, his body was already crisscrossed with old scars. Lightly she rested her fingers over his heart. The beat was steady and regular, as was his breathing, and satisfied, she turned to the cut on his head. This was the one that worried her and the one that bled the longest, each cloth that she pressed to it soon becoming soaked. Finally, by sunset, she was able to wrap her makeshift bandages around his head, had covered him with one of the blankets, and then sat back to wait. In the morning she would try to find the wild herbs to make a poultice to draw out the wound's poison.

She loaded all three guns and kept guard herself, wrapped in the second blanket with a musket in her hands. The night seemed very black to her, and very lonely, even with Kit lying beside her, unconscious or asleep she did not know.

She was far more frightened than she wanted to admit. Strong as he was, Kit's wound was still dangerous. She didn't know how long it would be before he could travel or how far they were from any English settlement. The Indians who'd abandoned this village could return. The Frenchmen Mattasoit had avoided might be searching for them, perhaps even Robillard himself. And Mercy, poor, innocent Mercy, could be a hundred miles closer to Montreal by now. Dianna placed another branch on the fire and huddled into her blanket. Last year in the fall she and her father had been in Paris, and she'd sung in the white-and-gold music room of the Vicomte de Thavenet . . .

It was mid-morning before Dianna awoke, with Kit muttering restlessly beside her. She followed Hester's receipt for the poultice, but by nightfall he was feverish and the head wound had become angry and swollen. He never seemed to know her, speaking disjointedly about his mother and father and other names she did not recognize. She cooled his fever with cloths soaked in the icy stream water, and tried to get him to sip the broth she'd made. She sang to him, too, for the sound of her voice seemed to calm him as gently she pillowed his head in her lap and stroked her fingertips across his forehead. No grand queen's laments this time, but old lullabies and wistful Scottish tales of forgotten lovers.

There was little more she could do, and she needed no great physician's skill to tell her that each hour he was drifting a little farther away from her and from life, nor did she need to be told what would become of her if the infection finally claimed him.

No matter where the dream began, it always ended in the same place, and in the same way.

He was on the old bay gelding, the autumn sun warm on his back. He had travelled this road to Wickhamton so many times that he and the horse could have done it blindfolded. As he rode he was thinking about a copper-haired tavern-keep's daughter in New London, and wondering if he could talk his father into letting him return downriver on business to see her again next week. He couldn't quite remember her name—Nell or Nan, he'd recall it soon enough when he saw her again—but she'd been quite generous in her affections, and at twenty-two, that was what mattered to him most.

Right before the bend in the road, low by the river, the horse had shied skittishly, and he had swatted its rump and called it a cowardly old noddy as they'd pushed on. And that was when he saw the body of his mother first, her skirts snarled against the red-and-

gold berries of a bittersweet vine, and then his father, face up and staring, surprised, at the cloudless sky, and finally Tamsin, who'd run the farthest before they'd shot her, too. There was a thin red line around her throat where they'd yanked away her coral beads, and she still clutched the arm of her calico doll, Sukey.

He should have been there to save them. That never changed. Nothing he ever did could make it different.

He should have saved them . . .

"You saved me!" said Dianna hoarsely. "Without you I would have died, and now, God forgive me, I cannot do the same for you!"

Confused, Kit realized it was her tears that were falling on his face. His mouth felt dry as a desert, but he forced himself to form the words, to make her understand. "I—I should have been with them," he said, half the words no more than breath without sound. "If I couldn't have saved them, I should have died, too."

"Nay, don't speak so!" she cried, her face close above his, and he saw how her mouth twisted to keep from weeping more. "You have been ill, and I thought—I was afraid—but you've come back to me now, and you'll live. You *will* live!"

Gradually his thoughts began to untangle, and his eyes began to make sense again. And Dianna: he'd never seen anything dearer than her face, her dark brows drawn together with concern as she watched him. But she looked too tired, bluish circles ringing her silver eyes, her face thinner than he remembered, and on her jaw, the last yellow patch of a fading bruise. She was the one who needed coddling, not him.

Gently she slid her hand beneath the back of his head and tried to raise him so he could drink from the little horn cup she held to his lips. He scowled, irritated by his own weakness, and too quickly tried to raise himself. The rush-mat walls of the wigwam spun wildly, and he feared his stomach would rebel and shame him. Desperately he clung to his bent knees, willing his own body to behave, until at last, covered with sweat from the effort, he could take the cup from her hand himself.

"How long have I been ill?"

She held one hand up, the fingers spread. "Five days."

"Damnation," he said softly. He touched his face and felt the rough beard that confirmed what she'd said, and then the bandage that swathed his head. He remembered everything now, how he'd let that damned Abenaki take him down neat as a babe in leading-strings. Unbelievably, unforgivably careless he'd been, and his head throbbed as though it still had the tomahawk in it. "Sweet, holy, hellfire, *damnation!*"

She shushed him gently. "Don't vex yourself, Kit, you're still weak."

"You don't need to remind me." He spoke too sharply and saw the surprise and hurt in her eyes. He should be thanking her, not swearing at her. But he couldn't bear to see her face go soft with love again. He didn't deserve her or her love, not the way he'd failed again. "In fact you don't really need me at all, do you? I came to rescue you and ended up half-brained instead. You'd have done better to stay with the French.''

''The French didn't want me, nor did the Indians. They only took me to get you.'' She ducked her head, feeling like a fool for wanting to cry again. Hadn't she wept enough for this man? She told herself that he was still in pain, that this wasn't really Kit talking to her like this, but his surliness stung, and so did the way he would not meet her eyes. ''I told them you wouldn't come after me, but it seems they knew you better than I do.''

''Aye, that's true enough,'' he said bluntly. If she knew what an incompetent coward he really was, she wouldn't have stayed with him a minute, let alone five days. He wondered why she hadn't realized the truth yet, when even the French were mocking his weakness: a man who could not protect the ones he loved most.

He saw Tamsin's plump little hand, never quite as clean as their mother wished, clutching at the chickweed where she'd fallen. . . .

''Where's Mercy?'' he demanded abruptly.

''A French priest took her away when we were in the village. I tried to keep her with me, I swear, but—''

''Asa was wrong to give the child to your safekeeping. Now that he's dead, she is my responsibility entirely, not yours.'' He paused, and Dianna noticed how he clasped one hand so tightly over the other that his knuckles showed white. ''You knew they killed him, didn't you?''

She nodded, but Kit's eyes were closed, his head bowed.

The still, small figure lying in the grass seemed more angular, was dressed more simply, and in place of the doll was a small, white cat named Lily.

The image was so vivid, Kit sucked in his breath as he fought it back, shaking his head fiercely with denial. Not Mercy, nay, not Mercy, too.

Fearful that the fever had returned, Dianna reached out to calm him. "Nay, don't even think it," he growled as he shook her hand away, his eyes still tightly shut. "Don't even think it!"

Swiftly Dianna drew back and stared down at her hands in her lap. He was right. She didn't know him, not when he was like this. When two days before she had found in his haversack all the torn red rosettes she'd left along the trail, she'd seen it as proof of his devotion. But now she wasn't so sure. Like too many other things he did, maybe rescuing her was simply one more test of himself, another chance to prove how invaluable Colonel Sparhawk was to the people who depended on him.

And not once in his feverish ramblings had he mentioned her name.

"Who is Tamsin?" she asked softly. "You called for her often."

He started so visibly at the name that Dianna's heart sank. "Someone very dear and special to me," he answered unevenly.

He'd grown pale again, his forehead glistening with sweat, and she worried that he'd faint. But she couldn't stop. She had to know. "You love her very much, don't you?"

"How could I not?" His voice had dropped to a hoarse whisper. "From the day she was born she seemed like another part of me. And then to lose her like that— God, Dianna, she was but seven years old!"

Dianna stared uncertainly, her own doubts forgotten before his obvious misery. "Tamsin?"

He had not meant to tell her, for he didn't think he could bear her scorn when she learned the truth. But to hear Tamsin's name on Dianna's lips seemed to shatter the last boundary within him and he could not have kept back the truth had his life depended on it.

"They came after the last war, after the treaties, only three of them, Mohegans. They—they murdered my mother and my father and my sister Tamsin and took their scalps, and when I found them, it was too late." He was shaking, his eyes red-rimmed and staring as he saw it all again. "If I had been there, I would have saved them. But I wasn't, and they died. They died because of me."

In horrified silence Dianna listened, and one by one, all the half-explained conversations and mysteries began to make sense. Asa and Hester and all the others had known. Only she, the one who loved him most, was left unaware of his suffering.

"Oh, Kit, my poor love," she murmured. "You should have told me before."

He dropped his head to his chest. "I know, Dianna. God forgive me, I should have told you long ago. But I was so afraid I'd lose you, and now look what it's come to. I've failed you and Mercy, too, just like I did my parents and Tamsin, sweet, silly Tamsin.''

His voice broke, and Dianna realized that tears were running down his cheeks to tangle in his half-grown beard. She threw her arms around his shoulders and pulled him close, and he fell against her like a weary child.

"Never say you failed me, Kit," she said as she rocked him gently against her, his face pressed against her shoulder as she drew her fingers through the snarls of his hair. "Never say it and never believe it. You came and you found me, and if you hadn't, I would have perished. And what of my uncle? If you had not come to his house that night, he would have killed me in his anger. I didn't think you were real, you know. You were too perfect, like a magic prince in an old story. But you saved me, and together, somehow, we'll save Mercy, too."

Kit listened without hearing what she said. The words didn't matter. Only the peace that came with her voice was real, and he didn't want it ever to end. She did not doubt him, did not scorn him. She still believed in him. His arms went around her waist and he clung to her in desperation.

"But think of what I am, Dianna," he mumbled against her. He had forgotten how soft her skin was. "A sorry, foolish creature who couldn't even protect his own family."

"Oh, Kit, I do not believe it," she said softly. "You always put others before yourself. 'Twill likely be the death of you, you know. To be the man you are, your parents must have loved you very much. I don't think they would have wanted you to blame yourself all this time."

He wanted so much to believe her. He had lived with the pain for so long that it was part of him, and there was no way he could simply let it go because she said so. But she was offering a way to ease it, and maybe, given time, she could help him forget. Why was it she was half his size, and yet had twice the strength? "Don't leave me, Dianna. God knows I've no right to ask you anything, but you can't know how I felt when I thought I'd lost you, too."

"Hush now, love," she said as she feathered a kiss on the top of his head. "I swear I'll not be going anywhere without you."

But he was already fast asleep.

Chapter Nineteen

"Your woman tried to kill me, Sparhawk," declared Attawan indignantly as Dianna followed him to where Kit sat by the stream, her musket leveled evenly at the Indian's back.

"I doubt it's much comfort, but she's said the same of you," answered Kit, trying very hard not to laugh. He wasn't sure which one, Attawan or Dianna, would be more upset with him if he did, and besides, it would probably not help his aching head at all. But the sight of Dianna in her tattered dress determinedly herding a disgruntled Attawan with a musket that was nearly as long as she was tall, was almost too much for him. Lord, how much he loved her! "Lower your gun, Dianna. Attawan's the best friend we have in these parts, and I'd prefer to keep him alive."

Reluctantly Dianna uncocked the musket and rested it back onto her shoulder. She hadn't expected to find Kit awake yet, let alone dressed and washing by the stream, and she wished she'd had a comb or brush to make herself look more presentable. She'd grown so accustomed to him ill and unconscious that to see his green cat's eyes once again watching her so attentively was somehow disconcerting. Despite all that he had told her last night, or maybe because of it, she felt oddly shy around Kit this morning, almost as if they were beginning all over again, and she tried to hide her skittishness by concentrating on Attawan.

"I suppose, then, I should ask your forgiveness, Master Attawan," she said stiffly, "but my experiences with Indians as of late have not exactly taught me to trust your people."

"Not *my* people. Abenakis." Attawan sniffed scornfully, confident that no more explanation was necessary. He touched his fingers to the bandage on Kit's head as he sat on the ground beside him. "Does your tiny woman carry a tomahawk as well as a musket?"

"You can't blame the damage on her, Attawan, only the healing." His smile flashing white against the dark beard, Kit looked past the Indian to Dianna, and she blushed with pleasure at the warmth in his expression and looked down, self-conscious in front of Attawan.

Attawan's eyebrows rose skeptically, not at all convinced this woman was worth the effort she'd cost. "I hope she does better tending your wounds than making your friends welcome, for you cannot linger here longer. Trailing that French priest was easy enough, but you, eh, you hide yourself away like a squirrel and I wasted three days finding you."

Anxiously Kit leaned forward, all trace of teasing gone. "Have you found Mercy Wing?"

Dianna rushed to Kit's side. "Is she well? They haven't hurt her, have they?"

Attawan shook his head. "The fat priest and the soldiers brought her to the mission at Deux-Rivières, and left her there with Père Vernet. They want her stronger before they take her to Montreal, but I don't know when that will be. A week or in the spring. They may have gone while I searched for you." He looked pointedly at Dianna, as if the delay were her fault alone. "We cannot wait."

Kit stood unsteadily, closing his eyes until the dizziness passed, and Dianna took his arm with concern. "You're not ready to travel, are you?" she asked softly. "It was only yesterday that the fever broke."

"I have no choice, dearling." Kit patted her hand on his arm to reassure her, but Dianna saw the strain etched around his eyes. "I have to get Mercy before they take her north."

"The mission is only a day's journey, Sparhawk, not hard travel for a strong man." Attawan studied Kit shrewdly. "But will you be any use when you get there, eh? Will your aim be true, your knife sure?"

"It will be, my friend, I swear to it. I'll be ready. I must. We can't very well rap on the door and ask them sweetly to give up the girl."

"Why not?" asked Dianna. "I'd think we'd have a better chance that way than to have you two go crashing in with knives and guns and God knows what."

"We'll hardly go crashing in anywhere." Kit frowned. "Dianna, love, you don't know how these things are best handled."

"Nay, you listen to me!" said Dianna urgently. "I'll tell them Mercy's my daughter, that Indians kidnapped her and I want her back. I'll pretend I'm

French, and you can be my guide. I'll say the Indians set upon us, too, so that's why we look so shabby. With the beard, no one would ever recognize you."

"True enough." Kit ran his hand across his jaw, thinking. He knew he'd be no use in a fight, but he hated to admit it, even to Attawan, and especially to Dianna. "I don't speak French, and they wouldn't understand why you hired an Englishman. Best I be your husband and Mercy's father. They can't quarrel with that."

Dianna smiled shyly, equally pleased that he would listen to her and be willing, even as a ruse, to be her husband.

"And Attawan," continued Kit, "you'll stay outside to cover us or go for help if we don't come out when we should."

"With the French, that's wise." Thoughtfully Attawan stroked his long scalp-lock. "Perhaps this woman of yours has merit after all."

Dianna groaned with exasperation and stalked off toward the wigwam to pack.

Kit grinned and slapped Attawan on the arm. "Watch your back, my friend. She not only has merit, but she's the very devil with that musket."

Uncomfortably, Père Vernet regarded the two people standing in the hall before him. Because the mission at Deux-Rivières was so deep in the wilderness, Père Vernet often went months without seeing another white face. And here, in less than a week, had first come Monseigneur le Abbé de Saint-Gilbert and now these two, an English settler and his French wife.

Even with her clothing shamefully torn, the young woman seemed graceful and modest, her genteel French a pleasure to hear, but the tall man was mistrustful, his hand never straying from the knife at his belt. So be it, decided the priest. If the sad tale they told of their missing daughter was true, the Englishman had reason to be wary.

Troubled, he thought of the child now sleeping in the kitchen. The monseigneur had described the girl's mother as a shrill, blasphemous Englishwoman, and Père Vernet had readily agreed to keep the child until she was well enough to go to the sacred sisters in Montreal. But the tears of the young woman before him touched his heart, and it would be clear enough if the child were hers.

Kit caught Dianna's arm as they began to follow the priest. "Has the little rascal admitted he's got Mercy?"

"He says there's an orphan in his keeping, and we must judge for ourselves," she whispered anxiously, chewing on her lower lip. "It must be Mercy, Kit. It must!"

"Attawan wouldn't have made that kind of mistake," he said thickly, hoping Dianna didn't realize how close to collapsing he was. Somehow he'd walked twenty miles this day, most of it hanging on to Attawan, and only sheer will and fear for Dianna and Mercy had kept him on his feet. "We'll take her from here as soon as you can make our thanks. I've no great taste for French hospitality."

The priest led them into the kitchen, where an old Indian woman with a conspicuous cross on her breast sat dozing over her knitting by the dying fire. To one side of the hearth was a small dishevelled pallet, and at once Dianna recognized Mercy's dark unruly hair poking from the mound of coverlets. With a little cry Dianna ran forward and lifted the sleeping child gently into her arms. Still too sleepy to comprehend, Mercy rubbed her hand across her eyes and muttered to herself before she slowly realized it was Dianna holding her, and Kit was there, too, bending over her. Without a sound she threw her arms around Dianna's neck and hung on as if she'd never let go.

Père Vernet wouldn't soon forget the sweetness of that reunion and the satisfaction of having done right by bringing it about. To witness such happiness, a child restored to loving parents, was a rare blessing, indeed. It had, then, been most unfortunate to see the poor father succumb to the shock of the ordeal and topple to the floor, his senses dead to the world.

Dianna undressed by the faint glow from the banked fire and climbed beneath the musty coverlet, being as careful as she could not to make the straw-filled mattress rustle and wake Kit. It had taken two of Père Vernet's Christian Indians to manoeuvre Kit's exhausted body up the narrow staircase to the mission's tiny bedchamber reserved for travellers, and he'd been asleep even before she'd stripped off his moccasins. Awkwardly she hugged the edge of the bed away from his body, listening to the even rhythm of his breathing. She had never slept with a man, and she wasn't sure what to do, whether to touch him or not.

But it was cold, and slowly she inched across the bed and tentatively snuggled her body against his back.

He was instantly awake, every nerve and muscle acutely aware of her imprint against his. Gingerly her hand crept around his waist, holding him, and he couldn't help groaning.

"Oh, Kit, I've wakened you," she whispered with disappointment, and he felt her begin to move away. "Forgive me, but I was cold. Here, I'll move back."

"Nay, stay." His fingers tightened around her wrist as he pulled her back, wondering how she could be cold when it seemed to him the very mattress was on fire from her nearness.

With a contented sigh she eased herself against him, her legs curled into his and her cheek turned against the broad muscles of his back. Her heart fluttered faster as her skin touched his where her tattered shift pulled up, and she inhaled deeply the special fragrance that was his alone. Sternly she reminded herself of how weak he still was, but her hand seemed to be moving on its own wanton volition, her fingers trailing through the curling hair on his chest.

"Did I really swoon away like a weak-kneed maid?" Kit asked, his voice strained. She had come to him innocently because she was cold, and in return he was randy as an old goat. If she'd only lie still!

"'Twas not your fault, Kit. The kitchen fire was too warm, that was all, and you've pushed yourself too far. Père Vernet understood. And the other priest, the one who took Mercy, isn't due back here for a fortnight, so we're safe enough here tonight." Safe enough from Frenchmen, thought Dianna guiltily, but not from her. "I sent the old woman in the kitchen to tell Attawan we were unharmed and would meet him in the morning."

"You've taken care of everything, haven't you, sweetheart?" said Kit softly. He said it proudly, without blaming or faulting himself, and Dianna didn't answer, smiling to herself in the darkness.

"You sang to me when I was sick, didn't you?" he asked. "I only now remembered it. 'Greensleeves,' and 'Hangman's Tree,' and 'Pray, Fair One.'"

"Would you have me sing to you now?"

"Nay, Dianna. I'd have you marry me. Now, this night, if that priest below didn't believe us already wed, but as soon as we return to Plumstead, if you'll have me."

Dianna froze, positive she'd misheard. "You don't owe me anything, Kit," she said in a tiny voice. "Not this. Whatever I've done for you—I expected nothing in return."

With a swiftness that startled her, he rolled over and trapped her against the pillows, his face so close to hers, she felt the hot urgency of his words upon her cheek.

"Listen to me, Dianna," he said. "When I thought I'd lost you forever, that I'd never touch you again, I knew then I could not go on living unless I found you. I want you in my arms by night and at my side by day, and I wish never to be parted from you again. Never, understand? I'm offering you everything I have, Dianna—my name, my home, my heart—and I pray to God it's enough. How I love you, sweetheart. How I love you!"

Dianna's throat constricted with emotion. "And I you, Kit. From the first, I've always loved you. Forever and always, Kit, my only love. Oh, Kit..."

She sighed his name as his lips met hers, a kiss that signalled a reunion, a pledge, a future for them as one. He kissed her tenderly at first, teasing with his tongue over the swell of her lips until they parted with a tiny catch of desire. He had forgotten how sweet she tasted, or maybe the velvety delight of her mouth was simply beyond remembering.

Dianna pulled away, her breathing already labored. "Your head, Kit," she protested weakly. "The wound—"

"The devil take it." His voice was more a growl, deep in his chest. "I'd sooner die than not love you now."

He pulled her shift over her shoulders, unwilling to have any barriers between them, and Dianna curled herself around him, marvelling again at the differences between them. His body was so lean and hard where hers was soft, his strength so visible in every muscle of his arms and back, and even when the fever had held him, he still had a power, a physical presence that she couldn't explain. He was unthinkingly confident in a man's harsh world of right and wrong and sudden death. Yet behind it all was the gentleness that touched her now, callused hands that caressed her with the tenderness that made her feel cherished and special. Then the gentleness fled before the passion, and their bodies twined together, wildly arching toward fulfillment. And when at last he cried out and called her name, she melted into him and knew such sweetness that she almost wept with the pure joy of loving him.

"In seven days by the river, we'll be home at Plumstead," he whispered happily as they lay still joined together. He swept her hair back to kiss her ear, and Dianna felt a contentment she'd never known before. Home, her home, with her love, her husband, her perfect Master Sparhawk.

The lantern's light was blindingly harsh as the door exploded open. The room seemed full of men, leering Indians with eyes like jackals, and Dianna shrank behind Kit.

"You see how completely these two sinners have sullied your good hospitality, Père Vernet," said François Robillard triumphantly, the curl of his mouth distorted by the lantern's upward glare. "But I'll teach them the folly of their wickedness. Aye, they shall learn, and learn well."

Chapter Twenty

Restlessly, Dianna paced the narrow length of the bedchamber that last night had been her sanctuary and now was her prison. The double-planked door was locked from outside, and the diamond panes of the casements were too narrow even for her to squeeze through. She wore the simple gown that had been brought to her, coarse grey wool fit for a penitent. But Dianna was neither penitent nor ashamed of what she had done. Instead, she was furious with Père Vernet's betrayal and frightened of what had become of Kit when Robillard and the others had dragged him away.

She stopped near the window when she heard the heavy footsteps echoing on the wooden stairs, and she didn't turn when she heard the key scraping in the lock. Whoever it was, she wouldn't give him the satisfaction of a greeting beyond the straight, proud line of her back. Absently she scratched the frost from the window pane and noticed the snow that had begun to fall. October still, and yet winter had already come to New France.

"Look at me, *mademoiselle!*" ordered Robillard crossly. "If we are to be friends, *ma chère,* I expect to see your pretty face."

"Friends!" Now Dianna wheeled around, hands clutched tight into fists at her sides. "How could I ever be friend to a vile creature like you?"

The Frenchman's face grew mottled above the grimy lace collar, his eyes narrowing into the pouchy folds beneath them. His expression was one that Dianna remembered well from her uncle: hungry expectation, as if she were a sweetmeat to be gobbled up in one sharp bite, changing to ugly belligerence with her refusal. Refusals were dangerous—she remembered that from Sir Henry, too—but nothing could make her give in. She belonged to Kit, and to Kit alone.

"There are other words to call you if *friend* is too fine," snapped Robillard angrily. "*Bonne ami,* mistress, whore—what you call yourself matters little. You *will* do whatever I ask, whenever I wish it. Why else would I have kept you here, warm and safe, instead of making you share the fate of that *bâtard* Sparhawk?"

"What have you done to him?" she demanded. "I swear, if you have hurt him—"

"Ha, and what would you do to me, eh? This time you don't have a gun to pretend you're a man." His laugh was a mean-spirited little bark. "Sparhawk is not so comfortable as you, *non,* but he still lives."

"Wherever he is, I'd rather be with him than you!"

"That is unkind, *ma petite fille.*" Robillard shook his head, the cool morning light glinting on the single earring he wore. "Let me tell you my plans for him, and then you will perhaps change your mind towards me, eh? The Indians with me are Mohawks, and I've promised them Sparhawk for their village *divertissement*. Already they wager over how much pain he will take before he cries out. They enjoy their torture, *oui!* Perhaps they'll burn him alive or cut out his tongue and make him eat it or slash at his belly until—''

"Stop it!" Dianna cried shrilly, her hands tight over her ears. "I won't listen anymore!"

"Have you heard, *ma chère,*" he continued, smiling, "that the Mohawks eat the flesh of other men?"

"Nay, stop!" She was trembling with what he described, knowing none of it was exaggeration, and she could not bear to think of Kit suffering that way. "Why do you hate him so? What has he ever done to you?"

The smile abruptly disappeared. "I hate him for what he is, *mademoiselle,* a Sparhawk and an *Anglais*. Sparhawks ruined me with their crops and their cattle and their little farmers everywhere I look. Sparhawks try to eat away at New France in the name of your fat Queen Anne, and Sparhawks drove the beavers away, and what did they leave me? An *indigent!*"

"That can't be so," said Dianna slowly. "Kit says there haven't been any beavers near Wickhamton for thirty years."

"Eh, what else would he tell you?" he asked furiously. "This Christophe is even worse than his father. He set the Pocumtucks against me and threatens me in my own house with his governors and soldiers. He won't even let me defend my honor and my name and

fight me like a man, but insults me and then runs back
to his grand manor house.

"But his fine living days are past, *ma chère.*" Robillard's smile returned, and he hooked his thumbs
into the fringed sash slung low under his belly. Almost swaggering, he gradually closed the distance between Dianna and himself. "At one word from me, his
blessed Wickhamton will be burned and looted like
Deerfield. I will claim the Sparhawk house for my own
and the Sparhawk land for New France."

Slowly he reached out to Dianna. He wore a gold
ring on his middle finger, the knuckle swollen above
it, and his nails were rimmed with dirt. "I know I will
have these things of Sparhawk's, because already I
have his woman."

"You don't have me," Dianna said with such ve-
hemence that his outstretched hand froze awkwardly
in midair, "and you never will, any more than you'll
have Plumstead or Wickhamton or the rest."

Furiously Robillard jerked back his hand, using it
to tug at the beard along his jaw. "Soon enough you
will see how wrong you are, *ma fille.* When you hear
the cries of the Mohawk braves as they drag your precious Christophe away, you will crawl begging to me."

Dianna drew herself up as tall as she could, folding
her arms across her chest to hide the shaking of her
hands. "I will never beg from you, *monsieur.*"

He scowled at her with disbelief. "Not even to save
Sparhawk's life?"

"Nay, I would not." It took every shred of self-
control to keep her voice from breaking beneath his
scrutiny. "I would not because Kit would not want me

to and because it would make no difference to you at all.''

Robillard slammed the door without bothering to disagree, and Dianna sank to her knees onto the bare floor. If there was a way out of this for her and for Kit and for Mercy, she must find it and soon.

Carefully Kit felt his way around the four stone walls of the cellar, trying in the darkness to make his fingers see what his eyes could not. Cold, damp stones chinked with earth and moss; a floor of packed dirt; stacked pyramids of hogsheads: nothing unusual and no way out.

Discouraged, he slumped to the floor with his head tipped back against one wall, staring up at the faint square of light that marked the trap door. The thick hewn beams supporting the floorboards creaked with footsteps overhead, and Kit could distinguish the rise and fall of conversations, though not the words, of the people in the rooms above him.

Dianna's voice was not among them. He hoped that meant she was still upstairs, and he prayed that Robillard was leaving her alone. Kit had hated the way that the Frenchman had watched Dianna last night, ogling her so blatantly while she had scrambled for her clothes, and the image twisted like a knife in his conscience. She'd looked so small, her silver eyes huge in her pale face.

Kit had wanted to kill Robillard then, and would have if the three Indians hadn't held him back. He rubbed the new bruises on his arms, the only marks on him to show how hard he'd fought before the three had thrown him and his clothes down into this cellar. They'd been careful enough not to injure him. Though Kit had no delusions about their gentleness, he had no intention of ending his days in some Mohawk squaw's stew pot, either. *Damn Robillard!* It seemed that the man had been there all of Kit's life, an irritating annoyance, a coward and a bully, but nothing worse than that. He should have stopped the man the way Attawan had advised months ago when the dying trapper had named his attacker. But Kit had believed that talking would be enough.

He sighed restlessly, staring at the trap door. Sometimes it seemed his whole life had been nothing but wrong choices made, an endless list of "should have done."

With a groan, he buried his face on arms crossed over his bent knees and thought about Dianna. Last night he should have—*God, there was another one!*—he should have insisted they leave the mission. And yet he wouldn't wish away the magic of their lovemaking. Nay, that was the one thing he'd done right! *She* was right. He could breathe her scent still on him, a comfort and torment at the same time. What he felt for her went beyond love, or love as he'd always defined it before her. She was part of him, in his blood and in his heart so completely that he felt the separation as a physical pain.

Somehow he had to get back to her. Somehow he would steal her and Mercy away from Robillard and his Indians, and together they would go home to Plumstead, and they would wed, and they'd never be apart again.

Somehow.

* * *

Père Vernet sat across the wide table from François Robillard, his unhappiness growing by the moment. As more and more of the mission's carefully rationed burgundy had disappeared down Robillard's throat, the heavy-set man came to seem less and less the gentleman he'd presented himself to be, and the more, too, that the little priest regretted his hospitality.

"And I tell you, *mon père,* that Lieutenant Hertel de Rouville himself has an interest in this affair." Robillard was bragging yet again. "You wouldn't know the lieutenant's power or influence, stuck back here where you are, but believe me, in Montreal, he is a man others listen to. When he learns how I've destroyed Christopher Sparhawk and that all the Sparhawk land can now be claimed for New France, he will be pleased. *Non, non,* he will rejoice!"

Père Vernet studied his hands clasped on the table. "I am, as you say, only a backwoods priest," he said hesitantly, "but still, this man Sparhawk did not seem to me to be quite the villain you portray."

"Then he has fooled you as he fools so many!" cried Robillard, slamming the bottle down on the table for emphasis. "He is *Anglais,* and that alone makes him an enemy of King Louis. But he is also greedy and cruel, with no morals. You saw how he pleasured himself with his woman even beneath your holy roof!"

Much as you would yourself, my friend, thought Père Vernet. For him the memory of the woman reunited with her child, the man bending tenderly over them, was a much stronger, much sweeter image than the one Robillard kept repeating. And although the priest had no first-hand experience with venal sins, he was astute enough to recognize them in others, and was certain Robillard desired the woman himself.

"His lands will all be mine," said Robillard with expansive satisfaction as he tipped the last of the wine from the bottle directly into his mouth. "All of it mine, *mon père!*"

"Then you will benefit from the Englishman's misfortune, *monsieur?*"

"*Oui, oui,* and New France, too, of course!" Robillard kicked the chair back from the table and rose unsteadily to his feet. "But it's time I took to my bed, *mon père,* I've—"

But once Robillard let go his grip on the chair, he tumbled forward to the floor and stayed there, snoring open-mouthed on his back. Slowly Père Vernet came to stand over the man. The priest reminded himself that vengeance belonged to God, not lowly men. But this, perhaps, seemed more a case of righting a wrong.

Swiftly he called to the Indian woman, giving her orders in her own tongue, and then hurried up the twisting stairs. He tapped at the locked door even as he fitted the key into the lock.

"*Mademoiselle?*" he whispered. The room was dark, no light showing beneath the door. "*Mademoiselle,* are you awake?"

He opened the door and ducked barely in time to avoid the crash of the earthenware chamberpot. "Stay back, *monsieur,*" warned Dianna tersely, grabbing the slat-back chair she planned to use as her next weapon.

"You betrayed us, and I'll have no guilt from serving you the same!"

Humbly Père Vernet bowed his head and nodded, acknowledging her reproof. *"Oui, mademoiselle.* I could beg your forgiveness, but there isn't time, not if you and your family wish to escape."

Dianna studied him warily. "Why should I trust you again?"

"Because you have no other choice?" asked the priest uncertainly. "Come, we must free your—your husband while that man Robillard sleeps."

Dianna didn't hesitate, but grabbed the blanket she used as a cloak and ran after the priest. In the hall she paused long enough to see Robillard stretched out on the floor, his mountainous belly gently rising and falling. How long would he remain like this, she wondered? With a shudder she rushed into the kitchen.

Père Vernet had already unlocked and lifted the heavy trap door, holding it open by its iron ring. Uncertainly he leaned over the edge, peering into the dark cellar. *"Monsieur?"* he called. "Monsieur Sparhawk?"

Suddenly Kit flew out from under the lip of the floor, attacking the priest like a great lion and rolling over and over with him in his grasp until they bumped into the trestle table. Kit grabbed Père Vernet by the throat, tightening his fingers while the priest began to gasp and clutch ineffectually at Kit's arms.

"Nay, Kit, stop it!" cried Dianna, grabbing Kit's shoulders to pull him away. "He's going to help us!"

"Dianna!" Abruptly he freed the priest and caught Dianna in his arms instead. "Praise God you're safe! They didn't hurt you?"

She shook her head. Briefly Dianna savored the comfort of Kit's embrace before she pushed back against his chest. "We must hurry, love, while Robillard sleeps!"

"Ivre, monsieur," croaked Père Vernet, massaging his throat as he pulled himself to his knees, and Dianna rapidly translated for Kit. "He's had too much wine."

"Then our lives may still be worth more than three hops of a louse!" Effortlessly Kit lifted the little priest to his feet and led him to a chair. "Forgive me, sir, I didn't realize—"

But Père Vernet waved his apology away. "It is no more than I deserved, *mon fils,* though I wonder that this man Robillard would dare to fight with you two. Your guns and other belongings are there on the chest." He shook his head sadly. "Such spirit, ah! No wonder you *Anglais* have prospered in this wilderness!"

Kit found his knife, his fingers tightening on the hilt in anticipation as he turned toward the room in which Robillard slept, but the priest called out and staggered to his feet. "In God's name, I beg you, no killing beneath His roof! That man has drunk enough to stop a bear. He can't harm you now."

Reluctantly Kit tucked the knife back into the sheath on his belt, and Père Vernet sighed heavily. "But you must leave now. Follow the river to the fork. There will be canoes waiting. You can trust the *sauvages* to

take you back to your territory. And those Mohawks—they will bring you no trouble, either."

"If ever you are in New England, sir," said Kit,
grasping the priest's hand, "you'll be welcome at my
home. Farewell and many thanks." The old Indian
woman appeared, leading Mercy, who ran to Dianna
as Kit urged them both out the door and into the
night.

The snow had begun again, or maybe it had never
stopped; fat, lazy, wet flakes that barely covered the
grass and fallen leaves. Because of the snow, the night
sky was pale with a yellowish tinge, and the trail was
clear, black trees outlined against the white snow. Although the journey before them—days in an open canoe in winter snow—would not be easy, Dianna
couldn't help but feel elated, almost deliriously happy.
They had escaped! Had Kit not ordered them to keep
silent, she would have begun to sing, something tri-
umphant, heroic perhaps, for Kit—

"You could not believe I'd let you go so easily, eh?"
demanded Robillard, his voice booming in the cold
air. His dark outline blocked the trail, and in the half-
light of the snow, the pistols in his hands glinted om-
inously.

Instantly Kit determined his alternatives. He could
stop one of the pistols, but not both, and he refused
to risk the lives of Dianna and Mercy. "Let the women
go," he said. "You have no quarrel with them."

Dianna stared up at Kit's impassive profile, the
snowflakes clumping on the brim of his hat and in his
hair. "I won't go," she said softly. "Even if he says we
can, I won't leave you again."

Robillard laughed harshly. "Don't worry, *ma chère,* I intend to keep you here to watch me regain my honor, and deal with this *bâtard* as he deserves!"

Kit didn't move. "You're still drunk, aren't you?" he said mildly.

"Be thankful that I am, *Anglais,* for it improves my mood. I won't slaughter you at once, eh? Now throw your guns in those bushes, and the knife, too. I know your tricks. Go on, now!"

One by one, Kit tossed Dianna's musket and his rifle and knife away, carelessly, as if they meant nothing to him. "So is this how it will be, Robillard? You will shoot me where I stand, without even pretending to make it fair?"

"That is what you wish to believe of me, isn't it, Sparhawk?" asked Robillard almost forlornly. "You and your father before you, you never would treat me like a *gentilhomme,* like yourselves. You have stolen from me and turned others against me, and with your smug *anglais* face alone you have shamed my king!"

"And to ease your pride, you've bullied and harassed my people for twenty years," answered Kit warmly. He knew he had to control his anger, but when he thought of all the misery that had come from this one man, he felt the blood pumping hot in his veins. "You've had men murdered and families torn apart, houses and farms burned, and worst of all, you've always been too great a coward to do any of it yourself."

"We will see who is the bigger coward, Sparhawk." Robillard stuck one pistol into his belt, reached into the bag he carried slung over his shoulder and pulled out a broadsword wrapped in an old blanket. To Kit's surprise, Robillard tossed the sword to him, and then the Frenchman drew his own, leaving the pistols and the bag on a rock behind him.

"You see, Sparhawk, I will give you your fair fight," crowed Robillard, already waving his sword in the air before him with excitement. "I will give you the honor of dying like a *gentilhomme,* and then your woman and your lands will be mine."

Dianna laid her hand on Kit's arm. "You can't mean to do this," she said urgently. "He could kill you!"

"And *I* could kill him," said Kit almost cheerfully, testing the weight and feel of the sword in his hand. The hilt was wood, the guard as battered as an old pot, but the blade was well balanced. He'd never carried a sword himself, finding them cumbersome in the forest, but his grandfather's long-ago lessons were still with him, as much in his arm as in his memory. He kissed Dianna on the forehead and gently disengaged her hand, feeling strangely calm. "Go now, sweetheart, take Mercy and stand clear. This should not, I think, take long."

"Then you're as mad as he is!" Dianna cried as she pulled Mercy back to the edge of the little clearing. The girl was crying silently, the tears slipping down her cheeks, and Dianna bent to hug her.

"Kit will be fine, you know he will," she whispered. "He's younger and bigger and—and, oh, he loves us too well to leave us like this!" And, she added to herself, she intended to help him win, manly honor be damned. She had watched where Kit had dropped their guns, and she meant to retrieve her musket. Slowly she began edging her way around the clearing.

She hadn't expected the harsh, scraping sound as the blades struck each other and the grunts of exertion from the men. Panting and snorting like a bull, Robillard held his sword with two hands, slashing large arcs that Kit always met and deflected. Around and 'round they circled, the blades swinging, as snowflakes drifted past them. Both men grew warm from the fight, and the steam rose from their bodies in the cold air.

Suddenly Kit lunged forward, his blade slashing deep into Robillard's shoulder. The man howled in pain and clutched at the wound, the blood rushing through his fingers and dripping crimson to the snow as his right arm now hung uselessly at his side.

Kit paused and wiped the sweat from his face with his sleeve, expecting the Frenchman to surrender, but instead Robillard lunged forward with the sword in his left hand, his thrusts now wildly uncontrolled, his feet staggering. Kit realized the fight's end was near, and he raised his arm to finish it.

Robillard's face stared up at him for the last time, his features distorted by hatred, pain and fear. "Your father fought like this, too, damn his soul," he gasped, "yet he could not save his women either, not even the *jeune fille* who tried to run."

Paralyzed, Kit felt the old nightmare wash over him again. *Robillard had watched his family die. Robillard had done it, and all these years Kit had let him go unpunished.* Kit didn't feel the pain as the Frenchman's sword sliced across his arm or hear the gunshot that jerked Robillard's body like a puppet. All his consciousness narrowed to the faint whistle of his sword through the air and through the snow and deep into Robillard's chest.

Then Dianna was running toward him, awkwardly, sliding on the snow with the musket still in her hand. There were others coming through the trees, Englishmen, soldiers from the fort at Northfield, and there was Attawan with them, and Mercy hopping up and down with excitement.

Dianna's arms were tight around him now, and when Kit slipped his hands about her shoulders, he realized she was covered with blood, his blood, but she didn't seem to care, and neither did he. She was all he wanted, and she was here.

"It's over, my love," he said hoarsely as he stroked her head against his chest. "It's finally over."

Afterword

Plumstead
July 1705

"Before I cleared New London last November, I kissed your bride farewell, and now when I return, I'm to kiss your babe, too," declared Jonathan as he peered down at the baby in Kit's arms. "You've wasted no time getting an heir, dear brother."

Kit only laughed, glancing across the room at how pink Dianna's cheeks had grown, while Jonathan bent dutifully to kiss his new nephew. Propped up on a mountain of pillows in the bed, Dianna happily watched the two brothers, one fair, one dark, admiring three-day-old Joshua John Sparhawk. At the foot of the bed perched Mercy, with Lily beside her, the little cat, too, basking in maternal splendor with five kittens tumbling across the coverlet.

Wincing, Dianna eased herself up farther on the pillows. The birth hadn't been easy—Joshua already seemed destined to equal his father's size—but she'd forgotten it all the moment the midwife had handed him to her. And Kit—Lord, she'd never seen a man so proud!

Jonathan presented his finger to be squeezed by Joshua's tiny fist as the baby squinted seriously up at his uncle. "Don't let them landlock you, boy. You come to sea with me, and I'll show you the world."

Kit snorted. "Ha, Jon, more likely he'll be leading you a merry chase for the wenches!" he scoffed. "Mark that hair! You can tell already he's a golden Sparhawk, and there's not a woman alive that can resist us."

"Mind I was a tow-headed lad, Kit, and look how I turned out. Nor do the ladies complain, either." Jonathan bent closer to the baby. "Ain't that so, young master?"

The young master's face crumpled, and he began to yowl with a surprising volume for so small a bundle. Quickly Jonathan stepped back, and Kit responded with all the experience of three days of fatherhood: he promptly returned the wailing child to Dianna.

"It's nothing you did, Uncle Jonathan," explained Mercy philosophically. "He be hungry, that's all."

"Then it's best we left him to his supper, poppet," said Jonathan heartily, relieved to have an excuse to flee. "Come, let's see if Hester's finished with those plum tarts." Eagerly Mercy hopped off the bed to join him, followed by Lily, her ears flattened at the baby's crying, and her kittens.

Clicking her tongue with sympathy, Dianna unlaced her gown, and soon the only sound from Joshua was a satisfied cooing. Kit sat on the bed behind her, and with her own sigh of contentment, Dianna settled back against his chest.

"Don't listen to Jonathan, Kit," she said softly, still in awe of her son's perfection. "Joshua's exactly in your image. He's got your hair and your eyes—or will have, once they change from blue to green—and even his ears look like yours. Though I believe the chin *is* mine," she added, touching a finger to the tiny cleft, now puddled with milk, that so mirrored her own, "and perhaps his brows."

Lightly Kit kissed the top of her hair, his arms encircling her as she embraced their child. "He's quite welcome to your chin and your brows and whatever else he pleases, as long as your heart belongs to me."

Dianna lifted her lips to his. "Forever," she whispered, "forever and always, my heart will be yours."

* * * * *

HARLEQUIN®

THE TAGGARTS OF TEXAS!

Harlequin's Ruth Jean Dale brings you
THE TAGGARTS OF TEXAS!

Those Taggart men—strong, sexy and hard to resist...

You've met Jesse James Taggart in FIREWORKS!
Harlequin Romance #3205 (July 1992)

Now meet Trey Smith—he's THE RED-BLOODED YANKEE!
Harlequin Temptation #413 (October 1992)

Then there's Daniel Boone Taggart in SHOWDOWN!
Harlequin Romance #3242 (January 1993)

And finally the Taggarts who started it all—in LEGEND!
Harlequin Historical #168 (April 1993)

Read all the Taggart romances!
Meet all the Taggart men!

Available wherever Harlequin books are sold.

If you missed *Fireworks!* (July 1992) and would like to order it, please send your name, address, zip or postal code, along with a check or money order for $2.89 (please do not send cash), plus 75¢ postage and handling ($1.00 in Canada) for each book ordered, payable to Harlequin Reader Service to:

In the U.S.
3010 Walden Avenue
P.O. Box 1325
Buffalo, NY 14269-1325

In Canada
P.O. Box 609
Fort Erie, Ontario
L2A 5X3

Please specify book title with your order.
Canadian residents add applicable federal and provincial taxes.

HARLEQUIN

AMERICAN ◆ ROMANCE®

HE CROSSED TIME FOR HER

Captain Richard Colter rode the high seas, brandished a sword and pillaged treasure ships. A swashbuckling privateer, he was a man with voracious appetites and a lust for living. And in the eighteenth century, any woman swooned at his feet for the favor of his wild passion. History had it that Captain Richard Colter went down with his ship, the *Black Cutter,* in a dazzling sea battle off the Florida coast in 1792.

Then what was he doing washed ashore on a Key West beach in 1992—alive?

MARGARET ST. GEORGE brings you an extraspecial love story next month, about an extraordinary man who would do anything for the woman he loved:

#462 THE PIRATE AND HIS LADY
by Margaret St. George
November 1992

When love is meant to be, nothing can stand in its way . . . not even time.

Don't miss American Romance
#462 THE PIRATE AND HIS LADY.
It's a love story you'll never forget.

PAL

HARLEQUIN®

I N T R I G U E®

INTRIGUE IS CELEBRATING ITS 200TH BOOK!

Remember all those great adventures you had....

The SHADOW OF THE MOON spills across the stained carpet
and the NIGHTWIND howls. You're stuck in a HAUNTED
HOUSE in which HIDDEN SERPENTS slither. There's a CALL
AFTER MIDNIGHT. It's THE LATE GENTLEMAN ringing to
see if that FACE IN THE MIRROR is SUITABLE FOR
FRAMING. "What do you mean?" you scream wildly into the
phone. But the only reply is WHISPERS IN THE NIGHT.

And the suspense continues! Don't miss Intrigue #200
BREACH OF FAITH
by Aimée Thurlo

Two hundred escapes into suspense and danger with
mysterious men brave enough to stop your heart.

IF TRUTH BE KNOWN, a trip through a Harlequin Intrigue
can be STRANGER THAN FICTION!   HI200

Capture the magic and romance of Christmas in the 1800s
with HARLEQUIN HISTORICAL CHRISTMAS STORIES
1992—a collection of three stories by celebrated
historical authors. The perfect Christmas gift!

Don't miss these heartwarming stories, available in
November wherever Harlequin books are sold:

MISS MONTRACHET REQUESTS by Maura Seger
CHRISTMAS BOUNTY by Erin Yorke
A PROMISE KEPT by Bronwyn Williams

Plus, this Christmas you can also receive a FREE
keepsake Christmas ornament. Watch for details in all
November and December Harlequin books.

DISCOVER THE ROMANCE AND MAGIC OF THE
HOLIDAY SEASON WITH HARLEQUIN HISTORICAL
CHRISTMAS STORIES!

HX92R